ALICIA'S FEAT

The Wards of Lamercier
Book 3

KATHY LEIGH

Published by Blushing Books
An Imprint of
ABCD Graphics and Design, Inc.
A Virginia Corporation
977 Seminole Trail #233
Charlottesville, VA 22901

Alicia's Feat
Kathy Leigh

EBook ISBN: 978-1-63954-466-0
Print ISBN: 978-1-63954-467-7

Cover Art by ABCD Graphics & Design

Prologue

LONDON, *1812…*

Alicia strode over to where her sisters were standing, a scowl furrowing her forehead. "I had not thought that supposedly educated gentlemen were so ignorant and biased. The men I have danced with expect women to say nothing but only nod in agreement to their superior knowledge and simper when they compliment you on the fashionable color of your ribbons."

"I like knowing what the latest fashions are," Cece protested. "But it's sad that most gentlemen simply expect us to smile prettily and agree with whatever false pearls of wisdom they cast before us."

Nell spluttered, "Are you saying that we are swine?"

Ali answered for Cece. "Of course not. We are able to discern that their pearls are nothing more than paste and paint, which means *they* are the swine."

Nell giggled and gave her twin a hug. "You are more intelligent than most of the men I have met, but if you suffer them for the fools they are, you will at least enjoy dancing."

Lord Robert and Jane arrived to hear Nell's advice. Jane

laughed. "There are some gentlemen who are not intimidated by intelligent women." She gave her husband a kiss on the cheek as he handed the others the much-needed refreshments they had gone to fetch. Ali pulled a face at the insipid, lukewarm lemonade but drank it anyway. She would have preferred ale that had been cooled in a cellar, but the only drinks on offer here were the horribly sweet orgeat or the watered-down lemonade. Ladies were not supposed to enjoy rough drinks like ale or whiskey.

As she sipped the despised lemonade, snippets of a conversation from a group of gentlemen drifted her way. Intrigued, she moved closer to hear what they were saying about the latest developments in the Peninsula War.

"Now that our army has Congreve's rockets, we'll send Napoleon and his rats running before you can say *Bonaparte*," declared one smug young man whose wispy hair flopped over his brow in a very fashionable fall. Alicia was fairly certain he had never fired a gun or tried to understand the mechanics of one.

"Their range is quite remarkable and the rockets are being used very effectively on the battlefield. I heard that three soldiers were killed with one shot," another gentleman explained, to the cheering of the others.

Alicia stepped right up to the group and pushed her glasses more firmly onto her nose. "The propulsion is remarkable, but the use of sticks for firing is very cumbersome. If the stick could be attached to the rocket, it would be much more efficient."

Five blank faces stared at her. She fell silent and stiffened her shoulders but did not back away. Eventually, the man with the wispy ginger hair raised his glass of punch in a mock salute. "Gentleman, we have a young fellow in disguise here. Next, we will hear her opinion about Mendoza and Molineaux's latest fight." The others joined in his jeering, all except one gentleman who looked at her with interest.

Alicia was too incensed to notice his intrigued gaze. Blood rushed to her head, blurring her eyes and making it difficult to see. "Unfortunately, I was not able to attend the mill, as ladies are barred from such events, but I have heard that Molineux displayed an excellent technique, using his uppercut to good effect and knocking Mendoza out cold with a decisive left," she snapped.

It was only when the firm hand of her guardian, Lord Medwell, gripped her arm that she fell silent. "Lord Keeton, gentlemen, I see you have met my sister-in-law and ward, Miss Alicia Goodwin." The earl's voice was smooth but held an edge that made the others back down and Alicia realize the extent of her *faux pas*, although fury still simmered beneath the surface as she seethed about the unfairness of society. Why couldn't she be interested in fighting, both the military kind and the pugilistic arts?

Lord Keeton, the gentleman who had watched her with fasscination, stepped forward. "It is an honor to meet you, Miss Goodwin. May I have the pleasure of the next dance if you are not already spoken for?" His voice was deep and warm, like cozy blankets on a cold winter's morning and she had a strange desire to want to snuggle close to him the way she did when she didn't want to leave her snug bed.

Lord Robert gave her a little prod in the back. She stumbled forward, pushing her glasses firmly up her nose and parroting the reply she had practiced with Nell. "Thank you, my lord. I have no partner for this dance."

It was only when Ali was standing opposite Lord Keeton, waiting for the music to lead them into the cotillion, that she looked at him properly. He was about the same height as Lord Robert, but his hair was lighter in color and it was a little longer than was currently fashionable. She liked the way it curled onto his collar and framed his face. It was a strong, sensitive face, she decided, with good features and a firm mouth that suggested sensitivity and humor. For the first time in her life, Alicia found herself feeling weak just from looking at a man. She pushed her glasses more firmly onto her nose and gave herself a scolding. Her reaction was nothing more than a response to his kindness. It was not actually possible for her knees to tremble and her heart to flutter just because of a man. That was scientifically impossible. And yet her heart was not convinced by the cold logic of reason.

The music began and she placed her hand in his, bracing herself against any charm his appearance or touch might wield. But the strength of her determination could not quell the jolt of electricity that surged through her when he held her hand just a second longer than was necessary.

In a brave attempt to be more conventional, she offered a conversational gambit. "The new vivid blue shades are most becoming for this year's fashions."

Lord Keeton hid a smile and responded gravely. "It certainly suits you very well, Miss Goodwin, but I am sure that you have better things to discuss than the latest fashionable colors, although I have it on the authority of my sister that this blue is particularly flattering to ladies of all complexions."

Alicia was more flustered than usual, both from the strange effect his proximity had on her as well as not wanting a repetition of the scorn she had endured earlier. She remained silent as they followed the intricate steps of the dance.

As he took her hand again, he asked, "Are you acquainted with Mr. Congreve?"

Alicia frowned, uncertain of his purpose in bringing up the very topic that had caused her embarrassment earlier.

"No, I have only read of his inventions," she answered abruptly.

He ignored her tone. "I ask because you mention an idea that he is, in fact, working on at the present time."

Alicia raised startled eyes to him. "Really? I wonder whether he has tried to use sticks of differing lengths for different sizes of the rocket?"

"I will be sure to ask him when next I see him." His hazel eyes twinkled, but his voice retained the grave tone he had used since the beginning of the dance.

Alicia stopped in the middle of an intricate series of steps. "You are acquainted with him?"

"He is a distant cousin of my mother's and I have been fortunate enough to visit his workshop."

"Oh, that must be fascinating. Does he use steam power to work his machinery? The potential for using steam power is endless and will change the world completely." Her stilted manner had been erased by her enthusiasm and the way he so readily accepted her ideas. Vivacity animated her and emphasized her delicate features and lithe figure. Her blue eyes shone and Lord Keeton felt a rush of blood through his body that had very little to do with her interesting scientific ideas.

He was intrigued by Alicia Goodwin but had never met her, even though he was acquainted with her guardian, the Earl of Medwell, because they belonged to the same club but they did not move in the same circles. "Is this your first time in London?" he asked.

"No, but my sister and I are making our debut this Season." Her forehead creased and she could not keep the irritation out of her voice.

"You do not wish to be a débutante and attend balls and soirées?"

"I prefer to spend time with my books and experiments."

He smiled. "That is not something many young ladies would admit to."

He cursed beneath his breath as Alicia stiffened and a mask of distant politeness descended over her features. Even her blue eyes lost their sparkle. He squeezed her hand, conscious as he did so that his body was responding in a very visceral way to this unusual young lady. "I, too, prefer the quietness of my study and the books that I keep there. I even have a laboratory set up in my house in Dorset." A flicker of interest sparked in her eyes but she said nothing. He continued, "I read science at Oxford and am fascinated by the advances that are being made which, as you say, will change the world. If you would allow me to, I would like to accompany you to the British Museum. There are many intriguing items on display and the library has some rare and wonderful books."

Alicia relaxed, and for the first time that evening, she really enjoyed dancing.

Lyme Regis, 1813…

Lord Keeton's head whirled as red-coated officers and other local gentlemen swirled ladies dressed in an array of pastel colors around the floor in time to a lively country tune. This was the first assembly he had attended in a year but he had no desire to join the mating rituals so obviously on display.

The dance came to an end and the dancers rearranged themselves, some leaving the floor and others changing partners amidst much simpering and smirking. Mr. Lewis, a local solicitor and self-appointed master of ceremonies for the local assembly, approached him. "Good evening, my lord. I trust this little entertainment is to your liking, although it is nothing like the grand affairs that are seen in the capital city and to which you are accustomed."

"Thank you, Mr. Lewis. It is a very pleasant assembly."

"And yet I have not seen you dance tonight, although there are many pretty young ladies I am sure you will find very agreeable." There was a hint of accusation behind the politeness of his words. Keeton smothered a sigh. He had only come to the gathering because a friend of his from his Oxford days was visiting and wanted a little entertainment. Masterson took one pretty lady back to her mother and led another into the set that was forming.

The solicitor stepped a little closer and whispered conspiratorially, "There are one or two young ladies who have not danced tonight and it would be such a pity if they did not enjoy themselves at such a pleasant assembly."

Lord Keeton was a gentleman who always did what was honorable and right. With an imperceptible shrug, he accepted the inevitable. Mr. Lewis clapped his hands. "Capital. Allow me to introduce you to Miss Bennet."

Mr. Lewis, satisfied that his duty was done, stepped away. Lord Keeton's eyes swept over the tall, lean figure of Miss Bennet. She was not beautiful or even pretty by fashionable standards, but her features were fine and her blonde hair, so pale it was like the shimmer of moonlight on the sea at night, drew attention to her pale blue eyes. But there was a set to her chin and a glint in her eyes that suggested she was not particularly ethereal.

She straightened her shoulders and looked at him directly, not intimidated by his status or the air of authority he exuded. Her posture verged on being hostile. Jasper Keeton found it refreshing and smiled with more sincerity than he usually used on young ladies at balls. She, however, was not charmed by his smile. Her frown deepened. She did not wait for him to speak. "It is not necessary for you to take pity on me and offer to dance simply because Mr. Lewis thinks I resent being a wallflower."

His eyebrow shot up. "Pity is not my motivation, Miss Bennet. May I ask why you attend an assembly if you have no intention of dancing?"

She was surprised by his question. Most gentlemen politely accepted her rebuttal and left her to her own devices. She was used to sitting on the side at social events, and, unlike so many of the eager young ladies who found themselves without dance partners, she was one by choice. She was not interested in finding a husband.

Lord Keeton had not moved and she looked more closely at him. She had never met him, or his late father who had employed her brother as a secretary for a short while, but Peter had liked old Lord Keeton, had admired the work he did, even though the Keetons were aristocrats and, like Belinda, Peter held very strong Republican opinions, influenced by their father's support of the ideals of the new French Republic.

Lord Jasper Keeton was good-looking, with hazel eyes a similar color to her own. But he was a large man, taller than most of the men in the room. There was no need of padding to make his superfine black coat sit so well across his broad shoulders. Altogether, he exuded an air of suppressed energy, as if he spent much of his time involved in outdoor physical activities. She held her breath. Never before had any man made her feel hot and bothered the way he did when he looked at her.

Against all logic, she wanted to hear him speak again. His voice was smooth and rich, like the cups of hot chocolate she sometimes indulged in. Instead of walking away as her common sense said she should, she answered his question. "My friend, Mrs. Wilby, urges me to attend at least one assembly or dinner a month." A rare smile lightened her eyes but her voice was still grave. "She fears that I am in danger of becoming a recluse."

"And are you?" Lord Keeton's question could have been impertinent but there was keen interest in his eyes that held no hint of judgment or criticism.

"I prefer to spend my time reading and collecting specimens to preening and acting like a doll with not a single thought in my head."

Jasper Keeton had a flash of memory of another young lady declaring a similar sentiment to him a year ago. He had seen Alicia Goodwin a few times after the Rushford's ball and had been beginning to form an attachment with her when the news of his father's sudden and unexpected death had brought him back to Dorset, bringing that promising alliance to an end. He did, however, often find his thoughts wandering to her, especially when he was working on various experiments in his laboratory, or when he was reading an article about a new discovery. Or even when he was riding out over the fields of his estate. In fact, he thought of her often and now that the period of mourning for his father was over, he wanted to return to London and find out if she still thought of him.

With a determined effort, he brought his attention back to Belinda Bennet. He offered her his arm. "I believe that if Mrs. Wilby were to see you dancing, she would be delighted at the success of her plans."

Belinda's mouth twitched as she tried not to smile, but she did graciously place her hand on his arm and tried not to be annoyed at the little jump her heart gave as a look of satisfaction settled on his face. It was no doubt only because he had won this tussle, not because he particularly wanted to dance with her.

Belinda was not surprised that Lord Keeton danced well, but she was surprised at how attentive he was to her, how easily he seemed to know just how to guide her, how to make her look like a better dancer than she was. His conversation was more interesting than that of most of the men she had encountered in her sheltered life. He did not boast about his prowess with his horses or bore her with stories of how he had bested another gentleman in a curricle race because he was such an excellent whip.

Lord Jasper gently persuaded her to talk about herself, something she seldom did because she was wary of the way most people were scandalized at her very unfeminine interest in politics and scientific discoveries. And yet she had a strange desire not to scandalize Lord Keeton.

"The musicians are most proficient," she attempted as a conventional conversational gambit.

The corner of Lord Keeton's mouth twitched, but he asked gravely, "And you, Miss Bennet, are you proficient on the harp or piano?"

Her mouth straightened and a small crease appeared between her eyes. "It is not one of my accomplishments."

Keeton's eyes twinkled and the twitch in the corner of his mouth became more obvious, but Belinda was not looking at him so she did not notice. She held her breath, waiting for him to censure her, and, like the last gentleman she had danced with, suggest that it was imperative for her to hire a music master and ensure that she could at least play a little or she would not find any suitor who would be willing to take her as a wife.

A deep chuckle made her jerk her head up to glare at Lord Keeton, but her ire subsided at the warmth in his eyes. He squeezed her hand gently as he guided her through the rondo, sending inexplicable shivers racing through her body.

"It is refreshing to meet someone who, unlike so many young ladies who force themselves into a mold of society's making, has chosen to focus on her natural talents and strengths. I have spent many an excruciating evening being entertained by young ladies who have no skill or talent and yet insist on performing in the hope of being seen as accomplished. I am not sure why a man should consider such a lady as the ideal wife."

She found herself laughing at his words. Her eyes sparkled with wit and intelligence, animating her delicate face and revealing an elusive loveliness that few people ever saw. Keeton took a deep breath. There was something very appealing about Miss Belinda Bennet. Her abrasive defensiveness was like a layer of varnish, hiding her vulnerability, and it aroused the deep sensitivity and compassion of his nature. He had a sudden desire to tilt that dainty face upwards and consume her lips in a passionate kiss, but such behavior would bring down the censure of the whole community on both of them. He needed to steer their conversation back into safer waters. Recalling something she had said earlier, he asked, "Have you read *The Monastery of St. Columb?* I believe it is all the rage right now."

She gave a look of such scorn, it could have burned his eyebrows. "It is not my preferred choice of literature. I have been reading Rousseau's *Social Contract* in the original French. I find that often the subtlety of ideas is lost in translation."

He was intrigued by her reading choice, but also reminded of his father's last secretary, Peter Bennet, who had a penchant for Jacobin ideas. "Belinda Bennet," he mulled. "Are you acquainted with Peter Bennet?"

A shadow fell over her face, obscuring the charm that had so recently animated her. "He is my brother," she said stiffly.

"He worked for my father for a while."

"I know." Her words were clipped, almost abrasive.

Jasper studied her for a moment before saying, "I never

met him but I know my father was pleased with his work, although their ideologies clashed somewhat."

"Which is why you had him dismissed without even speaking to him, just as you, out-of-hand, dismissed many other servants who had worked for your father."

Lord Keeton's eyebrow rose at the acrimonious words but his voice remained calm. "If that is what your brother told you, then there was some misunderstanding. Peter Bennet left Ashwood Park before I arrived for my father's funeral."

Further bitter words rose to Belinda's lips, but the movement of the dance prevented her from spewing them. Colonel Ross, bumptious and red-faced, with at least three chins and large white whiskers, skipped heavily beside her. "Ah, it is wonderful to see such a celebration in honor of our soldiers who sent those damn Frenchies scuttling back into their holes."

Belinda's face hardened and her eyes flashed, but Jasper Keeton, who was on her other side, gave her hand a squeeze and answered, "Our soldiers fought bravely and peace is always worth celebrating."

The dance brought her face-to-face with Lord Keeton again. She glowered at him. "You think it is commendable that we sent so many fine young men to be slaughtered in battle?"

Jasper Keeton was startled by her vehemence. "The death of so many young men is tragic, but they died defending the ideals on which our country is built."

Her voice became harder, colder. "The French have ideals that this country might do well to heed."

Jasper looked around the room and decided the best defense was retreat. This was not the place to hold such a discussion, but it was impossible to coax or goad Miss Bennet into a more congenial conversation again, and when the dance ended, she curtsied stiffly and stalked off without a word.

London, 1814...

Alicia sipped her wine and pushed her glasses more firmly up her nose. The guests at Prudence's wedding flitted around Lord Robbie's formal drawing room in Medwell House, fluttering from one group to another like butterflies and bees in a spring garden. She observed them for a while but soon grew bored of their flirting and simpering that never varied. It was much more fascinating to study the different kinds of algae, moss, and lichens that could be found around Lord Robbie's ancestral home, Lamercie Manor, in Derbyshire.

She scowled as one of the guests sauntered towards her. Sir Bigham was not put off by her expression. "So, Miss Goodwin, now that your guardian's niece is married, I am sure you must be looking for a husband for yourself." He leered at her meaningfully. "You came out in the same Season as she did and I am sure you don't want to be left behind in the marriage stakes."

"I have no intention of following Prudence into the bonds of marriage. There are other options for intelligent women to pursue," she declared decidedly.

Sir Bigham scowled and backed away, spluttering something about seeing someone he needed to speak to. Ali was grimly satisfied, but deep inside, there was a niggling feeling that her chosen path was a lonely one. Only one man had ever shared her enthusiasm for scientific studies but she had heard nothing from Lord Jasper Keeton in the two years since his father had died and he had left London so abruptly. It was far better to leave emotional turmoil to characters in novels and seek a rational, sensible approach to life. She had to forget about the one brief moment of wild love she had experienced.

"A wedding is usually considered a happy occasion," Louisa Halstead said with a laugh as she came to stand beside Ali, "yet you look as if someone had just declared that there will be no summer this year."

Ali turned to her with a wry smile. "That would be unpleasant. I am happy for Prudence although I never really liked her much, but I am tired of the emptiness of Society." She raised her wine glass to her lips and then realized it was empty. "I cannot agree with Samuel Johnson that *When a man is tired of London, he is tired of life; for there is in London all that life can afford.*"

Louisa Halstead laughed as she gestured to a footman who brought a tray of champagne to the ladies. It was only when she took a third glass that Ali realized there was a stranger standing beside Lady Halstead.

"Allow me to introduce Miss Belinda Bennet, who has just arrived in London for the first time, although she is a year or so older than you and Nell. Miss Bennet, my good friend, Alicia Goodwin."

Ali looked at the newcomer curiously. She was tall for a woman but very slender. There were hard lines on her face and she had a decided air as if she would not brook any nonsense. Her eyes were hazel and her pale blonde hair was pulled back in a severe chignon. Her blue dress, although made of good quality fabric, was without decoration, not even the simple ribbon edging she herself allowed the dressmaker to add to her dresses.

Ali liked her on sight. She smiled. "Miss Bennet, what brings you to London? Are you acquainted with Prudence or her husband?"

A flicker of uncertainty shot through her clear hazel eyes,

and then she rallied politely. "I know neither of them. I came to London to seek an appointment with Lord Halstead. I did not know that there was a wedding being celebrated here today."

Ali gestured to two chairs that were placed near the wall. "Let's sit. It will be more comfortable." As soon as they were seated, Ali asked, "Are you acquainted with Lord and Lady Halstead?"

Belinda gave a dry laugh. "No. I was given his name by someone who thought he might be able to help me."

Ali was intrigued. "You do not look like the kind of woman who has found herself in the kind of trouble Lord Halstead is used to sorting out."

Belinda's face sobered. "It is not me so much as my brother, Peter."

Ali suddenly realized that she was prying into the private affairs of a stranger. "Miss Bennet, please forgive me. I should not be so inquisitive about your affairs. When did you arrive in London?"

Belinda gave Ali a quick smile that lit her eyes and soft-ened her features, making her appear far more attractive than first impressions had given. "It is a relief to mention some of my troubles but it is perhaps better if I do not say any more just yet. I arrived this morning from Lyme Regis after two days of traveling."

"Lyme Regis! Oh, I long to go there. Have you ever met Mary Anning? She must be quite remarkable to have made such an extraordinary discovery when she was only eleven."

Belinda's air of despondency vanished and she answered keenly. "I have never met her or her brother, but I have made some small finds of fossilized sea creatures along the coast and have the beginning of my own fossil collection."

"Oh, I envy you. I would love to see what you have found. I would love to be able to discover fossils of seaweeds, algae and lichen." She looked a little abashed as she admitted, "I think I might have identified a species of moss that has not yet been documented."

The door on the other side of the room opened and distracted them both. A tall man, dressed somberly in black that enhanced his elegance and authority, entered the room and looked around with a determined air. The butler, Tomlinson, quickly made his way to Lord Medwell and spoke quietly to him. Lord Robbie nodded, glanced at the newcomer and then made his way to where he was standing.

"What is *he* doing here?" Belinda asked the question more to herself than Ali.

Alicia sat up straight, suddenly finding it very difficult to breathe. "Lord Keeton?"

Belinda looked at her darkly. "You know him?"

In spite of herself, Ali blushed. "He was very kind to me when I made a *faux pas* at a ball in my first Season and he accompanied me to some lectures and exhibitions."

Belinda's mouth tightened. "I wonder what he has to say to Lord Medwell?"

"Where do you know Lord Keeton from?" In spite of all Alicia's protestations that she did not want to marry, somehow Lord Keeton had woven himself into her dreams and wound his way through her thoughts. "He has not been in London for a while."

Belinda shrugged. "And nor have I. He has been in Lyme Regis since his father died and I encountered him at various assemblies and dinners." She shifted her gaze from the tall, handsome man to Ali. "He is at the center of my brother's troubles."

Chapter 1

LORD KEETON HESITATED JUST inside the door of the
large, formal drawing room in Medwell House, Lord Robert
Lamercier's London residence. He had not expected to see
the room crowded with guests. A quick glance at the large,
ornately decorated wedding cake on the long buffet table
confirmed that he had walked into a wedding celebration.
He surreptitiously wiped a piece of straw off his riding coat,
conscious that while his coat and breeches were stylish and
well-tailored, they showed signs of the hurried journey he
had made from Dorset. Amongst the brightly colored silks
and satins of the wedding guests, he felt like Hades rising
from the underworld, finding himself in the midst of a
Bacchanalia. His mouth quirked at his fanciful thoughts as
his eyes scanned the crowded room. For a brief moment, he
forgot the reason he had sought an appointment with the earl
in the sudden fear that he had waited too long and Alicia had
found someone else to love her, someone else to understand
her eccentricities and admire her intellect. He couldn't
breathe. And then the bride, a plain-looking woman in spite

of her wedding finery, came into view and he took a deep breath. It was not Ali.

His breath caught again when he glimpsed Alicia Goodwin through a gap in the crowd. His face softened and his cock hardened. Her dark hair was neatly arranged on top of her head, revealing the elegant curve of her neck and begging for his fingers to explore its allure. Her blue silk dress showed that she had grown from the slim schoolgirl he had met two years ago in her first Season into a woman with very attractive curves he wanted to embrace, whose pert pink mouth needed to be claimed. He resisted the desire to push through the guests and gather her up in his arms, taking those soft lips as his own. If he had any chance of renewing their acquaintance and convincing her to let him court her, he would have to woo her slowly. She did not trust easily and in spite of, or perhaps because of, her unusual opinions, she kept her distance from people, especially after her encounter with so-called gentlemen who had mocked her at her first ball.

She smiled at someone next to her, leaning towards a slim, fair woman. His eyes hardened even as his body responded viscerally to the image of the only two women he had ever truly found attractive and compatible with his desires in such close proximity.

What was Belinda Bennet doing here? She looked very intimate with Miss Goodwin. Were they friends? He frowned. Neither had ever mentioned the other. If the Bennets were intimate acquaintances of the earl, then it was possible Lord Lamercier would not consider his case objectively or seriously.

His thoughts were interrupted by the Earl of Medwell who greeted him affably. Keeton returned the greeting and apologized. "I would not have intruded if I had known you were hosting a private affair. Your butler let me in."

Lord Robbie smiled and handed him a glass of champagne. "It is my niece's wedding but you are welcome." His keen blue eyes studied the uninvited guest, taking in the shadows under his eyes, the fine lines around his mouth, and the rigidity of his shoulders. "I was sorry to hear of the passing of your father. He was a good man."

Lord Keeton relaxed a little but the shadows in his eyes deepened. "He was and I miss him. It is his death that brings me here."

The Earl of Medwell looked puzzled. "He died almost two years ago."

"Yes, but right from the beginning, there was something about the way he died that bothered me, and recently, I have come across some information that could suggest he was assassinated."

Lord Lamercier showed no change of expression at this statement. He sipped his champagne as calmly as if they were discussing the weather. "And you would like me to discover if that is true."

"That is part of it." He glanced around the room. "It would be better to meet in private. This is not the place to talk of possible treason."

Lord Jasper Keeton paced restlessly around the comfortable library as he waited for the Earl of Medwell. After his startling declaration in the drawing room, the very efficient butler had shown him into the library and asked him to wait until Lord Medwell was ready to speak to him. The butler had arranged for refreshments to be brought in while Lord Robert Lamercier continued to entertain his niece's wedding guests.

Jasper had been grateful for the hot coffee, ham sandwiches, and delicate sweet pastries which had been the first meal he had eaten since leaving his home in Dorset early that morning. But now the steady ticking of an ormolu clock on the mantelpiece reminded him that time was passing and he had not made arrangements for his accommodation in London, although he was fairly certain he would be welcome at his uncle's London house.

He stopped at the window and watched a young man race his curricle down the street. His mouth tightened as the young man, more intent on speed than the welfare of his horses, whipped the fine pair of greys and pulled at the reins, tightening the bits in their mouths. He watched them disappear around the corner. No other movement disturbed the street. The silence in the room was suffocating, as if a heavy blanket had been dropped over his head on a hot afternoon.

No carriages had left Medwell House for at least half an hour, yet there was still no sign of the earl. Had he forgotten about the unexpected, perhaps unwelcome, guest who was waiting to see him? The longer Keeton waited, the more dubious he became about the wisdom of bringing his problem to the earl.

Lord Keeton turned back to the room and tried to calm his turbulent thoughts. It was a pleasant room. Large leather chairs and couches were placed in inviting positions, urging people to sit and read or to engage in quiet conversation. He ran his fingers over the leather bindings of books that crammed the shelves, interested in the wide variety of subjects from history and science to the latest novels. Some books had been left in haphazard piles on tables next to the chairs, a ladies' fashion journal lay open on the window seat and two books on botany were open on a writing table alongside a notebook in which the reader had been jotting down observations and ideas. Near the fireplace, a chess set, exquisitely carved from ebony and ivory, had been left with the game unfinished. He studied the positions of the pieces, considering how the black knight could be moved to capture the white queen and bring about checkmate.

He resumed his restless pacing around the room but stopped when a large portrait of five young women hanging above the mantelpiece, attracted his attention. He recognized the Countess of Medwell and her sisters. The artist had captured each sister's unique quirks well. Although all of the sisters were attractive, his eyes lingered on Alicia Goodwin who, although identical in appearance to her twin sister, was distinctly different in character. He smiled as he read the title of the book Alicia was holding. *Linnaeus' Species Plantarum*. He wondered if she was the botanist who had been carefully making notes about different kinds of moss and algae.

The soft smile lingered and brightened the somberness of his face. He had caught only a glimpse of her earlier but it had been enough to show him that the slim girl he had met two years ago had developed into a very alluring woman. Her dark hair was just as thick and glossy as he had remembered it, with stray tendrils escaping her severe chignon to frame her face, and he had wanted to stride across the room, tug at those tendrils and watch her face flush with anticipation. He had not kissed her in those brief weeks when they had visited museums and lectures together, and the thought of taking possession of her soft mouth sent his blood surging through his body. His kisses would not stop at her mouth but trail down her throat and along her shoulders, nudging at the border of her dress and the promising curve of her breasts. In the silence of the library, he could almost hear how her breath would become uneven, ragged, as she let go of her control and yielded to pleasure and passion as he showed her that not everything in life could be understood through dispassionate science.

He ran his hand over his tight breeches, tighter now that

his cock was swelling at the thought of kissing her, tasting her, possessing her. As he gripped his shaft through the soft buckskin of his breeches, he pictured her as he had seen her earlier. Abruptly, his thoughts included the woman she had been talking to. Belinda Bennet. With her fair hair, pale eyes, and delicate bone structure, she had made a striking contrast to Alicia's vivid coloring. His blood heated even more at the thought of both of them together. They were the only two women he had ever found appealing, who had ever filled his mind when he jerked himself off. For a moment, he allowed his thoughts to linger on all kinds of impossible and forbidden temptations.

The clock struck again, bringing him back to his senses. It would not do to be found in the Earl of Medwell's library, his cock hard as he dreamed of the earl's ward and her friend. Deliberately, he gave his cock a squeeze, took a deep breath, and withdrew an exquisite gold watch from his fob pocket. The watch was a sobering reminder of why he was here and why he should not allow thoughts of Belinda Bennet to distract him, no matter how much he admired her intelligence and fervor. He was honest enough with himself to admit that her slim figure and pert breasts, which she tried to hide beneath her practical dresses, added largely to her appeal.

He turned the watch over in his hand, running his finger over the inscription on the back. *Virtus in arduis*. His father had given it to him when he achieved a first in science at Oxford. *Courage in difficulties*. He drew comfort from the words of his family motto but the thought of his father saddened him. It also reminded him of why he had to quell his interest in Belinda Bennet and her revolutionary ideas, and why he had to delay his wooing of Alicia. He frowned as he placed the watch back in his pocket.

He had been waiting for almost two hours. He had just decided that perhaps it was in his best interests to leave and find another way of dealing with his problem when the door opened and the earl entered, followed by Lord Halstead and another man who was introduced as Simon Barlow, the earl's secretary.

Robert Lamercier introduced them to Lord Keeton and then ushered them to some comfortable chairs grouped near the fireplace. He poured brandy into exquisite heavy crystal glasses from the decanter the butler always kept ready for just such occasions. When he was settled in a large, comfortable chair, he grimaced affably. "April is still such a blustery month. I do not know why my sister insisted that her daughter should get married at such an inconvenient time of the year."

Lord Halstead chuckled. "Perhaps she was nervous that if given too much time, Mr. Trimble might reconsider his offer."

Robbie laughed as he sipped his brandy. "That is probably it. Well, at last Prudence is safely married and I won't be called upon to host more events for her benefit."

Lord Keeton sat stiffly on the edge of his chair, holding the brandy glass but not tasting the drink. He had come here to discuss serious issues that could affect the nation and yet these men were gossiping about trivial matters as if they were at their club and had nothing to occupy their minds beyond social engagements and the latest gossip. Perhaps Colonel Ross had been mistaken and they were not actually an organization of men who worked to keep the country safe. He placed his glass on the table next to his chair and wondered how quickly he could politely extricate himself from the room and the house, and begin his own inquiries.

Lord Halstead noticed Keeton's uneasiness. He sat up

straighter, his casual air vanishing. His eyes conveyed the keen intelligence that had made him one of the most successful spymasters in England. "Keeton, you told the earl that you have some knowledge of a plot regarding treason. Would you care to give us the details, now that we are in a more private place?"

Jasper Keeton picked up his glass and swallowed a mouthful of brandy. With a deep breath, he decided to trust these men after all. "My father died about two years ago." Sadness clouded his hazel eyes. He had been very close to his father and still missed him.

"We are sorry for your loss," Lord Robbie said gently, "but how is his death related to a current possible act of treason?"

The others nodded but said nothing, waiting for Lord Keeton to explain. "The doctor gave a heart attack as the reason for his death and I accepted that at the time, although I found it odd." He hesitated. "Now, I am more inclined to believe that he was the victim of foul play."

"Why?" Lord Halstead was leaning forward, listening carefully to every detail.

"My father had never shown any signs of heart trouble. In fact, I cannot remember him ever suffering from any health problems at all, not even a cold in winter. He was fit and healthy, an active man, not given to excess, so his death was very unexpected." He looked at the three men. Their understanding and sympathy spurred him on. "I am not sure if you know that he was an advisor to the government, not in a military capacity, but as a negotiator for peace. Not many knew that he was making progress with some leaders in France who oppose Napoleon's plans."

A quick nod from the others reassured him that they were privy to information that was not publicly known. He continued. "His death delayed the peace negotiations."

Halstead looked puzzled. "This is all very interesting, but it has no bearing on current events. Napoleon has been exiled to Elba. Peace is being restored to Europe. There is to be a convention in Vienna later this year to finalize the peace treaty."

Keeton clenched his jaw. "There are warmongers who want the war to be rekindled because of how it will benefit them, both financially and for political power. Some of them will resort to any means, fair or foul, to achieve personal gain. There are others who support Napoleon's absurd ideals and are wanting to reinstate him and who would even like to see him rule here."

Barlow spoke for the first time. "All that you have said is true, but your suspicions about your father's death seem to be nothing but conjecture. Do you have anything definite on which you base your surmise?"

Keeton reached into his pocket and withdrew a letter which he unfolded and spread out on his knee, but he did not look at it. He knew the contents by heart. "I found this amongst some of my father's private papers."

Barlow took the letter, skimmed it, and handed it to Lord Halstead, who read it slowly twice through before passing it to the earl.

"This is addressed to you but was never sent." It was an observation, not a question, but Keeton nodded at Lord Halstead.

"It was the last letter my father wrote to me. He began it the day he died but never finished it." His eyes clouded over and he swallowed hard. "I found it in his desk amongst his personal papers that I had not touched until recently."

"I do not see any cause for alarm in its contents. He mentions an issue on the estate that had been resolved," the earl said smoothly, a touch of irritation coloring his voice.

"He also raises some concerns about his secretary, who

ardently supports the ideals of the revolution in France and ardently admires Napoleon and all he has done. I was initially under the impression that my father quite liked his secretary, but this letter suggests that there was some tension between them," Keeton countered.

The earl sounded a little cynical as he reread the relevant part of the letter aloud. "*Young Bennet and I had an interesting debate about Napoleon's ideals and whether or not they would benefit Britain. He is quite fervent in his beliefs about making education available to the poor, improving the roads, and advocating* libertie, egalite, et fraternitie. A*lthough I find him very diffident and timid in most other matters, he argues most powerfully when advocating these ideals.*" Robbie looked up. "A difference of opinion does not implicate Mr. Bennet in murder or treason."

Keeton leaned forward and spoke more quickly as he presented the arguments he had been forming over the last few days. "My father also mentions that he has been suffering from nausea and had developed a skin irritation along with heart pains, but the doctor could find nothing wrong and suggested it was likely an adverse reaction to too much rich food," Lord Keeton pointed out. "And the symptoms only appeared after the new secretary began working with him."

A light knock at the door cast a blanket of silence over the room.

"Enter," the earl called out.

The door opened and Keeton was surprised to see Alicia Goodwin enter. She looked around at the group of men, frowning slightly when she saw him. She pushed her glasses more firmly onto her nose and turned deliberately to her guardian. "I'm sorry, Lord Robbie, I didn't realize you had guests. I didn't mean to interrupt. I just needed my books."

He nodded at her and she quickly crossed to the table where her books had been left. She picked them up, hugging them close to her chest, and looked from the earl to Lord

Halstead, her eyes glancing over Lord Keeton as if she were hesitant to acknowledge his presence. "I didn't mean to listen to what was being said, but I heard something interesting just as I entered. It sounded like the symptoms of foxglove poisoning."

She stood firmly in her place, looking from one to the other, her chin tilted as if she expected them to reject her idea or scold her for eavesdropping. Instead, Lord Robbie nodded and Halstead leaned forward. "What did you hear?" he asked.

"Someone was describing the effects of ingesting foxglove. Is it a real case or hypothetical? Did the person also have tremors, vomiting, and eventually die of a heart attack? There is no antidote but few people would actually eat it. It is apparently quite bitter." She had lost all signs of diffidence and took a step forward in her eagerness. "I have been studying how different poisonous plants work and the effect they have on the body. Did you know that some plants have parts that are nutritious and others that can kill? For instance, rhubarb leaves can cause harm and yet for supper last night we enjoyed rhubarb and custard."

"Thank you, Ali. I might want to talk to you more about the foxglove later." Lord Robbie's voice was gentle but firm. Realizing she had been rambling and was now being dismissed, she held her head high and walked out of the room, trying not to look at Lord Keeton whose hazel eyes had been fixed on her unwaveringly from the moment she had entered the library.

She tried not to let his scrutiny affect her, tried not to notice his strong, sensitive face, and especially his firm mouth. And above all, his hands. She did not know why she was so fascinated by his hands, but even after two years, she could remember how pleasurable it felt when he placed them on her waist to guide her through the steps of a dance, how firmly he held her hand when they crossed the street, how a surge of pleasure jolted through her each time he touched her. She had no idea why he had suddenly reappeared in London or what business he had with her guardian and Lord Halstead, but she was determined not to let his presence affect her as it had done two years ago. If he had felt about her the way she felt about him, he would have contacted her as soon as the official period of mourning for his father was over, but he had not written or even sent a message to let her know he was in London. Two years was a long time, and she had probably deluded herself into thinking he had felt anything more for her than friendship. And any affection he might have felt for her had surely waned. She needed to get a grip on her own feelings, especially if he was going to be in London for a while. It would never do to let him know how much he affected her.

Once her footsteps receded down the corridor, Keeton, trying to focus on what was truly important right now and not be distracted by the vulnerability and hurt he had detected in Alicia's eyes, said, "What Miss Goodwin said makes sense and explains why the doctor believes my father died of a heart condition even though he had never suffered any such problems before."

"It would be extremely difficult to prove," Barlow mused. "How would it have been given to your father without his knowledge, and would it have been one large dose or several smaller ones over time? And above all, who would have had the knowledge and opportunity to administer it?"

The gentlemen sipped their brandy quietly for a few moments as they pondered this and then Lord Halstead put his glass down and said, "That is all speculation. None of what you have shared, Lord Keeton, shows any connection between the work your father did and his death or provides any indication that there are people actively opposing the peace negotiations and wanting to restore Napoleon, something that would be very difficult to do. There are people guarding him on Elba."

The earl added, "Besides, the information would be two years out of date and, therefore, no longer relevant."

"The letter is not the only reason I have come to see you. There were some other odd things among the papers I have only recently begun sorting through."

Halstead glanced at Robbie but they said nothing, waiting for Keeton to get to the point.

Keeton swallowed a mouthful of brandy before continuing. "It probably sounds like something from a fanciful novel, but there was a secret compartment in my father's desk which I discovered only a week or so ago. There were a number of documents in the drawer."

The earl raised an eyebrow. "Do you have those documents with you?"

Keeton bristled and then took a deep breath. It was a reasonable question. "I have stored them safely." He glanced at each of his listeners in turn, silently daring them to make a comment, but they simply watched him. He continued. "I wasn't quite sure how much of the story I could tell you. If I decide that you will be able to help, then I will show them to you."

Robbie shrugged as he replenished the brandy glasses. "Fair enough. Will you at least give us some indication of what is in them?"

Keeton sipped his brandy, looking from one to the other of his listeners, and then nodded. "Most of them are in some kind of code that I haven't been able to decipher. The ones I could read contained information about a few people my father believed were interested in prolonging the war and who consider Wellington a deterrent to their goals. The strange thing is that the pages are carefully numbered yet some pages are missing. Three, if page twelve was the last."

"He might have removed them himself for some perfectly logical reason," the earl pointed out.

Keeton set his glass firmly down on the table next to him and began to rise. He was halted by Barlow's asking quietly, "Who would have known about the secret hiding place?"

A flash of anger hardened Keeton's eyes. "Not even I knew about it. I can only imagine that someone must have spied on him and learned the secret and then later purloined the documents."

"Who?"

Keeton clenched his jaw. "Peter Bennet, of course, my father's secretary and whose sister was one of your guests at the wedding today." He spat the words out.

The other three looked at one another questioningly. Suddenly, Halstead chuckled. "Our assistance has been sought by more than one supplicant today. A young lady came to see me before the wedding. I was not available and Louisa must have brought her here. She must be the Miss Bennet to whom Keeton is referring."

"This could be interesting," Lord Robbie murmured, as he topped up the brandy glasses, "working a case from both sides."

Keeton's barely concealed temper flashed in his eyes but he kept his voice steady. "It is hardly a matter to provoke humor when gentlemen who have a reputation for aiding the government entertain traitors."

"Steady on, Keeton. Being the sister of someone you suspect might be involved in treason, is not a criminal offense," the earl said. "In our experience, things are seldom as cut and dried as people imagine them to be. What actual evidence do you have that Miss Bennet sympathizes with her brother or, indeed, that her brother really is on the verge of committing an act of treason? As yet, nothing you have said to us suggests that any new treasonous act is being planned."

Lord Keeton took a deep breath and swallowed a mouthful of brandy. "I have met Miss Bennet on a few occasions at some assemblies and dinners in Lyme Regis." He tried to eradicate the image of her slender figure and flashing eyes that intrigued and stimulated him, of her neat and precise steps as she danced, of her clear voice as she explained her opinion. He could not, should not, feel attracted to her, and yet he could not stop his mind from dwelling on her fascinations.

His contradictory thoughts made him harsher than he intended to be. "She is quite outspoken about her sympathies for the French and believes Napoleon has carried out, successfully, many of the ideals of the Revolution and desires to see similar changes in our country." Although he tried to keep his tone neutral, it was not possible to keep his personal aggrievement completely hidden. Much of his indignation rose from the attraction he felt towards Belinda Bennet. Her conversation was stimulating, her ideas invigorating, her attitude refreshing, but she spoke openly of her admiration for Robespierre's ideas of equality and freedom, ignoring the horrors he had perpetrated when he had ruled France.

Although Keeton had seen Belinda Bennet at various events in the last few months, he had not spoken to her privately since they had danced together at the assembly in Lyme Regis. But more often than they should have, images of the stately toss of her head when she defended her ideas, the flash of determination in her eyes, the stubborn tilt of her head obtruded into his thoughts. He gave himself a mental shake. He had just been contemplating Alicia Goodwin's attractions and now he was thinking of another woman. It was not like him to be so fickle.

Only by a flickering of their eyelids, did his listeners

betray their understanding of his attraction to Belinda Bennet. There was silence in the room for a few moments.

Simon Barlow asked, "Why do you suspect Mr. Bennet of nefarious actions?"

"Among the documents I found was a letter written by Mr. Bennet." He opened a dossier that he had placed on the table beside him and removed the top sheet of paper. His mouth twisted as he handed it to Simon Barlow.

The earl's secretary skimmed the page and then said, "This begins mid-sentence. Knowing what went before, might change the meaning."

"What does it say?" Lord Halstead asked.

Simon cleared his throat and then began reading. "*...a better society, based on the changes Napoleon has brought about in France. We cannot give up our hopes and plans for a better world, which will not happen while Wellington continues to oppose Napoleon.*" Barlow looked up, his eyebrow quirked as he waited for a response, but none was forthcoming so he continued reading. "*I agree that immediate action needs to be taken but with Lord Keeton's death, I can no longer remain here. Yours, P Bennet.*"

Jasper Keeton realized he had been holding his breath as the earl's secretary read the letter that had brought him to London. He purposefully forced his shoulders to relax and his breathing to even out. "It is all circumstantial so far, which is why I need your help." His voice was brittle and clipped as if he begrudged asking for their help. He was used to being in control of the circumstances of his life, but this was something much bigger, with much farther-reaching consequences than he had ever faced before.

"Did the secretary help you sort through your father's papers?" Simon Barlow's voice was gentle but insistent.

"No. He vanished before I arrived home. I never met him. But a few months ago, I heard he was working in the

Foreign Office. When I tried to contact him, he disappeared from there as well."

Halstead drained his glass and placed it decisively on the small table beside his chair. "So you suspect this man of being behind your father's death and complicit in an act of treason based on some missing papers, a few sentences in a letter, and because you never spoke directly to him."

Keeton drained his brandy glass, stood up, retrieved his letter, folded it, and began to walk towards the door. "I am sorry, gentlemen, for having wasted your time." He gave a stiff, curt bow.

"Sit down, Keeton. Don't be so hasty. We need to consider things from all sides if we are to find out the truth."

Keeton sat down at the earl's words, but his face was still set in rigid lines. His mouth tightened as he tried to control his anger. "I have spoken to some of the members of my father's, of my, household and their testimonies support my point of view about Peter Bennet. He had many opportunities to administer poison to my father, he had access to my father's papers and no one would have wondered if they had seen him looking through my father's desk. Furthermore, he did not even remain long enough in the house after my father's death to attend the funeral or discuss any of my father's business matters with me. And he has an extensive understanding of plants. It was only recently that I discovered where he has been. He has evaded any attempts I have made to meet with him."

"Why did you decide to consult us now?" Lord Halstead asked.

"Colonel Ross, whom I believe you helped out of a difficult situation some years ago, suggested that I should see you. He has heard some rumors that corroborate my suspicions. There are rumblings in the militia about Wellington's philosophy on war."

Simon Barlow leaned forward. "This is the first time you have mentioned Wellington. What has he to do with this?"

Keeton leaned back and ran his hand over his forehead. "Ross has heard rumors of assassination plots against the duke. Peter Bennet has been seen in company with some of those who oppose him and those who support Napoleon's release."

"That is not much to go on, but there is usually no smoke without fire," Halstead mused.

"If someone wanted to keep the war going, surely, killing Wellington would not be the best move," Barlow pointed out.

"He is a good general, but he does want peace as quickly as possible and he abhors violence. Some believe his ideals are counter-productive to victory and the British cause. Getting rid of him and replacing him with one of those who favor a longer war is not implausible," Keeton said, his voice milder now. "I believe there are those who are desirous of disrupting the peace negotiations and who seek a way to set Napoleon free from Elba to continue with his campaign. And Peter Bennet is somehow connected with this."

Halstead stood up. The calmness of his voice did not betray his troubled thoughts. "If you have decided that we can be trusted, we will look into this. We take any threat to the nation's security seriously. We will begin to investigate both the rumors of your father's murder and the threat to the peace efforts. To do so, you will need to let us have access to the documents you spoke of. Where can we reach you?"

Keeton also stood. His shoulders lost their stiffness as he decided to accept their assistance. "Thank you. I will be staying with my uncle, the Earl of Harcombe, in Grosvenor Square."

"Ah, yes. You are his heir." Lord Robbie's words were a statement rather than a question, but Keeton nodded as he shook hands with all three of the gentlemen he had spoken to.

As the earl rang the bell for the butler to call for Keeton's horse, he assessed him and gave him one of his charming smiles. "We have missed seeing you these last few years. Welcome back to London. My wife and I are hosting a small dinner party on Wednesday evening. It would be good if you could join us."

Chapter 2

"I'M GLAD THAT'S OVER," declared Messy, plopping herself down on the rug in the middle of the cozy, family sitting room that overlooked the garden at the back of the house and giving her dog, Ruffles, a hug. "It's tiresome having to be on one's best behavior for so many hours."

Her eldest sister, Jane, laughed. "Well, this Season, you will have to behave impeccably on many occasions. You will be joining the twins at many smaller social events in preparation for your debut next year."

Messy groaned. "Can't I wait until I am twenty-five before I have to think about all that sort of fuss and bother? Or at least until both the twins are married?" She sat up and tilted her chin, speaking with an air of grave dignity that was undermined by the licks Ruffles was placing all over her face. "I heard Lady Davenport say that younger sisters should not come out until all the elder ones are married."

As the others laughed, Ali turned from the window where she had been watching the clouds gather for a late afternoon storm in between reading her book and making notes. She had chosen her seat so that she could see when Lord Keeton left the house although, deep in her heart, she hoped that he would come upstairs to see her, to explain why he was here and why he had not bothered to be in touch with her sooner. Perhaps she should have spoken to him in the library or at least smiled at him instead of trying to ignore him. She should have given him some sign of encouragement, some indication that she still liked him, that she had never met any other man who suited her so well. She had spent most of the last half hour mulling over his visit to her guardian and wondering why he had been talking about foxglove poisoning. As she thought about Jasper Keeton, the strange comment made by her new acquaintance, Belinda Bennet, ran through her mind. How could he be at the root of Belinda's problem?

Ali had only just met Belinda, but she had felt an immediate connection with her, a strong bond that was difficult to analyze logically. She seldom made friends quickly, preferring to carefully consider the people she allowed to draw close to her, and yet she had the oddest desire for Belinda to like her. And even more odd, was that she wanted Belinda to like Jasper as well. All the rules of logic dictated that she should feel jealous of another woman's interest in the man she liked best, and yet, just before Belinda had made her startling declaration about Lord Keeton and her brother, Ali had noticed that Belinda's eyes had flashed with desire and she had held her breath. Ali was convinced that underneath Belinda's dislike of Jasper, she admired him, and she wanted him as much as Ali did. And that had made Ali's body heat in unexpected ways.

But all of this was moot right now. Lord Keeton had not shown any interest in either of them and Ali's feelings were more academic than practical. But still, she could not silence the whisperings of her heart that would not yield to rational thought. She was accustomed to seeking scientific reasons for whatever problems she encountered, but emotions did not submit themselves to scientific scrutiny or obey logical arguments. The secret admiration she had nurtured for Jasper Keeton for the last two years, known only to her twin, Nell, was no reason to begin making wedding plans or to indulge in exotic imaginings of how a woman she had only just met and the man she admired from a distance could be brought to like one another.

She heaved a sigh as she realized she was not going to find answers to these questions at the window. She gave up her vigil and answered Messy. "In that case, you will never come out into society because I am not going to marry, ever." She tried to prevent the image of Lord Keeton's hazel eyes and tall, lean body and Belinda Bennet's clear voice and pale, delicate face from filling her mind, but that required an effort of mind she wasn't quite sure she wanted to have.

Nell, who knew a little of Ali's feelings for Lord Keeton but not the depth of them, and who had not noticed his arrival at the wedding, sat up from where she had been sprawled on a rug in front of the hearth to face her twin. "Oh, Ali, I wish I could convince you that love is something glorious and transcendent. It brings a beauty to life that makes all the drudgery worthwhile." She quickly grabbed the notebook that was lying in front of her and scribbled something.

Jane laughed at her sister's words. "There has not been much drudgery in your young life that needs to be transcended. Mansions and manor houses to live in, delicious meals served regularly, plenty of pretty dresses to wear to balls and routs. And the freedom to indulge in your scribbles."

Nell sat up, smoothing the soft linen of the shirt she wore

over a pair of comfortable breeches. "No dress, no matter how pretty, is ever as comfortable as breeches, but you're right. We do live in luxury." She frowned. "A comfortable life does not give one very much scope for imagination. Stories are always more exciting when the heroine is inconvenienced in some way or another. I mean, Cinderella would not be nearly so dramatic if she had been pampered and spoiled."

Ali left her perch near the window and sat down next to Jane. "It's all very well for there to be excitement and drama in books, but I don't think living through it is very pleasant. Cece had a horrid time two years ago."

Cece, the second eldest sister, was pregnant and had left the wedding early, her husband, Daniel Eliot, insisting that she should not tire herself. But this reminder of her troubles sobered the sisters.

Nell shuddered at the memory of those horrible days when Cece had been kidnapped. "That was a frightening time. But," she said, brightening as her usual optimism took hold, "she did fall in love and marry and is now going to have a baby. I wonder if I could turn her experience into a novel. I'd change it, of course, make it even more dramatic, but it does have all the elements of a good story."

Jane laughed. "You'll have to talk to her about that."

Just then, the door opened and Nanny Browning brought in four-year-old Lord Gregory and his younger brother, Michael, who insisted on walking although he was not very steady on his feet yet. Gregory made a dash for Ruffles and began teasing the dog with a piece of wood from the basket next to the fire. Michael toddled up to Jane and clambered onto her lap, chatting in his baby talk about all the things they had been doing that day.

Gregory gave up teasing Ruffles when the dog snatched the piece of wood and scuttled under a sofa to gnaw at it. "We came to play with you, Mama," he announced loftily.

Soon, the room resounded to laughter and shrieking as they rushed around in a rowdy game of blind man's buff.

Belinda wiped her hand across her forehead. The slight headache that had troubled her for the last few weeks had eased a little as she shared her burden and it was a little easier to breathe. For the last hour or so, she had been sitting in a small, comfortable room with Lady Halstead who had listened sympathetically to her tale. Lady Halstead had nodded at the end of Belinda's description of the troubles Peter was facing and simply said, "I am sure this will all be sorted out soon. You have been carrying a heavy burden on your own, but you have come to those who will support you. Come with me now, and I will introduce you to the countess and the rest of the Goodwin sisters."

Lady Halstead had read beneath the surface of Belinda's words, discerning the isolation and loneliness of a young woman brought up by an intellectual and distant father and a self-absorbed elder brother. Louisa believed it was far more important for Belinda to spend time with the boisterous and affectionate Goodwin sisters than to try to get her brother out of a predicament that he had brought upon himself.

She stood up and followed Lady Halstead along a wide corridor, admiring the beautiful furnishings and exquisite paintings they passed, but her cynical nature was skeptical that anyone living in such luxury would be willing or able to help Peter. Lady Halstead stopped in front of a white double door, gave a light tap, and opened it. Belinda braced herself to enter a formal, sedate and elegant parlor, typical of members of the *ton* who carefully maintained their polite facades and never revealed their feelings. Belinda Bennet stared in bewilderment at the scene in front of her that was more like Bedlam than the drawing room of a fashionable and despised aristocrat.

She gaped as a little boy wearing a blindfold shouted loudly and ran towards a lady who darted behind a sofa. A number of other ladies were also dashing around the room and calling out to the child, laughing when they bumped into each other. The chaos was increased by a scruffy brown dog that yapped excitedly as he tried to catch the boy.

Another little boy, younger than the first, was clapping his hands and bumping into the others as they played. He laughed each time he tumbled to the floor and quickly scrambled up again. His nanny, sitting calmly in a straight-backed chair near the window knitting something in soft blue wool, was as calm as if she were in the night nursery and her charges were soundly asleep.

Louisa Halstead, who had entered the room in front of Belinda, was not perturbed by the chaos. She closed the door behind them with a thud and walked boldly into the fracas. The nanny was the first to notice her. She dropped her knitting and stood up, giving a quick bob, then stalked into the center of the group, scooped up the smaller boy, and stopped in front of a rather plain-looking lady who had just been caught by the blindfolded boy.

Over Lord Gregory's squeals of delight as he identified his mother, Nanny Browning announced, "My lady, you have visitors."

Jane kissed her son's cheek, ruffled his hair, and turned towards the door. Her smile lit up her face, making her eyes sparkle so that any observer who at first might have considered her plain, would now notice she was actually quite attractive. She moved forward, her arms held out in welcome. "Louisa, I did not know you were still here." Her hair was untidy from the game, but there was an air of assurance and dignity about her that convinced Belinda she was indeed the Countess of Medwell.

Nanny Browning bustled the boys out of the room, and the other girls arranged themselves into a silent line in front of a table. Even the dog now lolled quietly on the floor, his tongue hanging out as he watched the newcomers.

Lady Halstead laughed and hugged Jane. "Hugh is here, talking to Robert and some other people, and I also have a guest. I took advantage of your hospitality and used the green sitting room to talk to her but now I would like to introduce you to Miss Belinda Bennet, who has just arrived in London." Nothing in her voice hinted at the somber story Belinda had spent the last half an hour relating to her.

Jane tugged her skirt straight, patted her hair, and turned to Belinda, her face conveying the dignity befitting a member of the highest echelons of the *ton*, but her smile was warm and her eyes kind. "Welcome to Medwell House, Miss Bennet." Then she grinned. "You must think us terribly uncouth but we had promised to play with my sons and it is too rainy to be romping about outside."

Belinda's stiffness melted at the kindness in Lady Medwell's voice. "Thank you. I am sorry to intrude on your private time. I can see that you are not at home to visitors."

Jane shared a quick look with Louisa. The two women were aware of the clandestine work their husbands sometimes did for the government and often assisted them, especially when women were involved. Jane gave a thoughtful nod and turned to her sisters so that she could introduce them to Belinda. But before she could do so, Alicia stepped forward, a rare smile lighting up her face. She held out her hands. "Miss Bennet and I met earlier. Welcome. I had not expected to see you again so soon."

Nell looked at her twin quizzically. Ali was usually the least outgoing of the sisters and she did not make friends easily. Her skeptical nature made her wary of new acquaintances and it took her a long time to decide to trust someone. And yet, somehow, Belinda Bennet had broken through Ali's usual reserve.

With her head tilted to one side, Nell studied the newcomer. She was not conventionally pretty but her long lean figure looked very good in the current high-waisted fashions, although her dress, made from good quality fabric, had no embellishments. Her hair was straight and very fair, arranged in a simple chignon at the nape of her neck. There was something about her that suggested a woman who had thought much about issues and had formed very decided opinions of her own. But behind the air of confidence and competence, there were smudges under her eyes and fine lines around her mouth that hinted at the troubles Miss Bennet had faced and was still facing.

Ali gestured towards Nell and Messy. "Miss Bennet, may I introduce two of my sisters, my twin Eleanor, and the youngest, Esmeralda."

"And Ruffles," Messy chirped. "Well, he's not a sister, but he is an important member of the family."

It took all of Belinda's good breeding not to show her surprise at Nell's outfit of breeches and a man's shirt, her shoulder-length hair tied back in a loose queue and a pencil tucked behind her ear. Or at Ruffles. He was clearly a mongrel, not the kind of pedigree dog usually favored by members of the aristocracy. She took a deep breath. There was nothing conventional about this family. She relaxed and patted Ruffles who was sniffing around the bottom of her skirt. Perhaps her own peccadilloes would not be considered unusual amongst such people.

Jane ushered them all to comfortable chairs and asked Messy to ring for refreshments. "Is this your first time in

London?" she asked when Belinda was seated on the green sofa next to Alicia.

"It is. My mother died when I was young and my father preferred his own company. He never came to London and we seldom had visitors, but that suited me well," she quickly added when she saw the sympathy on Jane and Nell's faces. "I prefer the quiet of the countryside and my books to the social whirl, although I am looking forward to visiting the British Museum now that I am here."

A sensitivity born of years of looking after her sisters prevented Jane from inquiring further into Belinda's background. "London has many fascinating places that cater to all kinds of interests." As she poured the tea, she glanced at Ali, noting the brightness of her eyes and the flush on her cheeks. "Ali would spend all her time at the museum if we didn't drag her away from time to time."

Ali shot her sister a glare but took hold of Belinda's hand, "As Jane says, I know the museum well. I could show you around if you would like me to."

Belinda's shoulders lost their rigidity. "I would, thank you." A flicker of a smile softened her face. "I think your company would be stimulating." She was surprised at the warmth, the tingle of sensation that jolted through her when Ali took her hand. Only once before had she had such a response to someone's physical touch. She tried to banish the memory of the only time she had danced with Lord Keeton. No matter how her body had responded to him, her mind knew it was not rational or sensible to still yearn for a repetition of that moment.

Lord Keeton was the cause of her brother's troubles and not a man she should find in any way attractive. But her heart was not as easy to rule as her mind and his handsome face and excellent physique often filled her dreams. Seeing him earlier today, had been unsettling, arousing both desire and ire. Only now, when she was sitting beside Alicia, did the thought strike her that Ali had also responded to Jasper Keeton's appearance at the wedding. This shared admiration strengthened the bond that she felt with her new friend, but also shot a dart of jealousy through her heart.

Alicia Goodwin moved in the same circles as Lord Keeton, while the Bennets, although comfortably well-off, had never been members of the *ton*, or even aspired to be. Mr. Bennet had been a professor at Oxford University when, at the age of forty-two, his radical, anti-monarch views and outspoken support of the revolutionary French ideals led to his withdrawal from the university to a life of scholarly seclusion. Once released from the stringent requirements of the university, it suited him to finally marry. He chose for his wife an austere woman who had similar views on society. Soon after the marriage, she had given birth to Peter, and then a few years later, Belinda followed. Belinda was just a toddler when her mother had died, leaving the two children to the indifferent care of their father, who had educated both to accept his views of the aristocracy and how society should be restructured. Once Peter had gone to Harrow and then Cambridge, Belinda had been left to her own devices, but her cynicism about members of the aristocracy who, she believed, considered themselves superior to their fellow human beings simply because of the accident of their birth was deeply entrenched.

And yet, she begrudgingly admired Lord Keeton and was rapidly forming a strong attachment to the Goodwins. Perhaps she had been too hasty to tar all members of the aristocracy with the same brush. People were, after all, individuals who deserved to be judged on their individual merit.

With great effort, she put aside her thoughts and concentrated on the description Ali was giving of some of her favorite exhibits at the museum. She was relieved that Ali's enthusiasm meant that she did not expect Belinda to give more than vague murmurs of interest.

After a while, when the ladies were enjoying a second cup of tea and she was feeling more refreshed, Louisa Halstead said, "Miss Bennet, perhaps you would care to share some of what you told me earlier. The Goodwins might be able to suggest some ways to help you and your brother."

Belinda stiffened at this reminder of her problems and Ali took her hand again. The same rush of sensation flooded through her. She looked at Ali, a half-smile on her face but bewilderment in her eyes. She liked Alicia, was attracted to the steady focus of her eyes and the encouragement of her touch. She could not help noticing how attractive Alicia was, with her creamy skin and dark hair, her deep blue eyes, and her well-formed mouth. Belinda was familiar with and admired the poems of Sappho, mostly forbidden for young women to read, and she had sometimes wondered what it would be like to have the kind of physical closeness with another woman suggested in *Ode to Aphrodite* but she had never before felt such a visceral response to another woman. She would need to consider these odd feelings more closely at another time. For now, she had to focus on the difficulties her brother was facing.

She gave Ali's hand a grateful squeeze and took a deep breath. "For a short while a few years ago, my brother, Peter, worked as Lord Keeton's secretary."

Ali looked at her, her mouth open to ask a question, but Belinda squeezed her hand again and explained, "Not the current Lord Keeton, but his father, who died almost two years ago."

The others were all listening attentively, even Ruffles was sitting at her feet looking up at her inquisitively. "My brother was pleased to have the opportunity to work with Lord Keeton even though my father despised the aristocracy. But a few months after he began working there, Lord Keeton died and my brother was without work."

"Did the younger Lord Keeton not require his services?" Jane asked.

Belinda's voice hardened. "The current Lord Keeton has his own secretary and made it very clear that he did not approve of my brother's ideas and opinions. He had no letters of reference and it was only through the kindness of one of his friends from school that he was able to find a position."

"What ideas did Lord Keeton not agree with?" Nell wanted to know. She was leaning forward, her mouth open as she hung on to every word, imagining how she could turn the simple outline into a story.

"My brother and I were encouraged to read the works of Voltaire and Robespierre and we believe in their ideals of equality, liberty and fraternity. Robespierre helped black slaves and Jews when no one else would and he worked to provide opportunities for more people to own their own property and not be under thrall to the aristocracy." She looked defiantly at Jane and Louisa, her chin tilted and her eyes hard, but her hand clasped Ali's tightly.

Louisa Halstead's voice was gentle. "Those are noble ideals and yet Robespierre's methods were not as kind. Many people of all classes suffered terribly under his rule."

Belinda's eyes flashed. "That might be true, but I believe that if we ignore his ideas, we will do much harm to our own society. All people, whether street-sweepers or dukes, should be treated with respect." The lines of her face were set and she pulled her hand away from Alicia. "Those who are in positions of power simply because of the accident of their birth will eventually be toppled if they do not begin to accept the equality of all."

If she had expected the others to respond with horror

and dismay, she would have been disappointed. Messy tossed her curls over her shoulder and said mildly, "People in positions of privilege have a responsibility to do what is right and to help those who are in need, not with charitable handouts, but with the means to improve their lives, which is why we have schools for girls on our estates where they learn the same things that boys do." Then she added with a grin, "One of my best friends is a stable hand, Jed. He has taught me a lot about horses, and I even helped with a foaling last summer."

"And Lord Robbie, together with our other brother-in-law, Daniel, has invested in some factories where they are instituting reforms in the working conditions of the employees." Ali's pleading tone urged Belinda to consider her and her family as acceptable and understanding of Belinda's views.

Belinda looked both startled and abashed and then glanced from Lady Medwell to Lady Halstead. "But you are titled and wealthy. In my experience, members of the aristocracy want nothing more than to live idle lives of leisure and fashion being pampered and spoiled by their servants and living off the profits of the hard work of others." For the first time, her voice showed a little hesitation and uncertainty.

Lady Halstead ignored this slur on their status. "And Lord Keeton is such a man?" she asked.

"Yes." Her decided tone wavered as she amended, "At least, I believe so. I do not know him well, but he has made many changes on his estate since his father died that indicate he has no concern for the people who worked for his father. Some of the tenants were given notice even though their families had farmed that land for generations and he sacked quite a few servants who had been with the family for years."

Louisa Halstead spoke very calmly. "There might be very

good reasons for his actions that are not motivated by self-interest. Have you asked him about it?"

Belinda's mouth firmed even more and she sat up straighter. Her eyes glinted. "I have not, but I have spoken to some of the tenants, who are very upset. However, we are digressing from my brother's troubles. Thanks to his friend, Turner, he has been working in the Home Office, but a few days ago, Peter was asked to leave. The only explanation he was given was that he was no longer found suitable. At the same time, I found myself being ostracized in Lyme Regis. Mrs. Wilby, the doctor's wife and a friend of mine, told me that Lord Keeton has been making inquiries about his father's death and that Peter has been implicated in some kind of wrongdoing." She swallowed hard to hold back the tears. She never cried, especially not in front of other people, and yet since the beginning of her brother's troubles, she had often found herself on the verge of tears.

Jane's matter-of-fact voice helped her keep control of herself. "So, Lord Keeton believes there is something suspicious about his father's death and that your brother is connected."

Belinda nodded.

"How can we help you?" Ali asked.

"Mrs. Wilby said that I should seek Lord Halstead's help to clear Peter's name, which is why I traveled to London. I arrived this morning and went straight to the Halstead's house, but he was not available. Lady Halstead spoke to me and then brought me here." She looked a little uncomfortable as she added, "I did not know that there was a wedding. I would not have come had I known."

Jane dismissed this with a wave of her hand. "Why did Mrs. Wilby think Lord Halstead could help?"

Belinda straightened her shoulders. "Colonel Ross is a patient of her husband's and a few years ago he was in a difficult situation that Lord Halstead helped to unravel. Peter has disappeared and I do not know how or where to find him. Letters I sent have been returned to me and when I managed to contact Captain Turner, he sent a very disturbing response." She swallowed the lump in her throat. "Not satisfied with maligning Peter and suggesting he somehow killed his former employer, Lord Keeton has accused my brother of being part of a plot to assassinate the Duke of Wellington."

Chapter 3

THE DOOR of the drawing room opened just as Belinda made her dramatic announcement. Lord Halstead and the earl stepped into the room, stopping just inside, and looked at the gathered ladies, curious about the sudden silence. Louisa, the first to recover from the shock, rose and walked towards her husband, holding out her hands in welcome. "Hugh, have you finally finished your dreary discussions about business?"

He raised an eyebrow but simply said, "My dear, I am delighted to see you, but I thought you went home after the wedding."

She laughed lightly, taking his arm and drawing him farther into the room. "I was waiting for you. Besides, I've brought a new acquaintance to meet the Goodwins."

Alicia looked up when the door opened, peering behind her guardian to see if Lord Keeton was with them. Her heart beat faster than normal and blood warmed her cheeks. When she realized he had not come upstairs to join the ladies, a knot tightened her stomach and her skin turned cold. She bit her lip. Her usually ordered thoughts were buzzing in her head like a swarm of bees. Her admiration for Lord Keeton was unabated, but had she been fooled by his apparently amiable nature? Was he the kind, intelligent man she remembered, a man always respectful to anyone he encountered, from crossing sweeper boys to earls and dukes? Or was he really the monster Belinda had depicted, dismissing servants without a care for their well-being and accusing men of heinous crimes without any evidence? She glanced at Belinda, sitting next to her with rigid shoulders and her mouth in a straight line. Yet, how much did they really know about their new acquaintance? Perhaps Miss Bennet was maligning Lord Keeton for her own purposes and her brother really was a traitor. Ali's mind was in a whirl and a faint headache throbbed behind her temples.

She opened her hands which had curled into fists when Belinda had spoken so harshly about Lord Keeton. She would approach the matter in a logical and clear-headed manner, such as she usually used for conducting scientific experiments. Step-by-step. And she would draw the right conclusion. Such matters were best dealt with logically, not by letting her heart rule her head. But the ache in her heart betrayed her logical mind.

Louisa Halstead led her husband to the sofa where Belinda was still sitting next to Alicia. "I would like to introduce Miss Belinda Bennet to you. It was really you she wanted to talk to, but you have been busy with other things so I took her under my wing."

The earl, meanwhile, had crossed the room and was standing behind Jane, his hand on her shoulder as his fingers trailed along her neck and he quietly assessed the visitor, noting the pallor of her cheeks, the stiffness of her shoulders, and the mingled despair and hope that filled her eyes.

Belinda rose and gave a curt nod to the two gentlemen. "I am pleased to have the chance to discuss my brother's situation with you, Lord Halstead, Lord Medwell." She wasted no time in broaching the reason she was here. "I was assured that you could help him."

She resumed her seat on the sofa, but there was more distance between her and Alicia than earlier, not only because she sat farther away but because she had cloaked herself in a mantle of ice. The coldness that crept into Ali's heart was not very scientific. She pushed her glasses up her nose and tried to concentrate on the conversation.

Lord Halstead was saying, "Miss Bennet, I am sure you will not mind if the ladies remain while we talk about your brother. I gather they already know something of his situation?"

Belinda's answer was a curt nod and then she quickly outlined the details of her brother's problem. Her eyes looked haunted as she ended. "My brother is a fugitive at present and until I can clear his name, he will have to remain in hiding."

"Because he has been accused of being involved in a plot to assassinate Wellington?" Lord Medwell prompted.

"Yes. But he would never stoop to such villainy." Her voice was raspy as she tried to control her emotions. "Mrs. Wilby said that you would be able to prove that he is innocent."

Lord Halstead and the earl glanced at each other. "Who is Mrs. Wilby?" Lord Halstead asked.

"She is my friend, the doctor's wife." The stiffness in her shoulders eased a little as she explained, "Colonel Ross is one of the doctor's patients and he often talks of how you helped him solve a problem a few years ago."

"There must be some evidence, some reason that your brother has been implicated," the earl said. He gave no indication that for the last hour or so he had been listening to Keeton's perspective on the situation.

She bristled. "Only the insinuations made by Lord Keeton, who has blackened my brother's name simply because Peter does not kowtow to him the way peasants and laborers are expected to." Her words were clipped and her tone curt.

A vice tightened around Alicia's heart as Belinda spoke with such vitriol about the man she admired and yet she felt some sympathy for her new friend as well. She turned slightly and reached across the space between them, touching Belinda's hand gently. Belinda took a deep breath and, with a quick look at Ali that conveyed gratitude and something more that Ali could not quite interpret, she said more calmly, "Peter liked working for Lord Keeton's father. They disagreed on some philosophical issues but they had a common goal to bring about peace as quickly as possible. When Lord Anthony Keeton died, Peter sought employment with others who had the same goals. But now Lord Jasper Keeton has accused Peter of murdering his father and of being a traitor."

Alicia held her breath. What kind of tangled web had Lord Keeton woven?

Lord Halstead leaned forward. "We have just been talking to Lord Keeton, who has given us quite a lot to consider. This situation does need some careful thought and consideration but the main issue is to ensure that the duke is not assassinated and that the peace plans are not hindered. We need to discover who is behind the plot, if there is indeed such a plot, and stop whomever might be considering such a thing, before disaster occurs."

"In the meantime," Jane said in a matter-of-fact voice that eased the tension Belinda had been feeling for so many days now, "Belinda should spend time with us, visiting the sights of London and enjoying herself. Even though the Season hasn't fully started, she can join the twins on some of their excursions." She ended with a smile to Belinda. "We are hosting a dinner party on Wednesday and you must join us."

The drawing room was crowded and Alicia had sought her usual spot near the window. She really did hate having to make small talk, even when she knew most of the people present.

Nell, looking sylphlike in a cream dress with a diaphanous overlay in various shades of blue, joined her. "Are you all right, Ali? You've been out of sorts for the last few days." The sympathy in her voice wrapped around Ali like a hug.

"You know that I'd prefer to be back at Lamercie," she prevaricated. "I am never comfortable in London."

"That is true, but something more specific has disturbed you. Won't you share it with me?"

The door opened and Tomlinson, the butler, announced, "Lord Jasper Keeton."

Ali could not stop the flush that colored her face as she looked eagerly to where Lord Keeton had just entered the room, the candlelight limning him and bringing out the gloss in his thick, dark hair. His closely fitted coat of dark blue superfine and the simple fall of his cravat emphasized the handsome lines of his face and the strength of his body. When he smiled a greeting to Jane, Ali sighed softly.

Nell slipped her arm around her twin's shoulder and gave her a hug. "Oh, Ali, I should have guessed. He is perfect for you. Together, you will have the most intellectual brood of children the world has ever seen."

Ali flushed but said, "You are being ridiculous, Nell. He hasn't even paid me a visit since he returned to London. I think he has forgotten all about me. Besides, it's a little more complicated than that." She took a deep breath. "You were there when Belinda, I mean Miss Bennet, told us how Lord Keeton has treated his servants and tenants and her brother. Perhaps his character doesn't match his appearance."

Nell tilted her head. "There are two sides to the story, I think. In fact, I believe this story has a third angle that might just prove both parties are right."

Ali did not point out the illogicality in Nell's reasoning because the door opened again and the Halsteads entered with Belinda. "Oh, that is a complication," Nell breathed softly when Ali had almost the same reaction to Belinda as to Jasper Keeton.

Belinda had spent some time with the Goodwin twins, joining them at Somerset House to view an exhibition of paintings and enjoying their company when Louisa Halstead invited them for tea. She and Ali had played chess and debated at great length the ideas raised by William Charles Wells at the Royal Society about natural selection. But it was only now that Nell realized her twin had found more than a kindred spirit in Miss Bennet.

Ali grasped her twin tightly around the shoulders, a frown furrowing her forehead. "Am I very wicked, Nell?"

"No." There was not the slightest bit of hesitation in Nell's voice and relief washed over Ali. "Why would you think that? You are one of the kindest, most caring people in the world."

"Many people would consider it iniquitous or at least perverse that I am interested in a woman the way women are supposed to respond to men, and yet I feel the same way about both Jasper and Belinda. It's very muddled."

"Many people also believe that slavery is good and that women should not be allowed to study at universities. That does not mean they are right," Nell pointed out firmly. "Besides," she glanced across the room to where Simon

Barlow was standing very close to Felix Bellingham as they talked, "we all accept that those two love each other even though the law considers their relationship a crime and they could be executed if they were exposed."

Ali nodded. "It is absurd that people who are so good and kind are considered evil, just because of love." She gave her sister a watery smile and pushed her glasses more firmly on her nose. "I'm being foolish and not very logical. I agree with Sappho when she said, '*Love is a cunning weaver of fantasies and fables.*' It is only a fairy tale, not reality." Her voice was hard as she considered her own situation.

"How can you still be so cynical when both Jane and Cece have found love?" Nell gave her sister a kiss on the cheek. "I am looking forward to being your bridesmaid."

Ali laughed and shook her head but her breath caught in her throat as Lord Keeton made his way to her side. With a flutter of blue skirts, Nell wandered away, giving Ali and her beau some privacy.

"Good evening, Miss Goodwin. How are you?" Lord Keeton's voice was rich and warm. Like the amber-colored brandy Ali sometimes enjoyed sipping after dinner, it slithered through her veins, causing heat to pool in her stomach and then seep lower.

She tried to keep her face and voice dispassionate. "I am well, thank you, Lord Keeton. It has been a while since you were in the city. What brings you to London?" She couldn't quite keep an edge of aggrievement out of her voice.

"I apologize for not calling on you sooner." He stepped a little closer to her, close enough that she could smell the woody scent of his soap, the starch of his linen cravat, and the muskiness that was his alone. His eyes focused on hers and she could not look away as he ran his finger lightly down her cheek and traced her chin. "But I have thought of you often since we were last together."

She swallowed. His words and actions conveyed a tenderness that was difficult to ignore. Her voice was husky and her eyes flared with desire. For the first time in her life, she wasn't quite sure what to say. "I am glad to see you." A very unscientific tendril of pleasure unfurled in her innermost parts as the hazel of his eyes deepened to the color of bracken in autumn and his lips parted slightly.

Their moment of intimacy was broken by the sound of the gong and the butler's clear announcement that dinner was served. Lord Keeton stepped back, leaving her feeling a little cold, but he placed her hand on his arm and walked with her to the dining room, talking quietly about very unexceptionable things. Ali hardly heard what he said, her mind busy trying to analyze the look she had seen in his eyes.

She was glad that Jane had placed her next to Lord Keeton for dinner although she wished that Nell were a little closer to offer her support. Her face, however, lit up, when Belinda Bennet sat down opposite her. "Belinda, I am delighted to see you."

Belinda's eyes flickered towards Lord Keeton and then she focused on Alicia. "Good evening. It was kind of Lady Medwell to invite me."

There was a stiffness in her voice that rendered Ali at a loss for words. However, Lord Keeton stepped into the breach. "Miss Bennet, good evening. I trust you are well and are finding London to your liking."

Belinda took a deep breath. For the sake of politeness, she had to be civil to Lord Keeton. Lord and Lady Halstead had spoken at great length to her about Peter and his dealings with the Keetons. They had shared some of Jasper Keeton's concerns and Belinda's resentment had lessened a bit as she considered his position, but she loved her brother and could not forgive how Keeton had implicated Peter, making it impossible for him to work. She was honest enough with herself to acknowledge that much of her attitude to Lord Keeton sprang from her absurd attraction to him. She had enjoyed dancing with him in Lyme Regis, had found much to admire in the way he treated her, and had been stimulated by his conversation and sharp intellect. His good looks were also compelling. She was torn between admiration and resentment and this conflict of emotions made her voice sharp and hard.

She kept her eyes on Jasper Keeton, but she was aware of Alicia's drooping head, the way she had sucked in the corners of her mouth, and the shadows filling her brilliant blue eyes. She hadn't meant her coldness to hurt her new friend and her heart ached. This was all very confusing. Emotions had no place in a well-ordered mind and she had been brought up to be rational and sensible. There was nothing either rational or sensible in her feelings about both Jasper Keeton and Alicia Goodwin. She gritted her teeth and included Ali in her response to Lord Keeton's question. "I have not had the opportunity to see much of London as yet, although the Halsteads have been very kind and took me for a ride in their barouche in the Park yesterday and the concert I attended with Lady Medwell and her sisters was pleasant." She smiled at Alicia. "I am looking forward to visiting the British Museum with Miss Goodwin."

The delight that lit Ali's face sparked a warmth in Belinda's heart and began to melt the layer of ice that had formed around it. There was something almost startling in the sense of belonging and warmth that filled her when Ali was so thrilled at the thought of spending time together. She sucked in her breath, trying not to think of how much Jasper Keeton could be a source of contention between them, of how he could cause their new-found friendship to flounder. It was obvious that Ali admired him and he returned her feelings. She shifted on her seat. Neither of them knew how deeply she felt about Jasper, how much she longed for him to look at her with the same tenderness that filled his eyes when he focused on Ali. She wanted to feel the touch of his finger trace her lips, to be crushed against him as he took her in a kiss. But she wanted Alicia to be there as well. She wanted Jasper to turn from her to taste the joy of Ali's mouth. Glad of the distraction when the footman placed a bowl of cream of asparagus soup in front of her, she tried to banish such thoughts. Alicia would probably be horrified and the fragile thread of their friendship would snap if she knew that Belinda was thinking such wicked thoughts.

Lord Keeton began to eat his soup, enjoying the subtle and light flavor of asparagus flavored with dill, but he watched Belinda and Alicia keenly. He was attracted to both women and believed that neither of them was indifferent to him. But it was a complex and impossible situation.

He did not, like so many gentlemen, keep a string of mistresses or have liaisons with opera dancers, but he was not inexperienced in sexual matters. He often visited a discreet brothel, where his greatest pleasure was to be with two women at the same time, two women who unashamedly shared the pleasure of being together with him. He knew his tastes were peculiar, even wicked, but he had learned to accept himself. He had not, however, considered the possibility that he would ever find two women away from the brothel who would both attract him and with whom he could share his peccadilloes. He had resigned himself to believing that when he did marry, he would forsake his bizarre sexual appetites. But he was drawn to two women who were friends. He held his breath as his cock thickened and throbbed at the thought of kissing them both, of the two of them undressing each other and exposing the beauty of their nakedness to him and of how he would draw them onto his bed as he took first one and then the other. He had to slug half the water in his glass to cool the ardor that burned through him.

"Lord Robbie has arranged entrance vouchers for us to the museum," Ali was saying. "Are you available on Friday?"

Before Belinda could reply, Lord Keeton said, "I am planning to spend some time in the library at the museum on Friday." A slight frown creased his forehead. He wanted to research the effects of foxglove and other common household plants that were also poisonous, such as aconite. He swallowed. "If you would care to join me, we can examine some of the displays together."

Ali turned to him and his heart stopped for a moment. She gave him the same kind of look she had given Belinda, a look filled with barely disguised admiration and desire. "Are you interested in plants? I thought your interest leaned more towards mechanics and chemistry. I am investigating different species of moss and algae at the moment. I wanted to compare some of the specimens I have collected with those in the Clifford collection."

He smiled at her. "I have a particular interest in plants at the moment, although my usual interest lies more with chemistry."

Ali tilted her head. "The effects of foxglove on the human body. You were talking about that the other day."

He nodded his head, but out of the corner of his eye, he noticed Belinda lean forward slightly, keen to hear what was being said. Her mouth was in a straight line and hardness darkened her eyes.

Keeton placed his hand on Alicia's. "Perhaps we should discuss that some other time."

Belinda's eyes fixed on the way Jasper's hand was covering Ali's. Her thoughts were in turmoil. Why had Lord Keeton discussed foxglove poisoning with Alicia? Her father had loved the tall, stately flowers and they grew profusely in their garden. She and Peter had been warned from the time they were little never to touch them and as she had grown older she had read about the harm they could do. It had upset her that such beauty, such dignity, was a disguise for such danger. But it had been a lesson she had learned to apply to other situations. Lord Keeton, like the flowers, was very handsome and stately, elegant, and looking at him made her stomach feel as if it were doing somersaults. Yet his beauty hid just how dangerous he was, how callous and uncaring his nature. She had to remember that she could not succumb to his charm and should probably try to prevent him from luring Ali.

However, as she watched him with Alicia, the thought that was uppermost in Belinda's mind was born of jealousy and desire. She wanted Lord Keeton to touch her the way he was touching Alicia, yet she also wanted to be the one doing that touching. And more, she felt her cheeks heat as she imagined watching the two of them kiss, and then joining them as they all kissed each other and let their hands learn the feel of their bodies.

Her body grew hot at the thought and she fanned herself surreptitiously. Jasper Keeton caught her eye and gave her a knowing wink while his eyes held both amusement and a shared desire. Belinda was even more confused and she flushed under that steady gaze. Surely, Jasper Keeton did not share her strange longings. She must have imagined that look in his eyes.

With his eye still on Belinda, Lord Keeton turned Alicia's hand over and traced the shape of her palm with his thumb. Alicia shuddered. Belinda bit her lip. And then as Lord Eliot mentioned Napoleon's signing of the decree that banished him to Elba, he let go of Ali's hand and turned to face the other guests as if he had not just been flirting with the ladies on either side of him.

"This heralds peace and the defeat of Napoleon," Lord Halstead said.

"Twenty years of war finally ended." Lord Robbie raised his glass and offered a toast. "To peace and prosperity."

Lord Keeton had read the news with mixed feelings. Relief that the war was over, that peace would prevail, just as his father had worked for, but also concern. Would the matter of his father's death no longer be a priority for these men? Would he ever find out the truth and obtain justice for his father? And would any plots to assassinate the Duke of Wellington now be cast aside? That, at least, would be a relief. He glanced at Belinda. Did she share her brother's zeal to see Napoleon rule triumphant over all of Europe? He needed to remember that she had come to London to seek help for her brother, the very man who might have caused his father's death. His attraction to her must be overcome. And if possible, he needed to separate Alicia from her influence.

Lord Daniel Eliot was also skeptical about the decree, although for different reasons. "It is not enough for Napoleon to be given a little kingdom to rule over. He has, it appears, accepted the decision, but it will not change his character. He will never be satisfied with a small country to rule. His ambition was to rule the world. Being on Elba will simply give him time and space to plot and plan further havoc. There are, unfortunately, still many who support him and would follow him if he returned to France."

Fury flashed in Belinda's eyes. "The Coalition desires a return to the old regime, the one that suppressed and abused the people of France, just as the aristocracy of Great Britain suppresses the people of this country and they will undo all the good work achieved by Napoleon in the last twenty years."

There was silence for a moment and then Keeton asked,

his voice so icy cold, it sent a shiver down Alicia's spine although Belinda seemed unmoved by it, "That is a remarkably Jacobin sentiment. I suppose you believe all men, regardless of whether they have proved themselves to be valuable members of society, should be given the vote and our country should become a republic, overturning the aristocracy."

"Yes. And women, too. What gives certain men the right to vote other than their luck to have been born into a wealthy family that has owned vast tracts of land for centuries? Most of them do not care for the country or the people who have lived on the land and worked it. They seek only their own pleasure. They have not proved their value to society and so, by your own definition, they should not be entitled to vote." She cast a venomous look at Jasper Keeton as she spoke.

Lord Keeton clenched his jaw. "Your words are bordering on treasonous. You would like to see a revolution here just as there was in France. There was much suffering and despair under Robespierre and very little of the equality he so vociferously promoted."

Lord Robbie, watching his dinner party dissolve into a political barney, intervened. "I believe that many people are already planning to visit Paris. I wonder if the opera is still so excellent." He raised his glass. "To pleasure in Paris."

Belinda glared at Jasper, but both of them slowly subsided, realizing that their squabble was not appropriate at a dinner party. Jasper even served Belinda a portion of roast beef before placing some on his own plate.

Ali loosened her hands which she had grasped into fists on her lap during the contretemps. A headache was forming behind her eyes. She rubbed her temple. Much of what Belinda said made sense to her in general, but she had always found Lord Keeton to be a reasonable and fair man. She could not fit him into Belinda's category of idle, rich young men who had no interest in anything but their own pleasure. It was dreadful that the two people she most admired and liked in the world were at such odds with one another.

Jane took up the thread of her husband's diversion. "I have always longed to travel to Paris and am trying to persuade Robbie to take me there, but he says it is best to wait a while until things are more certain."

Cece laughed. "I spent a short time in Paris just before I married. It is a turbulent but beautiful and romantic city." She smiled at her husband. "I would love to return there in more comfortable circumstances."

The tension eased and conversation flowed along with the wine as the guests discussed the latest *on dits* and the new racecourse at Newmarket.

Belinda pushed the piece of tender roast beef around on her plate. Her appetite had completely disappeared. She would not look at Ali, concerned at the scorn and pity she might see in her eyes. Nor could she face the derision that was sure to be written all over Lord Keeton's face. She had humiliated herself, letting her anger get the better of her, and yet she could not remain silent when people spouted such nonsense.

As she sat musing, she couldn't help remembering how kind and accepting the people seated at Lord Lamercier's table had been to her. Most were titled members of the peerage and yet they were not the selfish, aloof, and idle people she had been led to believe made up that class. She was well-bred and her parents had owned a decent manor house set in a small park, but Peter and Belinda had been raised to be independent, to consider that earning one's living was preferable to living off the labor of others, and that positions of privilege made one responsible to improve the lives of those less fortunate.

The few days she had spent with the Halsteads had shown her that they held similar beliefs, in spite of their great riches and elevated position in society. It was difficult to reconcile her ingrained ideas with the new experiences she was facing. She eyed Lord Keeton out of the corner of her eye. Perhaps she had misjudged him as well. But then she remembered Peter's predicament and she banished such thoughts. If she had to choose between her new friends and her family, then family would always win.

"Miss Bennet, Belinda?" Ali's voice held only the warmth of friendship. She glanced up and her eyes were caught by Alicia's deep blue ones, brimming with sympathy and under-standing. The quick flash of a smile left Belinda blinking back tears, something she seldom had to deal with. "Are you all right?" Ali's question was asked gently, with real concern.

Belinda nodded and blinked again. She was made of sterner stuff than that. She straightened her shoulders and returned a tentative smile. "Do you often attend the opera when you are in London?" Perhaps if she conversed about more conventional subjects, people would forget her earlier *faux pas*.

Ali laughed. "We do, but it is more to Cece's liking than mine, although my sisters and I often sing together. I prefer to attend lectures at the Antiquaries Society or to listen to explorers who have traveled to different parts of the world than go to the opera, but sometimes it is pleasant to have a break from too many serious matters. Jane often reminds me that all work and no play makes Jack a dull boy, and me a dull girl."

"You are not dull, not at all," Belinda assured her. "You are quite the most fascinating woman I have ever met."

Ali's startled look and shy smile softened Belinda and she

relaxed. "I think I would like to hear explorers' stories, too. The world is such a big place, with so many different people and places. I wish I could travel to distant lands."

She had almost managed to forget that Jasper Keeton was sitting between her and Ali, although the sheer size of him was difficult to ignore. He had been quietly eating his dinner and listening to their conversation. When he spoke, the sound of his deep voice, mellow and amiable, surprised her. "I believe that Allan Cunningham is going to present some of his findings from Brazil at the Royal Institute on Monday afternoon. I have purchased tickets and would be very happy if you joined me."

Belinda held her breath. She would love to attend such an event, but surely, Lord Keeton meant the invitation for Alicia, not for her. Alicia had turned to Lord Keeton, her face bright and her eyes eager. "That would be marvelous. Belinda and I will enjoy it so much."

"Oh, I am sure Lord Keeton would prefer it if I did not attend." Even as she spoke the words, Belinda felt a longing to be there with both of them. In spite of the arguments she had with Jasper Keeton, or perhaps because of them, she yearned to spend more time with him. There was something quite invigorating about disputing ideas with him. Her heart was a very unruly organ that sometimes made no sense at all. And then she looked at him again, reminding herself that behind his sensitive, handsome facade lived a monster who was hounding her brother. She swallowed. It would be dangerous to spend more time with him.

Keeton watched Belinda as she struggled with her feelings. Her chin was set at a determined angle, but in her eyes, he could read her struggle, the hint of vulnerability, the touch of uncertainty behind the confident mask she showed to the world. An instinctive, almost primitive desire rose in him to see if he could coax her to trust him. To expose her vulnerabilities and emotions to him. His cock hardened at the thought, but then he hardened his heart, reminding himself that her brother was likely involved with his father's untimely death and she might be privy to the treasonous plot that was brewing. When he said, "On the contrary, Miss Bennet. Your company would be most welcome," he was thinking more about the possibility of discovering some indication of Peter Bennet's whereabouts from her than of seducing her.

Chapter 4

THE LADIES WITHDREW, leaving the men to their port and brandy. Lord Halstead pulled up his chair next to Jasper and the earl joined them. Jasper swirled the deep red port in his glass, watching the way the light reflected in it. "With the war ending and Napoleon surrendering, I suppose there is no longer a threat to Wellington, and what happened to my father is no longer important for the security of England."

Robbie and Halstead glanced at each other. The earl spoke thoughtfully. "I do not believe that all danger is over. The people who have profited from the war and who would like to continue to build their prosperity on the suffering of others will want to stir up conflict again."

"We have been making a little progress with your father's papers and it always feels so unsatisfying to leave a problem half-solved," Halstead added as he sipped his port.

Eliot nodded. "The coded documents are intriguing. Bellingham and I have tried various methods of decoding them and we think we might have found the answer."

Bellingham broke off his conversation with Barlow to explain. "They have used a keyword that unlocks the message. The problem now is to find the keyword or phrase that has been used for these documents."

"What I am interested to know is whether they were written by Lord Keeton or if they came into his possession by some other means," Eliot said. "Knowing the origin of the code will make it easier to discover the key."

"The handwriting looked like my father's," Keeton confirmed, "but I didn't look very closely because I couldn't make sense of the words."

Eliot reached into his pocket and handed a page to Keeton. "Look closely now. It could make a big difference."

Keeton studied the page as he sipped his port, and the others watched him. He frowned as he concentrated. "At first glance, it looks very much like my father's, but he had an odd way of forming e's that is not shown here. Also, he had an odd quirk of making t's as capital letters even in the middle of words, which is not done consistently on this page. It is possible that someone else wrote it."

Bellingham groaned. "That will make our task even more difficult. Did someone plant them, expecting us to waste our time decoding them or did Lord Keeton come across them and was he trying to decode them himself?"

Halstead shook his head. "There are people in the military who specialize in codes. If Keeton had come across these, he would have given them to the right people. It seems more likely that someone else placed them there, but who and why?"

"Peter Bennet." Keeton had no hesitation. "He hid the papers there and then forgot to take them when he left so abruptly."

The others looked skeptical. "Why try to mimic Lord Keeton's handwriting?" Barlow asked.

They all sat silently for a few moments, trying to find an answer to the puzzle. Finally, Halstead placed his glass on the table. "Putting that aside for now, what progress have you made with the list of names found in Keeton's desk?" He wanted to know.

Barlow finished his port before answering. "I have been putting together some notes on the names mentioned on the pages we could read. The most interesting is Captain Turner. He spent some time in Lyme Regis and was at school with Peter Bennet, but I can find nothing that suggests he is opposed to Wellington."

"Hmm, I think it will be a good idea to get closer to some of the people on the list." Lord Halstead drained his glass. "Robert, how do you feel about spending some time with Brigadier Wallace?"

"If I must. I do not particularly like him, but we are both members of Wattier's and I can find a way to get into some faro games with him. That's his game of choice. If I play with him, I can draw him into conversation and find out what he thinks of Wellington and the war."

Keeton looked at the earl. "I never go to Wattier's, but I am a member. I would like to join you there." Robbie eyed him thoughtfully, then nodded.

Eliot said, "Bellingham and I will continue to attempt to unravel the codes."

Halstead pushed his chair back and stood up. "Good." He looked at Keeton with a dry smile. "We're not giving up. The conundrum of your father's death is intriguing and there is something odd about the information you found."

Jasper felt relieved, but as the gentlemen rose to go and join the ladies, his thoughts were more about how this continued connection would give him more time to renew his attachment to Alicia than the need to find justice for his father.

Belinda stood stiffly near the window as the ladies gathered in the drawing room after dinner. She was still seething about the contretemps with Jasper during dinner which had reminded her of just why she did not belong here, with these people who were so different from her.

Ali had made straight for a comfortable love seat, but before sitting down, she turned to Belinda and held out her hand. "Come, let's sit over here. I wanted to talk to you more about the fossils you have found. I really wish I could visit you in Lyme Regis and go fossil hunting."

Belinda took a deep breath and walked slowly to where Ali was waiting. She placed her hand in Ali's outstretched one and felt a rush of heat shoot through her. Her smile was a little tight but the warmth that flowed from Ali to her softened her a bit. She turned to Jane, who was checking the tea tray that had just been brought in. She took a deep breath. "My lady, I am sorry for causing a scene at dinner."

Jane stopped what she was doing and turned around with a grin that went a long way to ease Belinda's awkwardness. "It makes a change from the overly polite conversations usually heard at dinners."

Messy, who had sat down in the window seat and was swinging her heels against the wood, chirped, "We don't usually have very peaceful dinners when we don't have guests. We argue about all kinds of things, such as whether Wordsworth is better than Cowper as a poet or if spaniels make better pets than pug dogs."

The others laughed and Belinda sat down next to Ali, feeling a little more comfortable.

Jane shook her head at her youngest sister. "It is not considered good manners to wash dirty linen in public. Besides, we don't actually argue. We just express our opinions clearly."

"And forcefully," Nell added as she picked up a well-read

book and flipped through the pages. "Of course, Wordsworth is good, but Byron has an ability to capture a depth of feeling and experience that is unsurpassed. There is such a melancholy air in *The Corsair*, such a sense of loneliness and mystery that haunts the reader."

Messy ignored her sister, knocking her heels against the window seat as she said, "Of course, I have noticed that when people really like each other, they tend to argue more."

The room fell silent for a moment and Belinda held her hands to her flaming cheeks. Jane, as usual, the first to recover, handed Louisa Halstead her tea and then looked at Messy. "That is an extraordinary point of view."

"Well, think about you and Lord Robbie. Before you married him, when you didn't want him to know how much you liked him, you were always taunting him with disparaging comments." Jane tried to object but Messy rambled on regardless of the suppressed giggles of her other sisters and Louisa Halstead's amused snicker. "And then there was Cece and Daniel. She cut him off, almost giving him the cut direct. It's a miracle they actually realized that they really loved each other."

Cece, who was leaning against the cushions of a comfortable chair, laughed. "I think Messy might have a point, but not everyone has the same experience." She glanced at Ali and Belinda. "Ali and Jasper are rapidly falling in love and they are very amicable towards each other."

Belinda felt both relieved and disappointed. Of course, Jasper liked Ali best. They were so well-suited, whereas she was the odd one out. And yet she wanted them to like her too. She tried to put aside the perverse thoughts that surged through her mind. All these women here, including Ali, would be horrified and disgusted if they knew how much she wanted both Jasper and Ali. She needed to remember that she was in London for her brother, and not to form attachments with people who could not understand her strange mind and heart. She would enjoy being with them for now and then retire to her quiet house in Dorset and live with the dreams of an illicit love.

The sisters all laughed at Cece's words but Belinda was quiet. Even though Ali had welcomed her, she still felt awkward. Jane looked thoughtfully at the two of them but it was Nell who, with the empathy that only twins can share, said, "True love never does run smooth. I think Shakespeare understood that when people face adversity together, their emotions are awakened and rise to higher levels." She tilted her head to the side and smiled softly. "The adversities that love faces do not have to be dramatic, like being kidnapped and whisked away to a war-ravaged France or facing a gunman. Many have to overcome the prejudices of society, which can be far more difficult."

Ali slipped her hand into Belinda's and squeezed gently. Belinda looked at the other women around her. Each one conveyed sympathy and understanding. She took a deep breath. Perhaps there was, after all, hope. But then she recalled the hardness in Jasper's eyes as she defended her brother. That obstacle was far more difficult to overcome than the issues Nell had raised.

The ladies sipped their tea and nibbled dainty delicious pastries. Suddenly, Cece paled and clutched her cup tightly. Jane jumped up and rushed to Cece's side. "What's wrong? Is it the baby?"

Nell had also hurried over and she took the cup from Cece's hand. Cece smiled at them both. "I am sorry, I'm fine. But there are times when being pregnant is very uncomfortable."

Nell tucked a cushion behind her back. "Is that more comfortable?" Cece nodded thankfully.

Jane took a deep breath. "It is quite a challenge carrying

another human being around in one's body for so many months."

Cece nodded fiercely. "They talk about being so brave and strong, but I'd like to see one of them try for just one day."

The men entered the room in time to hear this. Daniel strode quickly up to her, his face grim and his shoulders squared, but his eyes filled with tenderness and concern. "My little love, it's time for you to return to Gloucestershire. London is no place for you at the moment."

He placed his hand on the nape of her neck and Cece leaned into his touch, a dreamy smile on her face. "Will you come with me?"

His touch tightened. "Of course." He scowled at Lord Halstead who had been just about to protest. "I can work on the codes just as easily in the countryside as here." Lord Halstead backed down with a shrug.

Belinda had watched the interchange, unsure of how to understand the pang she felt in her heart. She had always dismissed the idea of love as a fallacy of logic, but when she saw the way these couples interacted, she wondered if that was just another idea she would need to reconsider. She glanced at Jasper, who was talking to the earl but who was looking towards her. Or rather, he was looking at Ali who just happened to be next to her. Her heart tightened. It was not her destiny to find the kind of love that Daniel Eliot so clearly shared with Cecilia. But the longing to have Jasper look at her with such fierce passion and tenderness filled her heart.

As if Ali had read her thoughts, she entwined her fingers with Belinda's and ran her thumb over her wrist. Belinda's tension flowed away but was replaced by a rush of guilt. Most women never found one person to care for them and yet she greedily desired the love of both Jasper and Ali. She had to remember that it was a dream beyond her reach. In all reality, it was far more likely that Jasper would eventually marry Ali and both would forget her as she buried herself in the country once more.

Jasper moved away from Lord Robbie and made his way swiftly to Ali and Belinda. Ali scooted closer to the edge of the seat, leaving a place between them for Jasper. She patted the cushion, inviting him to sit down. He grinned and settled in. Belinda flushed as his thigh pressed against hers. She stiffened and tried to move away but Jasper placed his hand on her thigh.

The rest of the guests wandered away to other parts of the room, leaving the three of them a modicum of privacy.

"Tell me about your brother," Jasper asked.

Belinda looked startled. "Why?"

Jasper moved his hand down her thigh. "My father employed him for a reason, but I never met him. And the more I know about you, the more fascinated I am to find out about you." His fingers kneaded the softness of her thigh. "I need to know what happened to my father, but I am not unreasonable."

Ali leaned forward to hear Belinda's quiet answer. "Peter is a few years older than I am and by the time I was old enough to spend time with him, he was already away at school for most of the year, so I didn't really know him well. But he was always kind to me when he came home. And after Father died, he turned to me for support."

Jasper nodded his head. "And so when circumstances brought trouble on his head, you felt responsible."

Jasper's summary of Belinda's situation was a statement that showed his insight and sympathy. She nodded and bit her lip. "He needs my help to clear his name." She straightened her shoulders and lifted her chin. "I do not believe that someone so gentle and tolerant could harm anyone."

Jasper's deft fingers continued to both stimulate and soothe. "From what you have said, he is very committed to the ideals and values of the French Revolution and deeply admires Napoleon."

"As do I," Belinda said, her eyes flashing.

Ali leaned across Jasper and placed her hand next to his on Belinda's thigh. "There are many faults in Society that must be rectified. All people deserve to find happiness and comfort, but Robespierre and Napoleon thought violence was the means to change the world. It has brought about much hardship for the very people they claimed to want to help."

Belinda gave her a watery smile. "That is true. But how do we change society?"

"Little by little," Ali stated. "And peacefully."

"In the meantime," Jasper declared, "I want to spend time with both of you."

Belinda had to blink against the sudden tears that gathered in her eyes. She was not used to being wanted.

Ali smiled in delight as the story of *La cambiale di matrimonio* unfolded on the stage of the Royal Opera House. The lively music and delightful story appealed to her. Belinda Bennet, seated next to her, giggled as Fanny snubbed every appeal of Slook for her hand in marriage. Ali leaned closer to her friend and whispered, "This is fun. We can learn much from Fanny about how to spurn unwanted lovers, and how to conceal real love from those who disapprove of it."

Both young ladies glanced involuntarily across the theater to the Halstead's box where Jasper Keeton was seated slightly behind Louisa Halstead and two of her aunts.

Ali and Belinda were distracted from the antics on stage

for a few moments as they admired the perfect fit of his dark blue jacket across his shoulders and the elegant but simple arrangement of his cravat in the style known as the mathematical. But both were more focused on his face. He was watching the performers, a slight smile curling his lips. He looked far more relaxed and happy than he had been for a while.

The first act ended and the audience immediately began moving around, seeking acquaintances and ensuring that they were seen by those they needed to impress. Lord Halstead came up behind Jasper, placing his hand on his shoulder to stop him from rising. "Before you pay your respects to those two pretty ladies who have absorbed your interest, I would like you to come with me while I talk to Brigadier Wallace."

Lord Keeton flushed slightly. He had thought he had been discreet in his feelings for both Alicia and Belinda, but Lord Halstead's keen ability to notice things that others did not see meant that not much could be kept secret from him. However, there was no hint of judgment or disapproval in his words and Jasper, with a reluctant glance across to Robert Lamercier's box where the two objects of his affection were leaning close to each other engaged in earnest conversation, followed Halstead into the crush of audience members thronging the corridors.

It did not take Halstead long to locate Brigadier Wallace. He was a tall man with a formidable presence. The bright crimson of his dress coat and his iron-grey hair were clearly visible over the heads of other audience members who were milling around. He was nodding to various acquaintances and greeting them as if he were an emperor holding court. Halstead slowly but inexorably made his way to him.

"Halstead," the brigadier acknowledged with a curt nod.

"Brigadier, it is good to see you back in London. Now

that Boney's been stopped, you military gentlemen will have much more leisure time." His voice was light, casual, and yet his eyes noted the slight tightening of the brigadier's mouth and the flicker in his eyes.

"Just so. I believe I promised to beat you at piquet the next time I was at Wattier's."

Halstead laughed lightly. "My game has had time to improve since we last played against each other. I wouldn't bet on your winning. Why, just yesterday, I won a considerable sum off a young officer who has a reputation among his fellow officers as a very sharp player who never loses. I believe he earned some prize money for capturing a French ship just before the war ended and so, was, I think a little careless about how much he dropped at the club."

"Ah, a naval officer, then." The brigadier nodded towards a younger man who was leaning against a column just to his left. "I don't believe you know my nephew, Captain Saunders. He captained a ship during the war and was so successful that he is now thinking of finding a wife."

Halstead's eyes flickered to the officer. He was only just able to disguise his distaste. Saunders had abandoned the uniform of the navy and was dressed in a foppish manner. His breeches were a virulent yellow, he wore two waistcoats of contrasting colors and his cravat was elaborately tied in one of the biggest knots Halstead had seen. The bored expression on his face was only alleviated by the salacious way he ogled two young ladies who were strolling arm-in-arm up and down the corridor.

"Well, that is something of a coincidence. Saunders was the man I played against last night. He didn't mention he was related to you."

The distaste in the brigadier's eyes was almost as intense as Halstead's. "My sister was overly indulgent with him. I hoped the navy would make a man of him, but that does not seem to have happened."

Jasper Keeton was standing quietly near the two gentlemen, listening to their conversation. He was not sure why Halstead had been so insistent that he meet the brigadier. He shifted slightly, but the movement was sufficient to draw Halstead's attention. He gestured towards Keeton. "Brigadier, allow me to present Lord Keeton to you."

The brigadier's mouth tightened and he drew a sharp breath but quickly regained his suaveness. He nodded, giving Jasper a cursory bow. "I knew your father. Sad loss. My condolences." Nothing in his voice conveyed any sympathy at all.

"Thank you."

"If you'll excuse us, Brigadier, I promised my wife I would convey a message from her to Lady Medwell." Halstead bowed and sauntered away, Keeton beside him.

When they were swallowed up by the hubbub of theater patrons enjoying the interval between acts, Keeton asked, "What was that about?"

Halstead casually glanced around, making sure they would not be overheard. He was, however, aware that the brigadier was still watching them.

"A whim, dear chap, nothing but a whim of mine. Saunders was in his cups last night and said some rather enigmatic things which I thought would be interesting to follow up on."

As they approached the Earl of Lamercier's box, Keeton said, "Neither Wallace nor Saunders is mentioned in my father's notes."

Halstead nodded. He and his team had spent many hours perusing the documents Keeton had found hidden in his late father's desk and were acquainted with their contents. "We are still analyzing those papers and are pursuing various ideas. But it is interesting that before Symes became your father's batman, he was a sergeant in Wallace's regiment." He opened the door of Robbie's box and gestured for Keeton to enter. "But now, there is just enough time before the next act begins to pay our respects to the earl and his guests."

Jasper had only just enough time to greet Ali and Belinda before the bell that signaled the end of interval sounded. As he and Halstead returned to their own seats along the corridors that were emptying quickly, they saw Saunders making his way to the broad staircase that led to the entrance. He had shed his languid air and looked far more determined. He was talking rapidly to a man of similar age. Halstead paused for a moment. "Interesting."

Belinda sat in Jasper's barouche, staring unseeingly at the vendors of meat pies and muffins who called out their wares, the maids shaking out rugs and young lads holding the reins of horses as carters delivered their wares.

Ali was chatting excitedly with Jasper about the exhibits at the British Museum. Neither seemed aware of Belinda's silence.

The carriage stopped in front of Hatchard's bookshop. Jasper swung himself down and offered his hand to the ladies. Ali jumped down lightly, but Belinda was still sitting staring blankly out at the street. Jasper and Ali exchanged glances and then Ali leaned back into the carriage. "Belinda," she called. There was no response. She called again. This time, Belinda gave a little start and turned, attempting a smile that did not reach her eyes.

"Oh, are we here?"

Ali pushed her glasses higher on her nose and looked at Belinda, her eyes dark with concern.

Some passers-by were beginning to stare and Jasper stepped forward. "Come along, Miss Bennet."

Belinda placed her hand in his and was grateful for the squeeze he gave her. She walked silently into the famous book emporium and looked around in awe. She had never imagined so many books in one place, but she could not linger in the entrance, as the other two had headed straight for the wooden staircase and were quickly making their way to the third level.

Ali headed straight for a shelf of books and ran her hand along the smooth bindings. She stopped when she found the title she was looking for. *Traité des poisons* by Mathieu Orfila had recently been translated into English and Ali was eager to study his views on toxicology.

Belinda wandered aimlessly along the lines of books. Jasper followed her and when she stopped near a window, he stood in front of her, placing his finger under her chin and tilting her face upwards. She tried to divert her eyes but it was impossible not to look at him.

"What is it, sweetheart?" His voice was low and gentle.

She blinked as tears stung her eyes but she shook her head as she bit out her answer. "Thank you, Lord Keeton, for your kindness, but my personal matters are none of your concern."

He raised his eyebrow and the corner of his mouth tweaked slightly. "I thought we were becoming more personally acquainted. And it does concern me when something has clearly upset you." His finger rubbed her cheek and he was gratified when she leaned into his touch, rather than pulling away.

A touch of remorse clouded the hazel of her eyes. "I am sorry for ruining your day. Perhaps I should return to Lady Halstead's house so that my mood doesn't continue to put a damper on you and Ali."

Jasper's grip on her chin tightened. "It is time for you to stop burying yourself. Alicia and I have both reached out to you and you have responded because, I believe, you like us both. And we both like you. But friendship only works if we are open and share our thoughts and feelings."

Belinda flinched slightly at the word friendship. She wanted so much more from Ali and Jasper, but she would rather have their friendship than nothing at all. She swallowed and noticed that Ali had come up alongside Jasper. She said nothing but her expression conveyed the same sympathy and concern that Jasper showed.

Belinda took a deep breath and tried to shake off the cobwebs that she had woven around herself. Jasper and Ali deserved better. "I received a letter this morning."

The other two looked at her in silence. They both knew that she was more likely to explain why the letter had upset her if they gave her time to gather her thoughts.

"From Peter."

A slight frown flitted across Jasper's face but he quickly regained control of his emotions. He should have realized earlier that only something to do with Peter Bennet could have upset Belinda like this. He had discussed the situation at great length with Halstead and Lord Robbie and was prepared to allow that his initial views might have been made too hastily. But he still had some doubts. However, his attraction to Belinda had been growing as he spent more time with her, and uppermost in his thoughts now was wanting to comfort her, help her. He traced his finger along her cheek and pressed the corner of her mouth. "What did your brother say in the letter?"

Belinda bit her lip and lowered her eyes. "Not very much. It's the first letter he's sent since he disappeared. It was very brief."

"At least you know that he is well," Ali pointed out. "And yet his letter upset you rather than bringing comfort."

"I'm not sure what I expected him to say, but he gave no indication of where he is, beyond saying that his friend Turner was helping him and he urged me to find a way to clear his name as quickly as possible so he could return to London."

Jasper studied her face and then gave a quick nod. "It seems to me that Turner holds the key, and perhaps we should find a way of contacting him."

Belinda looked a little less desolate as Jasper took charge. She had spent so much of her life focused on ideas and philosophies that she had not learned to be practical. "I have some letters from Peter back home in which he writes about Turner. Perhaps they will help us find where Peter is."

"Good." Jasper turned to Ali. "Did you find the book you were looking for?"

Ali grinned and held up the book. "Here it is."

"Then we should pay and be on our way. We are already a little late. Lady Medwell was expecting us to join her and your sisters about a quarter of an hour ago." Jasper ushered the two ladies down the stairs to the counter. As Ali waited behind two ladies who were trying to decide whether to buy *Mansfield Park*, written anonymously or Fanny Burney's *The Wanderer*, Jasper picked up another novel, also by an unnamed author. He showed it to Belinda. "I know that you were brought up to disparage novels but I would like to encourage you to try reading this one. I think you will sympathize with the characters as they fight for social progress. Sometimes, deep truths are found in fiction."

Belinda looked skeptical but then relented as her eyes caught the words on one page. *But I would have vengeance to fall on the head, not on the hand; on the tyrannical and oppressive government which designed and directed these premeditated and reiterated insults, not on the tools of office which they employed in the execution of the injuries they designed you.* She laughed. "Perhaps I will enjoy reading this."

The two ladies had finally decided on Fanny Burney's latest novel and Ali was searching in her reticule for the five shillings needed to pay for her book. Jasper took the book from her and placed it on the counter with Belinda's novel. "My gifts to the two of you," he insisted as Ali tried to protest.

A few minutes later, they were out in the sunshine that flooded Piccadilly and were making their way up Bond Street to Gunther's Tea Shop. The tea shop was crowded at this hour as shoppers sought to refresh themselves after a busy morning of shopping and it took them a few moments to find where Jane was sitting with Nell, Messy and Louisa Halstead.

Ali made straight for the empty chair next to her twin and sat down, talking rapidly about what she had seen at the museum. Belinda hesitated. The only other empty seat was on the other sie of the table. She glanced behind herself and saw that Jasper was sitting down at a table next to this one, where the earl, Lord Halstead and Bellingham were enjoying a cup of tea and cream pastries.

Belinda took a big breath and sat down. Messy immediately grinned at her. "Ali obviously had a good time. Did you?" Her eyes dropped to the book wrapped in brown paper and tied with string that Belinda was holding. Without waiting for an answer to her first question, she asked, "What book did you buy?" Her nose wrinkled. "I think there must be something wrong with me. All my sisters love reading but I would much rather be running around outside and learning things about animals and nature from actually seeing what they do rather than reading about it. Mind you, there are some books that are interesting. I think Wordsworth writes exquisite poems about the countryside, although I wish he included more animals rather than daffodils."

"Esmeralda, do stop," Jane said with a laugh. "You are bewildering Belinda." She looked across at Belinda and asked, "Would you like an ice or do you prefer a pastry? Ali will probably want a peach ice cream."

Belinda looked at Ali who had finally stopped telling Nell about the specimens she had spent time examining that morning. She smiled at Belinda. "The peach ice cream is delicious but they also make a very tasty strawberry one."

Belinda's smile was close to the kind of grin the Goodwin sisters so often gave each other. "I'll have the same as you. It sounds delicious. I haven't ever tasted ice cream."

Jasper sat down at the earl's table. He could see Ali and Belinda enjoying the ices that they had ordered. Belinda was looking less tense and Ali looked happy. He smiled softly.

"Have you and Miss Bennet put aside your differences?" Lord Halstead asked.

Jasper frowned. "The issue of Peter Bennet is still very much an issue, but I am able to separate him from my feelings for Belinda."

Consternation flashed through Lord Robbie's eyes. "Have you decided which of those two ladies you prefer? If you choose Belinda over Ali, my ward will be heartbroken."

Jasper gritted his teeth. The dilemma facing him was very difficult to resolve. "At the moment, all three of us are enjoying each other's company."

Robbie's face relaxed. "Good." The strange arrangement was something they would have to discuss at a later date. For now, they needed to focus on the investigation.

"Did you have any success with Brigadier Wallace?" Halstead asked him.

"Not really. He is not a very careful card player and I

won a fair sum off him. He misses the action of the war but said nothing about Wellington."

Halstead's mouth twisted. "I am not sure where his loyalties lie, but I am concerned about his nephew, Saunders. He is not quite the empty-headed dandy he pretends to be."

Bellingham nodded. "It is difficult to get into his little clique. He doesn't play cards with anyone not in his inner circle. He spends a fair amount of time with Captain Turner. But he's even more taciturn than Saunders. We know almost nothing about him."

Keeton sat up straighter. "Turner keeps popping up. He is friends with Peter Bennet. Belinda thinks Peter might be staying in a cottage that belongs to Turner. Belinda has some letters back home that have details about Turner."

Halstead was thoughtful. "It might be worthwhile to spend some time in Dorset. Keeton, how do you feel about having a house party descend on you? The more we know about Peter Bennet, the more likely we are to find the answers."

Chapter 5

ALICIA WALKED around Lord Keeton's workspace as quietly and reverently as if she were in a church. She paused at a table where a microscope had been set up and peered through the lens, examining the tiny oval seed, smaller than a fleck of pepper that was on the slide. The magnifying lens revealed the intricate openwork patterns and the tiny fronds that were invisible to the naked eye. She adjusted the lens and bit her lip as she studied the new view and then began sketching what she saw, making notes as she did so.

Jasper stood in the doorway of his private laboratory, watching her. Usually, he used this space to conduct chemistry experiments, attempting to isolate elements and analyze the effect they had on each other, but recently, he had focused more on botany, hoping that if he could unravel some of the secrets of the foxglove, he would be able to uncover the truth of his father's death as well. But at the moment, all thoughts of science had fled. He was more interested in observing Alicia and considering the effects she had on his body.

Her curiosity about all things scientific fascinated him. But as she bent over the microscope, he was not thinking of her mind. Rather, his eyes were focused on the rounded shape of her buttocks and the outline of her thighs clearly visible beneath the blue dress that clung to her body as she bent over the table. His eyes traveled upwards, over the long, lean line of her back to where errant curls kissed her neck. He took a step forward, impelled by the desire to run his finger along her exposed skin and twirl that strand of hair around his finger, tugging it as he kissed her nape and the slope of her shoulders.

He moved across the room until he was just behind her, so close that only a breath of air separated them. She straightened and turned around, her eyes bright with discovery. "Do you think we could identify something in the structure of the plant that would show why it is poisonous?" Her voice trailed off as she realized just how close Jasper was standing to her and how fiercely his eyes were burning with desire.

The tip of her tongue peeped out of her mouth and moistened her suddenly dry lips. She pushed her spectacles up her nose but kept her eyes locked with his. They stood silently for many heartbeats. Eventually, Jasper touched the corner of her mouth with the tip of his finger.

It was a light touch, as soft as a baby bird's feather drifting from a bird's nest, yet Ali felt it ricochet through her body like lava flowing from a volcano. She gulped. His finger pressed a little more firmly and then he outlined her lips slowly, as if memorizing their shape and feel.

Ali's knees trembled and the only way she could steady herself was to clutch Jasper's jacket. She lifted her face to his, urging him to kiss her. He did.

His mouth descended to hers and brushed the softness of

her lips, savoring the feel and taste of her. Her body softened and she leaned into him, pressing her lips against his, mimicking his movements.

He cupped her head, twisting the loose curls in her nape through his fingers. He tugged and used the leverage to move her head where he could access her mouth more easily. A low moan rumbled in her throat as she clung to him more tightly, pressing her body against his and rubbing against the hardness of his chest and stomach. Her fingers curled into the soft strands of his hair.

His mouth took possession of hers, claiming her, owning her, loving her. He slid his tongue past her lips and entered the warmth of her mouth. He inhaled deeply, memorizing the scent of her, the elusive fragrance of apples and cinnamon, the suggestion of autumn afternoons, and the headiness of moss on trees.

His one hand slid down her back, pulling her closer to him as he explored her mouth more thoroughly. He cupped her bottom and squeezed it, enjoying the feeling of her soft, tender flesh beneath his fingers. She moaned as he pulled his mouth away from hers and tilted her face up, exposing the slim column of her neck. He kissed his way down to the little hollow at the base and flicked it with his tongue.

She pressed closer to him, murmuring, "More, please, more," over and over again.

Her breasts had swelled and were tight and heavy, pressing against her dress and pushing upwards. Her nipples were as hard as ice but much hotter.

While they were kissing, Jasper had moved her slowly backwards so that she was now leaning against the wall near the open window. A soft breeze blew the curtains and brushed against her sensitive skin, causing more sensations to ripple through her body. Now that she could balance against the wall, Jasper moved his thigh between hers, pushing her legs apart. Heat pulsed in her private places and the only relief she could get was from rubbing herself against the hardness of his thigh.

He responded by pushing her harder against the wall and taking her mouth more insistently, while his hands pulled the soft material of her dress up, leaving her legs exposed. He stroked the bare flesh of her upper thighs and the smoothness of her buttocks. Sweet moans filled her mouth. Jasper's hand slid between her thighs, through the slipperiness of the juices that were sliding from her pussy. Using the wetness, he stimulated the swollen flesh and sought the core of her pleasure.

Ali surrendered to the sensations that raced through her. She forgot all her scientific findings, all the facts she had been gathering, and focused on the pleasure Jasper was drawing from her body. She drowned in the aroma of woody spices, heat and hardness that radiated from him. His cock pressed against the softness of her stomach and roused her desires even further.

Her breasts felt swollen and her dress was suddenly too tight. She wanted to pull it off but her hands were too busy exploring the delight of Jasper's body. She unbuttoned his waistcoat and loosened his cravat so she could mold her hands against the hardness of his muscles. When he pulled away from her mouth, which was swollen from his kisses, she placed her lips on his chest and swiped her tongue along the ridge of his muscles.

She smiled when he emitted a low groan. It felt good to have such power over him. But before she could revel for long, his clever fingers resumed their stimulation of her pussy. He ran his fingers between the inner and outer folds and then circled the opening to her most intimate places. She held her breath and absorbed the sensations.

His thumb pressed the nub where her pleasure was

centered and sent the sensations soaring beyond anything she had ever thought possible. Her knees trembled and she couldn't keep herself upright. She leaned her head against his shoulder and steadied herself with her hands against his chest.

Jasper prodded her opening with his large finger, stretching the muscles. She gasped at the sudden sharp pain and then breathed deeply as the thickness of his finger filled her. She wiggled, trying to adjust to the intrusion while she reveled in the pleasure that ricocheted through her whole body.

As her body relaxed, Jasper began moving his finger, plunging it into her and pulling it out slowly at first, and then as her body accepted him more easily, he moved faster and faster. It became impossible to isolate the sensations as they melded into a perfect storm of pleasure. A second finger joined the first and stretched her even wider.

Juices were pouring from her body now and his fingers were slick as they plunged into her. He pumped his fingers in and out, becoming more and more forceful with each thrust. He went deeper and deeper until he could feel the barrier of her maidenhood.

Ali was breathing heavily and her body tensed. She was standing on her tiptoes as she yielded to the pleasure. She could think of nothing except the hardness of Jasper's body, the scent of his manhood, the heat of his closeness. Every inch of her skin tingled and felt stretched. Parts of her body were as soft as moonlight, but her nipples were hard and scratched against the linen of her stays.

Jasper's thumbnail scratched across the top of her clit and she exploded with a scream of pleasure.

Lord Robbie, his jacket removed and his cravat hanging loose, swallowed a mouthful of brandy. His eyes scanned the notes he and his secretary, Barlow, had made as they interviewed members of Keeton's staff. On the whole, Peter Bennet had been liked by the staff although some of them were a little shocked by his revolutionary ideas. He was polite, affable and showed a genuine concern for others, no matter their rank or position in the household. He had even started teaching some of the younger footmen to read and write, which had alarmed some of the older employees who did not hold with all this book knowledge that stuffed the younger generation's heads full of nonsense that made them unfit for a decent day's work. He chuckled as he turned to the next page. "Bennet knows a lot about plants and botany, much to the grudging admiration of the head gardener, Jack Legg, who believes that his own knowledge of flowers and gardens is superior to anyone else's," he commented. "I spent a tedious half an hour with Legg, being taken around his greenhouses and lectured on the best methods for propagating tomatoes and cucumbers before he spoke about Bennet. He even insisted that I taste his tomatoes, ensuring me that they are not toxic, in spite of common opinion."

Barlow looked up from the notes he was writing. "Was it worth the risk?"

Robbie chuckled. "It's not the first time I've tasted them. My gardener has been experimenting with this new fruit as well. I actually quite like the taste." He brushed his hand over the page he had been reading. "And I did find out some interesting information, which doesn't make things look good for Mr. Bennet who seems to have spent a lot of time in the still room, concocting different potions as he experimented with herbs and flowers."

"That is interesting, but all-in-all, the staff liked him. He doesn't seem to have struck anyone as nefarious."

"Only one person seemed to have actually disliked Bennet," Lord Robbie added. "The late Lord Keeton's valet, Symes, is fiercely loyal to crown and country and disparages anyone who in any way criticizes anything the king or militia do."

The earl skimmed over his notes of the description Symes had given. "He describes Bennet as a rebel and a disgrace to his country who has no sense of rank and hobnobbed with anyone, including stable boys and scullery maids. He suggested that Bennet had *inappropriate relations* with one of the still room maids. Symes believed that Lord Keeton was bitterly disappointed in Bennet and was sorry to have employed him. He says Lord Keeton was going to let him go at the end of the quarter."

"That is hardly a reason to want him dead, even if Keeton had mentioned dismissal to Bennet," Barlow mused.

"Not likely. It isn't as if he has benefited in any way from the death. Some of what Symes said could just be petty jealousy. No one else mentioned any tension between Keeton and Bennet," Lord Robbie added. "Besides, if the motivation for the assassination was political and military, then we need to look more deeply into Bennet's political views and philosophies."

"Although, if he sympathized with the French, why would he want to prolong the war?"

"Because by doing so, the British militia would be weakened, their focus would be on the continent and it would be easier to create disturbances, even revolution, here." The earl's voice was very somber as he considered the possibilities.

The two men contemplated this idea silently for a few moments. The door of the study opened. Lord Robbie's hunched shoulders relaxed as he looked up to see Halstead and Bellingham enter.

Barlow grinned and dropped his pen as he rose to greet Felix with a kiss. "I didn't think you'd be here before the end of the week," he said when they finally sat down.

Halstead, who had sat down at the table, answered. "We thought we'd come and join you two on your holiday at the seaside."

Robbie threw a scrunched-up piece of paper at him. "We've hardly left this room in the week we've been here." He blinked at the window, as if he were only just aware of the bright sunshine streaming through the open curtains. "Ah, the rain must have stopped."

The others laughed as the earl quickly reported on their findings about Peter Bennet. When he drew to an end, Halstead took the page where Robbie had recorded his interview with Symes. "Perhaps Symes had a clearer insight into Lord Keeton's misgivings. They do say that a gentleman's valet knows more about him and his thoughts than anyone else."

Barlow laughed. "Not having the luxury of a valet, I cannot say, but I have heard that no gentleman is his valet's hero."

Robbie raised an eyebrow. "Mycroft says it is a pleasure to ensure that I am properly dressed. He claims that I have the perfect figure to wear the most fashionable coats and that my calves are shapely and look excellent in the new pantaloons. He rules my wardrobe with an iron fist but, without him, I would not look half the gentleman I am." The others laughed as he stretched out his legs and studied his gleaming Hessian boots with a satisfied smile.

Halstead was the first to return to business. "I thought Keeton had dismissed surplus staff when he took over the estate. Why is Symes still here? He doesn't seem to have any definite function."

Jasper himself, who had arrived in time to hear the end

of this conversation, answered. "I did cut back on the staff here because I do not need twenty footmen or two dozen housemaids, but I kept on two or three of the older members of staff, those who were unlikely to find employment elsewhere. Symes is a crusty old bugger who spent his younger years in the militia but my father relied on him, so he is now assisting the butler." He poured himself a brandy and sat down, nodding at the papers in Robbie's hands. "Have you discovered anything of note?"

Lord Robbie glanced at Halstead before saying, "Nothing that implicates Peter Bennet, but we agree that the circumstances of your father's death do appear strange."

"Bellingham and I have been following up on the names we found in the dossier you showed us." Halstead grimaced. "I have subjected poor Louisa to countless tedious dinners with majors and colonels who have regaled us with endless stories of their exploits in the war. Bellingham and I have also been wading through floods of papers, letters, documents and so on. I believe that the people mentioned on the pages you found are not involved in any plots. However, my investigations have raised suspicions about some other people whom we are looking into."

Keeton nodded, relief mingling with sadness as he realized his father had probably been murdered, but that he would be able to take revenge against his killers.

"In the meantime, we have these documents to read, to see what connections we can find between these people and Lord Keeton's death and how that relates to any current plots of treason," Barlow said.

"What about the letters Bennet sent to his sister? Have any of them given any insight into where he is or whether they are involved in any treasonous plots?" Halstead picked up a bundle of letters that Robbie had placed on the table.

"I find it odd that someone like Bennet should be such close friends with a man who has made his career in the militia. Turner even spent a few days here, visiting Bennet."

Jasper frowned. "Why did Bennet not introduce Turner to his sister? I find it odd that he was living so close to his own home, to his sister, and yet he hardly saw her during the time he worked for my father."

"That is odd," agreed Halstead. "And it suggests that Belinda is not in any way involved. I think her only crime has been loyalty to her brother and a fierce commitment to family."

"Which is understandable when you consider that she has spent so much of her life alone. I can understand why she wants to feel connected to her brother, even if he seems to have ignored her except when he needs her help," the earl said.

"Well, let's continue sorting through these documents," Halstead said.

Jasper watched as they settled down and then left them to their work. There wasn't much he could do to help them and Alicia had spoken of going for a walk along the shore and maybe visiting Belinda. Joining them, would help calm his mind.

A few hours later, Robbie pushed back the hair that had fallen onto his forehead. "We need Eliot for this work. He is meticulous and doesn't mind hours of poring over minutia."

Bellingham commented, "He took the coded pages with him and is seeing if he can decipher them, but he has not had any success as yet. We've both been trying various keywords and phrases, but so far, nothing has worked."

Halstead looked up from the document he was reading. "I don't suppose he would come now. He won't leave Cece when she is so close to giving birth."

Robbie huffed. "No, he won't. But this is relentless work." He got up and stretched his arms over his head. "I think I'm going to take a break." He glanced out the window to where Jane and his sons were playing with a cricket bat and ball in the garden.

Halstead smiled understandingly, but as Robbie started walking towards the door, Barlow said, "Wait a moment. This looks interesting." He had a notebook open in front of him. A slip of paper had been tucked into its pages.

Robbie stopped behind Barlow's chair and read the list of names that had been scrawled there. Next to each, were letters and symbols that, at first glance, made no sense.

Halstead reached for the page and looked at the list. "These are all names of high-ranking military officers," he observed. "And none of them are the ones who were on the pages we've already looked at or even considered."

Robbie nodded. "What connects all of them and what do the signs next to their names mean?"

Barlow turned over the pages of the notebook and then groaned. "These pages are also written in some kind of code, different from the other one. It seems odd that one person would use two completely different codes."

The earl reached for another piece of paper and began jotting down these names and the others they had found, writing them in different groupings depending on the information he knew about each one. "There is something that links all of these people. I will work on finding the connection while you work on the code." He reached for a book on one of the shelves that contained the listings of all officers and their service records. He began flipping through the pages and scrawling notes on various sheets of paper. Halstead helped him while Barlow and Bellingham began copying the coded pages of the notebook.

They worked in silence until, about forty-five minutes later, Jane came in to remind her husband that he had promised to spend some time with his sons and that it was almost their bedtime.

Chapter 6

THE DAY WAS perfect for a picnic. Fluffy white clouds floated slowly across the deep summer blue sky, creating a panorama of shifting shapes and images. A gentle breeze wafted over the meadow from time to time, keeping the picnickers cool, and birds sang merrily as they flitted from tree to tree.

Alica stretched out on the green and blue plaid blanket and sighed happily. "I much prefer this kind of life to the hustle and bustle of London."

Nell smiled dreamily as she weaved daisies into her hair that was hanging loose around her shoulders. "It is glorious here. Nature provides so much inspiration for creativity. I think I have written some of my best poetry in the last few days." She reached for a rich, red-skinned peach and bit into it. "Fruit tastes much sweeter in the country than in London and nothing in the city can rival the majesty of trees and the glory of meadows resplendent with wildflowers on a summer's day. It is almost an insult to compare the beauty of the wildflowers to jewels. They are far more beautiful."

Messy, who had been wading in the nearby stream with

Gregory and Michael, wandered to where the others were sitting. The bottom of her dress was wet and her shoes and stockings were missing. Jane sat up straight, looking somewhat alarmed. "Where are my sons? Have you left them alone at the river?"

Messy plopped down onto the blanket and selected a little cake, then swiped her tongue across the delicious buttercream icing. "They're enjoying using their nets to catch tadpoles and didn't want to leave." When she saw Jane's alarm increase and her elder sister began to rise, she relented. "They're with Nanny. Don't be such a fusspot."

Robbie and Lord Halstead, who had been fishing for trout with Lord Keeton, sauntered up to where the ladies were sitting chatting. Robbie kissed Jane as if he had last seen her weeks ago instead of having left her here an hour or so ago. "Did you save me some cakes?"

"Of course." She studied his face carefully. "Being in the fresh air has been good for you. You are looking far more relaxed than you have been the last few days."

He finished the mouthful of cake he had been eating. "Mmm, this is good. I wonder if our cook would be offended if we took her the recipe." He tucked a loose strand of Jane's hair behind her ear. "We have been working hard but we haven't really made any real progress. If we could get some kind of breakthrough, it would help."

His sons, hearing his voice, came hurtling towards him, showing him the pollywogs they had caught with their nets and which were swimming slowly at the bottom of the glass jars they were using to collect them. Robbie admired them and asked if they had the right kind of food to give the tadpoles.

Jasper Keeton leaned against the trunk of the spreading oak tree which sheltered the group from the sun. He was an only child and had a somewhat lonely childhood, with few friends nearby, and this raucous, lovable family filled his heart with wonder. His eyes sought out Alicia, who was still lying stretched out on the blanket, an open book resting on her stomach. He admired her graceful form, the curve of her hips and the swell of her buttocks and his breath caught in his throat as he suddenly imagined her surrounded by her own children, *his* children, as they romped here in the grounds of his home exploring all the wonders of the natural world. His vision enlarged to include Belinda holding a beautiful baby with soft blonde hair.

Ali felt his gaze on her and sat up, looking at him quizzically. He smiled and sat down next to her, reaching for a bunch of grapes.

Her eyes followed his hand as he plucked one and popped it into his mouth. She swallowed and the tip of her tongue slid out of her mouth as if she were the one tasting the fruit. Her moist, pink lips were like a berry waiting to be tasted. The sounds of the others faded and all he could see was her deep blue eyes, wide behind her glasses, and the desire that simmered in their depths.

He pulled another grape from the stalk and raised it to her mouth. He ran it softly across her lips. She opened her mouth and he placed it inside, her tongue just brushing his finger as she bit down on the succulent fruit and he gently swiped his thumb over the juice that moistened her lips.

A low clearing of a throat nearby brought Jasper back to his senses. He glanced up to see the earl watching him, a glint of amusement and understanding in his eyes. Jasper was not usually easily embarrassed but he felt his cheeks heat. Then he looked at Ali again and he squared his shoulders. He was not ashamed of his admiration for her. And he knew she returned his affection. In time, that affection would blossom into love and when all this trouble about his father was over, he would ask her to marry him. And somehow, against all the odds, Belinda would be included in their relationship.

He gave Robbie a curt nod, but before he could say anything, the sound of horses' hooves echoed through the glade where they were enjoying their picnic.

A large black stallion, at least seventeen hands, crashed through the trees. The rider brought the horse to a halt a few paces from the group of picnickers.

Jane, her face pale, was on her feet, Michael in her arms. "What the hell do you think you're doing? There are children here." Her voice was shrill with fear for her children's safety. Robbie had also risen to his feet, his one arm protectively around her while the other rested on Gregory's shoulder.

The rider raised a sardonic eyebrow at her, a slow mirthless smile assessing the termagant who stood before him. He doffed his hat. "My apologies, ma'am. I am not used to finding people in the path of my afternoon ride." His smooth voice conveyed arrogance and disdain, a criticism of people who disrupted his usual routine rather than any hint of apology or contriteness for the harm he might have caused. He glowered at Michael who was sobbing from the fright.

Jasper stepped forward, holding out his hand in welcome. "Xander, it's good to see you. As always, you know how to make a dramatic entrance."

The harsh lines of the rider's face softened slightly. "Jasper, I did not know you were back in the country." His eyes skimmed over the party, pausing when they took in Nell who was staring at him with wide blue eyes, her hands clasped in front of her. Even though she was dressed in breeches, her loose-fitting shirt could not disguise the fact that she was a woman, a very attractive woman. His dark eyes raked over her, taking in her dark hair crowned with daisies, curling softly onto her shoulders, the creaminess of her complexion, her lithe figure and her bare feet.

Lord Keeton gestured towards the earl. "Summerson, may I present Lord Lamercier, the Earl of Medwell and his wife, Lady Medwell, Lord Halstead and the Misses Goodwin."

Messy, undaunted by the imposing stranger, walked up to the large horse that was tossing its head impatiently. She ran her hand down its neck, whispering soothing words. The horse nickered, nuzzling her shoulder gently.

Lord Summerson showed the first sign that his composure could be ruffled. "Lucifer is not usually friendly to strangers. I am the only person who can handle him." Messy ignored him and continued to talk to the horse who was behaving more like a kitten than a majestic steed.

Jane, who, now that the danger for her sons had passed, shifted her concern to her sisters. Lord Summerson had a reputation as the worst kind of rake, and many unsavory stories circulated in the *beau monde* about his exploits. Messy did not seem affected by him but Nell was staring at him as if he were a demigod who had deigned to descend from his lofty height to mingle with mere mortals. Jane stepped in front of her younger, very impressionable sister.

Her horror increased when Jasper said, "Xander, I am having a small dinner party on Thursday night. Please join us."

With another sweeping glance over Keeton's guests, his lips turned up mockingly, especially when he saw the fierce protectiveness on Jane's face. He focused on Nell when he answered. "It would be my pleasure." With a crack of his horsewhip, he urged his horse forward and disappeared into the trees on the other side of the glade.

"You are acquainted with Summerson?" Robbie asked Keeton. He deliberately avoided using his title.

Keeton seemed oblivious to the undercurrents Summerson's appearance had created. "We played together when we were little and he has always been a good friend to me. We don't see much of each other now, as he is more often in London, but he is still my closest friend." He looked around, suddenly aware of the impression Summerson had made on his guests. "I do apologize. I am sure he didn't mean to frighten you and he certainly wouldn't harm anyone, but he does carry himself with a degree of hauteur that can make him appear unfriendly."

Michael was still sobbing in Jane's arms. "There is no excuse for his behavior. A simple apology costs nothing and goes a long way to easing a difficult situation. I don't care who he is, I will not let him harm anyone in my family."

Alicia put her empty tea cup down onto the table. "That was a delicious scone."

"It was, indeed," agreed Jasper. He and Ali had walked down to the village after a late breakfast to bring Belinda a copy of *An Enquiry Concerning the Principles of Morals* that she wanted to read.

"Do have another one." Belinda offered her the plate.

Jasper reached over and also took one then, quickly, almost half the scone disappeared into his mouth. "Hmm, that is good." A smear of cream was left on his upper lip and Ali, who had been watching him and not taken a bite of her own pastry, swiped her finger over his lip and then licked the cream off her finger.

Time seemed to stand still. Nobody breathed. Ali pushed her glasses up her nose and gave a self-conscious laugh. "I'm sorry," she whispered.

Jasper took a breath and placed his hand over hers, turning it palm up and rubbing circles over it with his thumb.

"I'm not." His voice was husky. Shivers ricocheted through Ali's body and she shifted on her chair.

Belinda, watching them, also fidgeted as her body heated and her skin felt tight. It was difficult to breathe and her lips tingled. As if he knew exactly what she was feeling, Jasper quirked his eyebrow at her. He held her gaze with his as he raised Ali's hand and kissed her palm. Then he let go and continued his tea, a smirk in his eyes as they talked about the novel he had bought for Belinda in London.

When they had finished tea, Ali pushed back her chair and said, "There is a wonderful beach between here and Jasper's house. Can we go down there? It's ridiculous that we're so close to the sea and yet we haven't spent much time on the beaches and I haven't looked for any fossils yet."

It didn't take long for the three of them to make their way to a quiet cove with high cliffs above them and blue-green water stretching beyond them. Unlike most beaches in Dorset, this one had golden-brown sand that stretched in a lazy curve to a rocky outcrop of rocks about half a mile away.

The early afternoon sunlight sparkled off the sea as waves whispered along the beach. The only other sound was that of three seagulls squabbling over some mollusks on the rocks. Ali bent down and let a slow wave break over her hand.

"It's not cold at all." She stood up and gazed out at the clear water. "Is it very deep? Is it safe to swim?"

Jasper was standing close to her. He placed an arm around her shoulders. "It is reasonably shallow and the current is not too strong."

Belinda came up on Ali's other side. "We cannot swim." She sounded a little shocked. Even though she had been raised in a home where liberal ideas were propagated, that liberalism had not stretched to include an openness about physical matters. "We do not have bathing dresses or a bathing machine."

Ali laughed and slipped out of Jasper's hold. "When my sisters and I were growing up, we never bothered with bathing dresses. We often swam naked in the river near our house." She looked around the beach. "Besides, there is no one here. Only us."

Jasper grinned. "This is a private beach, not open to the public. No one is likely to disturb us here."

Ali removed her straw bonnet and light pelisse, dropping them onto the sand above the tide line on the beach. The other two turned to watch her as she unbuttoned her sprig muslin dress and shrugged it off, leaving it in a heap on the sand. She bent down and untied her half boots, tugging them off, and then, with a glance at Jasper and Belinda, untied her garters and rolled her stockings down, revealing shapely calves and well-turned ankles.

She stood up and pulled off her petticoat and stays, leaving only her shift to cover her nakedness. It was made of very thin linen and, with the sun shining through it, became completely transparent. Jasper and Belinda both raked their eyes over Ali's pert breasts, her narrow waist and down to her curvy hips. The dark shadow of hair at the juncture of her thighs made them both hold their breath.

Leaving her clothes in a heap and her glasses on top of them, Ali straightened her shoulders, walked between the other two and waded into the water, squealing when a wave broke over her thighs, wetting her shift which clung to her body. Jasper held his breath as he admired the very pretty roundness of her buttocks. He wanted to cup it in his hands, to trace his fingers down the line in the middle and tease her pussy as he had that day in his laboratory. A quick look at Belinda's face showed that she was thinking similar thoughts.

He shucked his coat, loosened his cravat, and pulled his

shirt over his head. Ali was standing thigh deep in the sea, waves swirling around her as she watched him. Belinda had also turned towards him. Both women held their breath as they saw, for the first time, the clear outline of muscles on his arms and chest that rippled with power.

Jasper grinned at them and then strode into the water to join Ali. The bulge of his cock in his fitted breeches became more pronounced as the heat of his body adjusted to the cold water that splashed around him. He faced Ali, placing his hands on her hips and pulling her closer so that he could kiss her. She placed her hands on his chest, reveling in the hardness of his muscles and the fineness of the dark hair that was now flat against his chest as it tapered to a V that disappeared beneath the water.

Belinda watched them uncertainly for a few moments, her arms crossed over her chest. She bit her lip and then made up her mind. If this very strange menage was going to work, then she would have to be as bold in these matters as she was when she defended her philosophical and political opinions. With a deep breath, she began to take off her clothes. Jasper and Ali brought their kiss to an end and turned to watch her. She folded each piece of clothing, placing each item in a neat pile next to Ali's scattered garments. Then, with a determined tilt of her chin, she waded into the water. Ali broke away from Jasper and met her halfway, taking hold of her hand and leading her deeper.

Meanwhile, Jasper had plunged into the water and was now swimming with strong strokes through the waves, his arms and shoulders powerfully propelling him forward. When he was deeper, he stood up, pushing his wet hair off his forehead as water dripped down his chest, and beckoned the others closer.

They raced over to him, Belinda an arm's length ahead of Alicia. She stood up and shook her head, spraying water over the others. Ali squealed as spray from Belinda's hair sprinkled her. She scooped up water and threw it, aiming at Belinda but missed. It hit Jasper's face. He spluttered, wiped his hand across his mouth and then caught her arm and yanked her closer. "Naughty, naughty."

She giggled but then fell quiet as she saw the stern expression on his face. She dropped her head, and even Belinda took a step back. Neither of the women noticed the twinkle in his eyes as he said, "As soon as we finish our swim, I'll have to teach you how to show more respect, young lady."

He ruffled her wet hair and placed a kiss on her forehead. She breathed deeply and leaned closer to him. Jasper looked over Ali's head to where Belinda was standing two feet away from them. "Come closer," he instructed.

Ali made a place for Belinda and the three of them hugged one another as the sun shone down on them, warming their heads while the cool water swirled against their legs.

Jasper brushed a kiss against Ali's lips and then she moved behind Belinda, while Jasper cupped Belinda's chin and lowered his head to her lips. To keep her balance, Belinda placed her hands on his shoulders and leaned closer to him, enjoying the feel of his smooth skin and hard muscles beneath her hands. Her mouth tingled as his lips pressed against hers.

Ali pressed her body close to Belinda's and slid her arms around her waist, fitting them between Jasper and Belinda. She moved them up and cupped Belinda's breasts, kneading and molding them until Belinda moaned against Jasper's mouth. Jasper responded by prodding her mouth open and sliding his tongue into her mouth, penetrating her warmth and tasting her sweetness.

Belinda gasped. Ali began kissing her shoulders and trailed her tongue along the curve of her neck, nipping lightly as she moved. Her own breasts felt swollen and tight and she rubbed the hardened nipples against Belinda's back. Her right hand traveled down Belinda's stomach, brushing against Jasper's as well. She paused when she touched his swollen and heavy cock. She rubbed her thumb against it and smiled when he groaned as he pressed himself against her hand and his tongue deeper into Belinda's mouth.

Her hand continued down beneath the water until she found the juncture between Belinda's thighs. The gentle swell of the sea had lifted her shift up around her hips and Ali's fingers traced circles against the silkiness of the skin just above her mound. She tugged the soft hair and slipped along the outer folds that covered her pussy.

Jasper, still kissing Belinda, moved one hand to take hold of Ali's waist and slid the other down to join her hand between Belinda's legs. He guided Ali's hand as they parted her folds and discovered the sleekness of the inner whorls. Her nubbin was hard and poking up and Jasper slowly led Ali's finger around its base and along the sides, finally letting Ali's hand go as he flicked his finger along the top while Ali continued to stimulate the sides. Belinda caught her breath as sensations whirled through her body, centering in the core of her private parts. She had fingered herself some nights when she lay in her bed, especially when her thoughts were focused on Jasper and Alicia, but never had she felt anything as powerful as the sensations that rocked through her now as she yielded to their combined touches.

Jasper and Ali's fingers worked faster and faster until Belinda knew nothing except the three of them surrounded by the endlessly swirling sea. In spite of the coolness of the water, her body was hot. Her nipples were hard and she pressed against Jasper's chest, creating even more sensations.

She closed her eyes. Every muscle in her body felt like the softest silky syllabub and if the other two had not been holding her, she would have melted into a soft heap under the water. She moaned as the sensations increased. Jasper's finger circled her hole and then plunged into it, causing a burning sensation for a moment but, quickly, the sharp pain mutated into a rush of pure pleasure. Her back arched and she cried out, her cries joining the mewing of the seagulls swooping overhead.

She collapsed against Jasper's body and she only murmured softly when he lifted her into his arms. He carried her out of the sea to the hot sands.

Belinda sat on the sand, letting the sun dry her. She ran her fingers through her loose hair, lifting it off her shoulders. Jasper used his shirt to rub his torso dry and Ali was squeezing water out of her shift.

When they were all partly dry, Jasper turned to Ali. "Now, little one, it's time to discover the consequences of your earlier disrespect."

Ali turned to him, blinking her eyes, which were suddenly very wide and as blue as the sea. "But we were just having fun. I didn't really disrespect you." She glanced at Belinda. "I was trying to splash Belinda. If she hadn't moved, I wouldn't have splashed you."

He shook his head in mock severity. "That's no excuse." His voice dropped lower as he continued. "Besides, Belinda had her reward. It's time for yours."

The warmth that flooded Ali had little to do with the sun. Jasper sat down on a flat rock and patted his knees before he beckoned to her. "Come here, miss. If you delay, the consequences might be very severe."

Belinda was sitting up straight, her eyes wide as she looked from one to the other. She could not imagine what was about to happen. But Ali suspected. Instead of feeling horrified, she was startled to realize her body was tingling with anticipation. She wanted to know what it would feel like to lie over his lap and have his large hand smack her bottom.

She swallowed and then walked slowly over to him. She stood a few paces from him, staring at his hands that were resting on his thighs. He tilted his head to the side and patted his thighs again. She moved closer, her knees brushing against his. Slowly, she lowered herself over his lap, trying to pull her shift over her bottom, but Jasper took hold of her hands and moved them in front of her. She used them to brace herself but he shifted her so that her bottom was more central and both her hands and feet were dangling. She had to clutch his calf to stop herself from falling.

Belinda was fascinated. She moved closer until she was in front of Ali's face. Jasper stroked his fingers through her hair. "If you hold Ali's hands, it will help her."

Belinda nodded and did what Jasper had asked. She held Ali's hands tightly and Ali smiled at her. Jasper, satisfied that everything was ready, ran his hand over the roundness of Ali's bum. His strokes became firmer and firmer and the skin warmed under his touch. He scrunched up the drying linen of her shift so that he could see the nakedness of her bottom. He paused a moment to admire the firm heart shape and then brought his hand down on the whiteness of her skin.

"Ow! That hurt," Ali called out but she wriggled on his lap and pushed her bum up, ready for the next strike. He responded to her silent request, this time bringing his hand down on the other cheek. He was not spanking her very hard. This was, after all, a fun spanking, not a punishment one. Ali squealed. He settled into a rhythm of spanking first the right side and then the left, high and then low. The rhythm was soothing and the smacks were stimulating. It was a strange combination and Ali was lulled by the waves of sensations that flowed through her.

Belinda caressed her arms and began kissing her face

while Jasper continued to spank her. Her body softened, melting against her two lovers. She had never imagined such delight and pleasure.

She was unaware that her pussy was soaked with her juices. She closed her eyes and rode the carousel of delight. She soared on the wings of pleasure. Jasper brought his hand down in a final hard strike and her body shattered.

She did not know how much later it was when the world around her began to resume its normal functions. She was sitting on Jasper's lap, cuddled against his bare chest. Belinda was kneeling with her head against his knee and her hands on Ali's legs. There was a glorious intimacy that could not be explained. Somehow, Ali knew that if it had been only her and Jasper, it would have been good, but she could never have reached the sublime heights that Belinda's presence had brought.

"How are you feeling, little love?" Jasper's voice was deep and satisfied.

She nodded. "Good." Her voice was raspy as if she had been screaming. With a blush, she realized that was exactly what she had been doing.

She shifted on his lap and suddenly stopped.

"What is it, little one?"

"Nothing. Only. Well." In spite of all that she had shared with both Jasper and Belinda, it was suddenly impossible to articulate what she was feeling.

Belinda's hand moved in a gentle sweep up her thigh and bumped into the hard bulge of Jasper's cock that was pressing against Ali's bum. She quickly pulled her hand back. Jasper chuckled.

Ali found the courage to say what was worrying her. "Belinda and I have been pleasured, but you haven't."

He chuckled again. "I enjoy bringing you pleasure."

Ali shook her head. "That isn't fair." She had recovered

sufficiently to know what she wanted to do. What must be done.

She slid off his lap and knelt next to Belinda, who slipped her arm around Ali and kissed her cheek. "Are you all right?"

Ali nodded. "Very well. But I will be even better when we've taken care of Jasper." She reached up and cupped his bulge, squeezing lightly.

He tensed and swore softly. Ali looked up, alarm in her eyes. "I'm sorry. Did I hurt you?"

It was impossible to speak. He shook his head and breathed deeply. He placed his hand over hers and guided her to his cock, showing her just how to touch him the way he liked best. Belinda watched for a moment and then placed her hand tentatively next to Ali's. Jasper groaned. Encouraged by this reaction, Ali became even bolder. She unfastened the top button of his falls and slid her fingers against the hot flesh of his crotch.

The next two buttons followed quickly and his hot, hard cock sprang out, jutting lewdly out at the two women. They both paused for a moment and then Belinda touched the slit which was weeping clear liquid. She traced it around the head of his cock that was so swollen, it was almost purple.

Ali admired the glistening mushroom-shaped head and then leaned forward and placed her tongue on the slit, lapping the juices that were gathering there. She sat back, her lips now misty with him. "It's strange. Not quite bitter. A little musky."

Belinda needed to taste for herself. She opened her mouth wide and took the head fully into her mouth, exploring it with her tongue. Ali gripped the stalk with her hand and squeezed. She began to lick the sides, following the throbbing vein to the base where his balls were tight and drawing up against his body. She kissed one and then drew it into her mouth, sucking softly.

Belinda let go of the head with a popping sound and then also ran her tongue down the side.

Jasper was usually able to control his responses but the sensations of having these two women explore him were overwhelming. He could hardly breathe. He retained only just enough sense to realize that neither had ever seen a man's seed spew out as he climaxed. Ali had covered the head with her mouth but he pushed her back a little more roughly than he intended. She sat back and stared at him. He placed his hand on his cock and Belinda also sat back to watch as he stroked himself rapidly. His body tensed. His balls tightened. Long ropes of sperm jetted out of him in long spurts, gathering on his stomach and thighs.

Chapter 7

BELINDA ENTERED the drawing room slowly, behind Dr. and Mrs. Wilby. She had never before entered Ashbourne Hall, even though Peter had worked here. It was an elegant house and yet comfortable and welcoming, with large windows that let in the light during the day and looked out over the wide sweep of land that surrounded the house.

She wasn't sure that she was welcome in this splendid place and yet, as her eyes wandered over the brightly colored silks and satins of the ladies' dresses and the candlelight glimmering off exquisite jewels, her mind was busy trying to analyze Jasper Keeton, to categorize him and understand him. She had, for some inexplicable reason she had never been able to understand, found the masterful way he had insisted she dance with him at the assembly over a year ago very arousing, alluring. And the last few weeks had been remarkable. She blushed as she remembered the way she and Ali and Jasper had pleasured each other on the beach. Perhaps there was a way for her to fit into this world, a way for her to learn to love Jasper and Ali. And perhaps they would welcome her into their lives, perhaps they could love her too.

And yet, she reminded herself as she looked around at the rich furnishings and elegant decorations, both Ali and Jasper lived in a world that she had been taught to despise. Would she betray all of her values because of the fleeting pleasure they brought her? With an effort, she reminded herself that Lord Jasper Keeton had been very highhanded with tenants and staff and he had treated Peter badly.

She had received another letter from Peter that morning. This time, her brother had warned her about becoming too attached to a scoundrel like Keeton and to be careful not to trust anyone who was not family. There was even a hint of criticism because she had sought the assistance of Lord Halstead and his spymasters to clear Peter's name. For someone who was in hiding, her brother knew a lot about what was happening in her life. But he had also begged her to believe in him, to trust him. And to help him in any way she could. He was her only family. She looked across the room of elegantly clad guests. This was not her milieu. She needed to help her brother as she had promised to do and then she would return to her solitary life, where she could think about ways to make the world a better place.

Which the people in this room were doing every day. She was honest enough to realize that the Goodwins and Lord Keeton had far more of an impact on society, were doing far more to ensure that all people were given opportunities to fulfill their potential, than she had ever done. And they showed far more compassion and kindness to people of all backgrounds than her father or brother ever had.

When they had been walking back from the beach the other day, Jasper had stopped to talk to one of the fishermen, listening to his long list of ills and woes with patience and compassion. He had arranged for the doctor to visit the old fisherman. Although he hadn't said so, it was clear that he would pay for the costs. And when he and Ali had visited her, he had been kind and considerate to the elderly Mrs. Gibbs who looked after her house, thanking her for the scones she had made and offering to carry the tea tray to the kitchen. Belinda had also heard a different side to the stories of tenants who had been removed from their holdings. Lord Keeton had offered to assist those who were interested in becoming more profitable but had pensioned off those who were either too old or too lazy to work the land. The older ones had been settled in cottages. The two or three tenants who had been sponging off the estate for years had been sent to find work on the docks or elsewhere. Lord Keeton was not the cold-hearted aristocrat that she had first thought him to be.

Her eyes sought him out and her breath caught in her throat. He was so tall, so imposing, and yet there was compassion on his face as he listened to Lady Sitwell describe her latest pains and ills.

Alicia joined Jasper and the light of the candles from a chandelier above them looked like halos. Belinda's heart beat faster and she had to grip her hands tightly. In spite of her determination to keep her distance from Jasper Keeton, to dislike him, her dreams in the last few weeks had been a tangled web of images of his hands, his mouth, his hair. It didn't help her equilibrium and rationality that Alicia's smile and shapely chin, deep blue eyes and curvy figure formed an integral part of those dreams.

Alicia, who was describing her find of some unusual moss to Jasper, stopped mid-sentence. Some instinct, like a magnetic force, tugged her gaze towards the door where Belinda had just entered. Jasper's eyes followed hers. Alicia was aware of the gleam of admiration that deepened the hazel of his eyes, even as she was watching Belinda. How was it possible to be so aware of two people at the same time? To be attracted to both of them? When she was with each of them separately, tenderness and affection filled her heart, but when they were all together, it was as if a scientist had found a potent chemical combination that bubbled and boiled, ready to explode. The afternoon on the beach had been a glorious hint of the possibilities of the future the three of them could create.

Belinda, after a whispered consultation with Mrs. Wilby, took a deep breath and made her way through the crowd until she was standing in front of Jasper and Alicia.

Alicia took her hands, aware even through the silk of their gloves, of her warmth and the firmness of her grip. "I am so glad to see you. I was worried that you might cry off."

Belinda glanced at Lord Keeton. "My lord, thank you for inviting me tonight."

He nodded his head in greeting, a smile teasing the corners of his mouth. "Welcome to my house, Miss Bennet."

Alicia placed her hand on her hips in a very unladylike manner. "Why is everyone being so formal? Considering the intimacy we have shared recently, it is absurd to go back to being *Miss Bennet* and *Lord Keeton*."

The other two laughed at her words and relaxed. "You are right," Keeton agreed. He reached for Belinda's hand. "I am glad that you are here."

There was no mistaking the sincerity in his voice and Belinda felt her cheeks heat, especially when he kept hold of her hand. She tried to dismiss the sense of reassurance and comfort she drew from his touch that was so at odds with her usual determination to be independent and self-reliant.

She was relieved when the butler announced that dinner was served and the guests began to walk to the dining room. Jasper looked from Alicia to her, uncertainty clouding his eyes. He did not let go of Belinda's hand, but he brushed

Ali's arm with his other. She shivered as goosebumps formed where he touched her. Then she smiled and stepped back. "I'll walk with Nell. She's on her own."

Ali joined her twin who was hovering behind most of the guests. "Come, Nell, we need to go."

Nell looked thoughtfully at her sister. "Are you happy?"

"I am, truly, I am. There is something satisfying about seeing the two people I love together, especially when there is so often tension between them." As they began walking, Ali continued, "I am not sure if there is any possibility of a future for us, but until we have to think of such things, I will take the joy of each moment as it comes." She glanced at Nell. "And you, are you all right?"

Nell's smile was too bright and it didn't reach her eyes. "Of course. Everyone Lord Keeton has invited is very pleasant."

"And yet the one person you hoped would be here, isn't." Ali slowed her steps and slid her arm around her twin's shoulders. "Nell, I really want you to be happy, to find love and joy. But Lord Summerson is the kind of man who breaks women's hearts as carelessly as little children discard sticks they have used in their games."

Nell's only response was a watery smile and a flick of her head as she and Ali sought their places at the table.

Ali was thrilled that Lord Keeton, eschewing convention, had placed himself at the middle of the table with her on one side of him and Belinda on the other. He looked very smug when he sat down and gestured to the butler to begin pouring the wine as the footmen served a light cream of mushroom soup. They had only just tasted the soup when the door opened and Lord Summerson sauntered into the room, as casually as if he were returning to his own home after riding in the fields. He wore his black dinner jacket and breeches with the kind of casual elegance that spoke of his self-assurance and arrogance.

Keeton grinned at him. "Glad you could make it, Summerson."

Summerson showed no indication of remorse or apology for his tardiness as he strode around the table to the place set for him between Jane and Nell. As he sat and gestured for the butler to fill his wine glass, he said, "You have an exceptional cellar and if you have kept the chef your father had, then the meal is sure to be excellent." A footman had served him some soup which he now began to eat with a satisfied air.

The guests had fallen silent during the last few moments, and Keeton showed his impeccable manners and his competence as host when he turned to the earl and asked, "Would you let me know where you get the flies you were using today? They were much more effective than mine."

Robbie raised an eyebrow but answered smoothly, "I make my own. It's one of my hobbies and I have spent many hours perfecting the perfect ones for different conditions. I will gladly show you how to do them."

The rest of the guests relaxed and began chatting again as the footmen removed the soup plates and brought in the next course, which included the fish the gentlemen had caught that afternoon.

Summerson turned to Jane. "I trust, my lady, that your children are well?"

Jane had to respond, but her voice was very icy as she drew on all the dignity of her position as a countess and an elder sister. "They have recovered from their fright, although I had to coax my younger son to approach his father's horse without fear. I trust, my lord, that your horse has not been inconvenienced by any other inconvenient passersby in his path."

Nell drew in her breath at Jane's words but was surprised when a low chuckle emerged from Lord Summerson. He raised his glass. "Touché, madam. You are a formidable opponent and completely wasted on your husband who is far too affable for someone with your asperity. If ever you wanted to seek more inspiring company, just send me a note."

Nell gasped and Jane began to bristle again but Robbie slipped his arm around his wife's shoulders. He left Jane to answer, though. "My husband offers all the excitement and stimulation I need." The slight emphasis she gave certain words made it very clear that she was talking of far more than just conversation.

Nell bit her lip, her face coloring lightly. She was not usually tongue-tied or very shy yet she had no idea what to say to the man seated next to her. His very presence intimidated her. This close, she was more aware of just how tall he was, just how hard his muscles were beneath his smooth satin breeches. With each breath she took, she was conscious of the spiciness of his cologne, the heady male smell that clung to him. She was so deeply lost in her thoughts that it took her a moment to realize he had turned from Jane and was now asking her a question. She had no idea what a pretty sight she was, her dark hair arranged softly on top of her head with gleaming curls daintily framing her face, her cheeks flushed a soft pink and her white muslin dress giving her a fairy-like appearance. The rest of the guests were chatting quietly although Jane was trying to hear what Summerson said to Nell, who was far too impressionable and with a romantic disposition that was far too likely to be impressed by someone as dangerous as he was, rather than keeping her distance.

Lord Summerson tilted his head as he addressed Nell. "Miss Goodwin, you look so very different this evening from when I first encountered you that it took me a few moments to recognize you."

Nell bristled but could think of no appropriate response. She silently cursed her awkwardness, wishing she had the suaveness of the character she created in her books who always knew exactly how to respond to urbane insults.

Lord Summerson was amused by how flustered she was and entranced by the pretty pink of her cheeks. He had not heard her speak and tried again to goad her into answering him. Surely, with a sister as quick to speak as the countess, Eleanor Goodwin should have learned something about repartee.

His eyebrow shot up but she did not see because she was studiously examining the empty soup plate in front of her. His mouth tightened. Perhaps she was the fool of the family. Jasper was clearly interested in the other twin and he could hear her talking about Prichard's *Researches into the Physical History of Man.* He had read the book and was fascinated about the idea that in spite of the differences between people, essentially all humans were united by a common origin. Perhaps she shared her sister's interest in scientific subjects.

He swallowed down the last of his wine and signaled for the butler to refill his glass and then tried again. "Miss Goodwin, what is your opinion of Prichard's book?"

Nell was furious with herself for behaving like a school-girl who had never been in company, especially because this man was the one above all others she really wanted to impress. She took a sip of wine before saying, "I have not read it, although Ali has explained some of his thoughts to me."

Her voice was just as low and sweet as Summerson had expected it to be. Now that she had broken through her reserve, she was able to speak more confidently. She turned to face Summerson, her deep blue eyes wide with enthusiasm. "I don't think his ideas are all that original. Shakespeare said something similar more than a hundred years ago."

"*Hath not a Jew eyes? Hath not a Jew hands, organs, dimensions, senses, affections, passions?*" Summerson quoted.

Nell's eyes grew wider. "Yes." She could think of nothing else to say.

Summerson was growing bored. It was not as much fun to tease and provoke Eleanor Goodwin as he had expected it to be. But he tried one last rapier thrust. "I have heard that in all families there are those who think and those who are merely decorative. Your sister clearly thinks about many things, so I imagine you pass your time in the vague pursuits of ladies who have nothing better to do than embroider more cushions than any household could ever need and paint watercolors no one wants to look at."

This did rile Nell. She forgot to be a polite, demure society miss. "It is my sister Cecilia who sews. She used to make all our clothes. None of us paints. My time recently has been taken up with making the revisions to my book that Egerton has asked for."

She was serving herself a portion of roast chicken and did not see the start of surprise on Summerson's face or how the mocking glint in his eyes faded. He looked at her with renewed interest but his cynical demeanor was so entrenched that there was an undertone of irony in his answer.

"So you spend your time scribbling nonsense that presents ladies with impossible depictions of gentlemen who are nothing more than the figment of a lady's dreams and that suggest those who sow their wild oats are villainous and dangerous."

Nell turned the full force of her brilliant blue eyes on him. She studied him for a moment as she thought through his words. "Perhaps such views are the result of the way ladies are expected to turn a blind eye to their husband's peccadilloes. Women deserve to be treated as valuable."

He chuckled dryly. "And you, a young lady who has no real experience of the world, are going to write a book that will change the way men and women interact." There was a bitter edge to his voice as he said, "Women are far more interested in their husband's riches and status than in the love and passion they could bring to their lives. And so women will continue to marry for titles and jewels and their husbands will continue to seek pleasure away from home in spite of your very noble efforts to suggest that love is possible." He leaned a little closer to her and lowered his voice to a tone that ladies usually found irresistible. "Of course, if you wanted to know about passion, I would happily give up a few hours of my time to show you what it really means."

Jane had been growing increasingly alarmed as she overheard parts of this conversation. She clutched her knife and fork so tightly, her knuckles were white. Robbie placed his hand over hers and rubbed softly. "Don't worry," he murmured. "Nothing is going to happen at the dinner table."

She let out her breath. "You're right, and I think Summerson has shown his real colors and Nell is no longer quite so infatuated." Her eyes drifted to Ali, who was seated across from her. "However, it seems we have another situation developing that might need more immediate intervention."

Robbie chuckled. "My little mother hen," he said affectionately, busking a kiss on her cheek before leaning back to allow the footman to clear their plates. "Should we intervene and bring it to an end, or support Ali?" he asked, taking a sip of wine as he watched Jasper place his hand on Ali's while he leaned towards Belinda to hear what she was saying.

Ali shifted closer to Lord Keeton, so close that she could feel the heat of his body and breathe in the smell of sunshine and sea that characterized him. Her hand was so small beneath his large one and she pushed her glasses up her nose, remembering just how powerful his hand was and how her body had responded to his spanking.

She had to drink half the water in her glass to cool down a bit before she could concentrate on the discussion Belinda and Jasper were having about Prichard's theory that all of humankind was connected.

Belinda had lost her air of desolation, the grievance that usually hung about her like a cloak. She was relaxed and looked very attractive in the candlelight that lightened her hair to the color of spun sugar. It lit the delicate lines of her face and made her eyes larger and more vivid. Ali smiled as Belinda's eyes rested on where Jasper's hand covered her own, bringing a soft flush to her pale cheeks. She, too, was remembering their wonderful afternoon on the beach.

Jasper and Belinda were quite heated as they each expressed their views but there was none of the vitriol that had so often characterized their discussions in the past. Ali was so lost in her thoughts that she had almost forgotten there were other people at the table. She had a brief, fanciful image of the three of them sitting like this every evening, sharing a meal and discussing the ideas and discoveries they had come across that day. And then they would go upstairs and their explorations would become far more physical. Nothing could be more perfect. She shifted on her chair as the images caused her core to heat and swell.

Jasper smiled and winked at her as if he knew what thoughts ricocheted in her mind. To make matters worse, he placed his hand on her thigh under the table. The warmth of his touch sent blood to her cheeks and pussy. She pushed her glasses up her nose and tried to focus on Belinda, but Jasper's fingers began a slow, lazy movement that, even through the layers of her clothes, felt like the glow of a fire that made it impossible to concentrate.

Jasper was enjoying his evening, enjoying focusing on Ali and Belinda, but he was still aware of his guests. He had been surprised when Alexander Summerson had accepted the invitation to dinner. Although he often visited Keeton for a casual game of chess when he was at home, he preferred not to attend local dinner parties and assemblies. His reputation made mothers and elder sisters wary of letting him near impressionable young ladies.

As Lord Keeton continued his attention to both Ali and Belinda, he was aware that both of Summerson's dinner partners had deliberately turned from him. He felt sorry for his old friend. "Xander, it is good to see you in Dorset. I had not expected to see you until the beginning of September at the earliest."

Summerson shrugged one elegant shoulder and swallowed a mouthful of wine. "Certain events in London made it necessary to rusticate for a few weeks." His voice was smooth, impassive, but a slight emphasis on the word *events* hinted at some salacious scandal that had brought him to the quietness of the country when he was usually to be found at the center of the social whirl of London.

Jasper chuckled. "Well, I'm sure you will find much to occupy you on your estates. This is always a busy time of year."

Summerson cast a look at Nell. "The company here is certainly better than I had expected, but as to my estates, apart from riding out and a little shooting, there's not much to do." A slight shudder rippled over his body. "I have bailiffs and stewards who see to my concerns. I have no interest in tenants and yields and other rustic matters."

Belinda was incensed. "Why should someone like you, *my lord*," her tone was scornful, "own vast properties simply because of a quirk of birth while others labor and make your lands prosperous so that you can indulge your idle habits?"

Summerson was not moved by her impassioned question. He raised an eyebrow and looked at her slowly before saying, "Your father did a great disservice by inculcating republic ideas in you." His tone suggested that such ideas were the worst kind of crime or moral outrage.

Belinda brushed off his scorn. "I believe that property should belong to those who work it. One of these days, power to rule this land will fall into the hands of the farmers and merchants, and aristocrats like you will face the same fate as those in France."

There was silence around the table as everyone looked at Belinda. She blinked her eyes a few times but tilted her chin defiantly. Jasper broke the silence. "In the future, things might look very different, but for now, it behoves those of us born to privilege to ensure that those under our care are given the assistance they need to live good lives, and now that the war is ended, we will all prosper." He placed his hand on Belinda's thigh and stroked gently to sooth her, and to remind her that such outbursts were not polite to his guests.

Summerson tapped his glass, asking the butler to refill it, and the rest of the guests relaxed, beginning to chat about less controversial issues. But Halstead heard Symes, the under butler, who was standing just behind his chair, mutter, "Bah! Peace! It is war that proves the mettle of a man."

Chapter 8

THE LADIES WITHDREW, leaving the gentlemen to their brandy and port, as usual. Halstead pulled his chair up next to Robbie's. Bellingham and Barlow joined them while Summerson and Keeton caught up on local news with Dr. Wilby, making it easier for the members of the Spymaster's Alliance to talk about the reason they were in Dorset.

"Felix reckons he has figured out something important from the notebook," Barlow started eagerly, with an affectionate glance at his lover.

The earl quirked an eyebrow. "That sounds hopeful. What did you find?"

Bellingham, trying to look suitably humble, explained, "There were some notes that I managed to decipher which relate to the signs and symbols Lord Keeton placed next to the list of names Jasper found. He was listing those he could trust and those who were working against Wellington." The others exchanged quick glances while Bellingham took a sip of port. "I also think there might be some clue in the notes that could help decipher the code."

"We need to get that to Eliot as quickly as possible,"

Halstead said, "and we also need to follow up on the names on the list, especially those we have not already investigated."

"I can take the notebook to Eliot. I know Jane wants to visit Cece," the earl stated. He looked at Bellingham. "If that's all right with you?"

Bellingham nodded. "Of course. I'll show you what I found."

Halstead nodded. "Excellent. Then Bellingham and Barlow can come with me to London and help follow up on the officers and other names on the list. I don't think there is much more we can do here for the moment."

They lapsed into silence, each thinking over the details of the case. In their silence, it became possible to hear what the other gentlemen were talking about. Dr. Wilby swallowed the last of his brandy, set the glass heavily on the table, and declared, "Well, peace has finally been achieved. All of Wellington's good efforts have paid off. He deserves the dukedom."

"Indeed, peace will ensure a much better chance for all of us to prosper and plan for a better future," agreed Lord Keeton. His voice became a little softer. "My father would have been pleased. I am sorry he is not alive to see this day. He would have enjoyed being part of the peace talks that are going to be held in Vienna."

All of the gentlemen raised their glasses as Summerson made a toast to peace and prosperity. As Halstead joined the others in raising their glasses, he noticed the under butler who was standing just behind Jasper Keeton. His face was twisted into a sour expression, his shoulders were stiff and he glowered when Keeton spoke. It took Halstead a moment to remember his name. Symes. The former Lord Keeton's valet. Halstead tucked away the incident. It was probably nothing, just an insignificant moment. After all, the man had a reputation for being grim and unpleasant. And yet his instincts warned him that nothing was ever really insignificant and he didn't believe in coincidences. He drained his glass and followed the other gentlemen as they went to join the ladies.

———

The ladies settled down in the drawing room after dinner. Jane picked up a letter she had received with the evening mail and which she had not had a chance to read earlier. The twins and Messy crowded around her.

"What news? Has the baby arrived?"

"When can we go and see it? What's its name?"

"Is it a boy or a girl? I do hope it's a girl. Boys are all very well, but we need some girls to balance out all the boys."

"Girls, girls, quieten down. The noise you're making is likely to wake the dead, never mind my babies." Jane laughed as she drank a mouthful of tea and then began to read the letter to her sisters.

Dearest Jane, (and the rest of you)

I was never sympathetic enough with you during your pregnancies, and you have done this twice. I have told Daniel that one baby is enough but he just laughs and tells me I will change my mind when the baby is here, but I do not think so. I cannot believe how huge I am, all puffed up like a hot air balloon, only I could never float. It is hard enough to get out of a chair on my own. The midwife says the baby will arrive very soon. Daniel is as solicitous and caring as always, but, Jane, as the time draws nearer, I long for you to be with me. I know Lord Robbie is busy with something very important, but if he could spare you, I would be very happy if you could be here with me when the baby is born. Of course, there is plenty of room here for the girls as well. I'm sure they will want to see their new niece or nephew as soon as possible.

I loved the poem about the sea and the seagulls that Nell sent me. I can't wait to receive a copy of your book. It will feel so grand to know a real author.

Messy's description of the horse that almost ruined your picnic made me laugh although it must have been frightening at the time, especially for Gregory and Michael. Ali, I am sure that you will find dozens of remarkable fossils.

Hugs and kisses,

Cece

Belinda sipped her tea quietly while Jane read Cece's letter to the others. Ali sat right next to her sister, trying to see the words on the page while Messy hung over the back of the chair and Nell sat on the armrest, her arm around Ali's shoulders. The girls giggled and commented, pushing each other playfully and poking each other at various points in the letter.

A little slither of envy uncurled in Belinda's heart. Although she and her brother cared for and supported each other, they had never enjoyed the camaraderie these sisters shared. Furthermore, the exuberance and enthusiasm they so freely exhibited had been quelled in her from a young age. Her father had insisted on silence in the house at all times so that he could work without being disturbed and she had learned from a young age to suppress all her enthusiasm and excitement.

When Jane finished the letter, she folded it slowly, her expression thoughtful. Messy and Nell began clamoring about beginning to pack so they would be ready to leave. Jane answered their enthusiasm with a smile. "You don't need to rush off right now. We won't go until the day after tomorrow. I will talk to Robbie tonight and let you know what the arrangements are."

Messy and Nell clapped their hands with excitement, but Ali was more subdued. As much as she wanted to see Cece, her heart was torn. She looked at Belinda, who was looking at her at the same time. She bit her lip and pushed her glasses higher on her nose.

Nell stopped mid-clap, suddenly aware of her twin's lack of enthusiasm. She slid her arm around Ali's shoulders. "You'd prefer to stay here a little longer, wouldn't you?"

Jane heard and studied her sister's face, her own becoming more thoughtful. "It wouldn't be proper for you to remain in Lord Keeton's house without us."

A great aching emptiness opened in Belinda's heart. She could not bear to be separated from Ali just when they were beginning to understand one another and there was a slight possibility that they could share something deeper, an illicit connection but one that would satisfy a yearning they each had. And if Ali left, she would probably not have any contact with Jasper, either. The thought of returning to her lonely life emboldened her. She cleared her throat and spoke above the clamor of the Goodwin sisters. "Ali could stay with me for a week or two. My house is not as grand as this one, but it is comfortable and pleasant. And it has been a little lonely since Peter left." She couldn't quite keep the wistfulness out of her voice.

The forlorn look vanished from Ali's face and her smile outshone the glow from the candles. "Please say yes, Jane. I haven't had a chance to look for fossils yet and Belinda knows some good places to find them." Her conscience compelled her to add, "I do want to see Cece, of course, but she won't want all of us bothering her before the baby arrives. I will be there soon afterwards and will make a great deal of fuss over the baby, because I will be the last to see it."

Jane laughed. "That is a compelling argument." She looked thoughtfully from Ali to Belinda. She tilted her head.

"I am sure no harm can come to you here. If Robbie agrees, then you may stay for two more weeks."

Ali hugged her sister. "Thank you, thank you."

Jane held Ali close for a moment, her dark head tucked against her shoulder. "It will not be easy, the path you have chosen, but true love is worth all the challenges that you will face. I want you to be happy."

An unexpected tear trickled down Ali's cheek at her sister's words. She swallowed a lump in her throat but said nothing as the door to the drawing room opened and the gentlemen sauntered in. Robbie made straight for Jane and her sisters. He placed his hand on Ali's back as he leaned down to kiss Jane. "Is everything all right?"

Ali nodded and Jane smiled at him. "It will be difficult, but love will triumph," she assured her husband.

Robbie squeezed Ali's shoulder. "Always remember that we love you and support you, whatever happens in your life."

Ali nodded, straightening her glasses, but activity at the far end of the room drew their attention and she did not reply.

"Oh, good. Mrs. Wilby is opening the piano and we're going to dance," Messy exclaimed.

Ali sat up, pulling her skirts straight and slipping her hand into Belinda's, who took Jane's place on the sofa when Robbie led Jane onto the dance floor while Messy claimed Simon Barlow's hand for the dance. Nell, after looking long-ingly in the direction of Lord Summerson, accepted Dr. Wilby as her partner. She tossed her head, hoping that Summerson, who was leaning against the mantelpiece, one elegant leg crossed over the other while he sipped a cup of tea, would notice that she didn't care if he did not ask her to dance. In spite of his insulting manner at dinner, she still admired his good looks and the air of self-assurance that sat so easily on his broad shoulders.

"I will miss your sisters," Belinda commented as the dancers formed two circles to begin the dance. "But I am glad we will have time to be alone together."

Jasper Keeton came into the drawing room after the other gentlemen because he needed to discuss a few matters with his butler. As soon as he entered, he headed straight to the sofa where Ali and Belinda were sitting, just in time to hear these last words. He frowned. "Is the earl planning to leave? I thought he was going to stay until he had..." He trailed off, not sure how much the ladies knew of what Halstead and the others were investigating. Ali glanced at him but his hazel eyes were shadowed and showed none of his feelings.

Belinda stiffened and her hand gripped Ali's so tightly, she thought her fingers might be crushed. She stared straight ahead as she spoke, her words like hard pebbles clattering to the ground. "You are disappointed that they did not find any evidence against my brother."

Jasper had almost forgotten Belinda's connection to his father's death. He frowned, not sure how to redeem the situation and convince Belinda that he had begun to think differently about her, that he found her radical ideas refreshing, and that he was no longer quite so sure that Peter Bennet had played a part in his father's assassination.

Ali slipped one arm around Belinda's shoulders while keeping her other hand holding Belinda's on her lap. Jasper's cock hardened as he looked at the two of them so close together on the small sofa that their thighs were touching. How was it possible to be aroused by two women at the same time? Unlike so many of his contemporaries, he had not indulged in hedonistic pleasures. He had, from time to time, visited a discreet bordello but had never indulged in the wild exploits his friends often boasted of. But here he was, contemplating something so wicked, so perverse, that even his most lascivious friends would scorn him for it. These two ladies were genteel members of the *Beau Monde* and yet he wanted to bed them both at the same time. He wanted to watch them undress each other and kiss and then join them in discovering the pleasure of expressing love physically. He swallowed, suddenly realizing that what he was feeling for them went far beyond physical attraction. His admiration and attraction had slowly evolved into the realization that without these two women, his life was incomplete.

He wanted to kiss them one after the other and declare his love without delay. But he had to control himself. His drawing room was filled with guests and he did not want to plunge Ali and Belinda into a scandal that would destroy the precarious relationship they were forming.

Ali responded to Belinda's comment. She glared at Jasper and pursed her lips. "I am sure that Lord Robbie and Lord Halstead are doing all they can to uncover the *truth*, even if it does not match anyone's preconceived notions," she admonished pertly.

Jasper had the grace to blush. "I did not mean to offend you, Belinda. There is more at stake than just the circumstances of my father's death, and if we could talk to Peter, he might be able to shed some light on what happened." His eyes darkened, reflecting the sincerity in his voice. "Belinda, believe me when I say that I have no desire to see your family disgraced or you hurt. I found, amongst my father's papers, a notebook your brother left here. He had been making notes about Plato's *Republic*, and I found some of his observations about the ownership of land and property interesting." Belinda looked at him, hope dawning in her eyes, but the light dimmed when he continued. "I am not sure that I am ready to accept such radical ideas, but some of his ideas could improve the lives of tenants and the profitability of my estates."

Ali shook her head. "That's all very well, but this evening is about enjoyment and amusement. I think you should show Belinda just how sorry you are by dancing with her."

Aware of the quandary facing him, Jasper looked from one to the other of the two women. He would love to dance with both at the same time, but that was not possible. Ali's expression was hopeful and determined.

"You won't mind that I dance with Belinda first?" he asked. If they ever found a way to pursue their unusual arrangement, this kind of question would always arise. But there would be no place for jealousy if they wanted to make this work.

Ali grinned and shook her head. She felt Belinda tense next to her and ran her fingers over Belinda's wrist. Tension stretched between all three of them, taut and tangible, like water poised to drop onto sodium and potassium in one of Sir Humphry Davy's experiments. Without words, all three were aware of the possibility of a dangerously explosive reaction if they followed their hearts and allowed their feelings to interact. Yet all three were prepared to take the risk needed for this kind of experimentation of the heart.

Jasper caught Belinda's gaze. He had only ever danced with her once before, but he could still remember the feel of her hand in his, the way her body had brushed against him, and the elusive fragrance of green and growing things that was unique to her. Now, her expression wavered between desire, anticipation, and uncertainty.

Ali was the first to break the knot of tension. She placed her free hand on Jasper's arm. "Dance with Belinda, Jasper. Please." When he looked at her uncertainly, she added, "I want to watch the two people I lo-like most, being close to each other."

The momentary discomfort she felt at her daring was washed away when Jasper placed his finger under her chin and tilted her face upwards, holding her eyes with his, and said, "Thank you." He held out his hand to Belinda. "Miss Bennet, would you do me the honor of dancing the next set with me?"

Belinda let out the breath she had not realized she'd been holding. She gave a final squeeze to Ali's fingers and placed her hand in Jasper's, following him onto the dance floor as Mrs. Wilby brought the lively reel to an end and began the prelude for a more sedate quadrille.

Ali sat forward, pushed her glasses firmly onto her nose, and watched Jasper guide Belinda in the steps. Lord Keeton moved with a casual grace that conveyed an easiness with himself and an assurance of his place in the world. His dark blue jacket and dove grey breeches outlined his broad shoulders and drew attention to the length of his legs. His thick, light brown hair brushed the top of his collar and Ali had a sudden urge to run her fingers through it and hold him close in a kiss. A kiss she wanted to share with Belinda, who looked so right in Jasper's arms. Ali intercepted a heated look between the dancing couple and felt a twinge of jealousy which was quickly burned away by the flare of desire. There was something thrilling and arousing about watching the two of them dance and thinking illicit thoughts that simmered beneath the polite drawing room atmosphere of members of the *haut ton* enjoying an evening amusement.

Jasper and Belinda moved to the end of the line and Ali's attention was drawn to Nell. She frowned. The pale blue chiffon of her sister's overdress made her look even more ethereal than usual and she moved with such a light step that she was almost floating above the ground as if she were a fairy come to enjoy herself with these mortals. Ali shook her head. It was not like her to be so fanciful, but Nell was dancing with Lord Summerson, her expression even dreamier than usual. He, however, in his severe black coat, with his dark hair worn longer than was fashionable, looked as lascivious as the Big Bad Wolf about to devour Little Red Riding Hood. Ali bit her lip. It would be rude to walk up to them and extract her sister from the dance. Besides, such an action would probably incense Nell, making her more determined to spend time with the renowned rake. Ali's only option was to keep Nell as far as possible from the wolf and try to coax her into a better sense of reality before she was hurt and damaged her reputation. As Ali watched them, she remembered a whispered story about the younger Miss Quinn who had been ruined by her association with Lord Summerson. Ali did not know any details but she didn't want her sister to end up ostracized and brokenhearted. She was relieved that her sisters would be leaving Dorset within a day or so and Nell would be removed from Lord Summerson's influence.

This thought coincided with the end of the dance. Jasper led a flushed and glowing Belinda—who was attempting to appear indifferent—back to the sofa, but the heat in her eyes could not be doused. However, rather than asking Ali to dance, Jasper suggested, "It is quite warm inside. Would the two of you care to join me on the terrace for some fresh air?" His words sounded fairly innocuous but there was something in the way he spoke that hinted at more than a polite walk outside. Belinda was still standing next to him, her hand resting on his arm. The heat in the room increased and Ali nodded her head. She rose and placed her hand on Jasper's other arm.

As they headed out the door, she was aware of Jane's quick nod and Nell's smile, but she was beyond caring what others might think. Her whole body tingled with anticipation. A full moon hung in the sky, casting a silvery light over the garden. Jasper, without a word, led the two of them down the stairs at the center of the terrace to a little alcove that gave them a modicum of privacy. The sound of the piano drifted down, like distant music from the heavens, and with a smile, Jasper bowed to the two ladies. "Would you care to dance?"

Ali and Belinda looked at each other and then Belinda took a step back, making room for Ali. Jasper tilted his head but decided that perhaps it was best to begin slowly. He took Ali's hand in his and they began to dance. Jasper drew Ali closer to him than was usual and she leaned into the warmth of his body, finding assurance in the strength of his arms. She breathed deeply, satisfaction suffusing her body with warmth. She was very conscious of Belinda standing only two or three feet from them, of the intense way Belinda watched them, of the heat that flared in Belinda's eyes as Jasper pulled her even closer and brushed his lips over her forehead in a light kiss that sent ripples of arousal through her body.

As they danced, Jasper moved them closer to Belinda, and when he held his arm out for Ali to circle around him, she passed behind Belinda, capturing her between the two of them. Ali could hear Belinda breathing heavily, see the flush on her cheeks even in the moonlight, and smell the green woodsy aroma that always surrounded her.

On the next circle, Jasper dropped Ali's hand and took Belinda's, urging her to join them. She hesitated for a moment and then took a tentative step. Ali twirled around her, so close that her breasts brushed the soft sateen of Belinda's dress. By the time the dance came to an end, all three were laughing and breathless.

Ali was in the middle of the group, facing Jasper. They looked at each other, heat simmering in their eyes. He cupped her chin and tilted her face upwards, bending his head to claim her lips in a searing kiss that lasted for a long while and left Ali breathless. When Jasper released her, her eyes were glazed and her glasses were misted. She was panting hard but she turned to Belinda and pulled her closer. "Kiss her!" she demanded.

Jasper chuckled. "You really do like to watch us."

Ali nodded, then a small frown creased her forehead. "Do you think I'm perverted? Wicked?"

Jasper and Belinda immediately exclaimed, both putting their arms around her shoulders. "Not at all." "Of course not."

"If you are perverted because you like to watch then we must be too, because," Jasper explained with a glance at Belinda, "we like to be watched by you."

Ali nodded and settled her glasses on her nose. "Then you'd better kiss Belinda."

Jasper moved closer to Belinda, slipping his arm around her shoulders and clasping the back of her head with his other hand. She stiffened. She had only been kissed once before, and it was still strange to feel his muscles press against the firmness of her slim body. But it was not unpleasant, and as she relaxed, she absorbed his warmth and leaned against him, particularly when his mouth brushed over hers, gently, firmly, savoring her taste. Everything around her faded until all she knew was the hardness of his mouth against hers, the press of his body, the fragrance of wood and sea, and something undefinable that was uniquely Jasper.

Jasper pulled back slightly so that they could take a breath and Belinda was aware of Ali leaning against Jasper's side, her arm around his waist. Her eyes were wide and a blue as deep as the ocean on a clear day. Her scent mingled with Jasper's, creating a harmony of sea, wind, and earth that filled Belinda with hope and possibility.

Chapter 9

ALI LOOKED around at the beautiful, secluded cove with appreciation. She had not spent much time at the shore and the whole experience thrilled her. The sun sparkled off the greenish-blue water, seagulls swooped down calling to one another when they found a fish, and the white-capped waves chased each other over the rocky beach. She raised her face to the sun, like a mermaid soaking up the warmth.

Belinda secured the little rowing boat she had used to row the two of them here for their fossil-hunting expedition and then took out the picnic basket and blanket which she placed on the only sandy part of the beach. Looking around to see where Ali had disappeared to, she began to laugh when she spotted her friend enthusiastically bashing a pile of rocks with a little hammer.

Quickly, Belinda clambered over the rocks and came up behind Ali. "It is clear that your knowledge of plants far exceeds your understanding of geology and paleontology."

Ali dropped her hammer and spun around, her bonnet askew and her hair awry. The sun had brought out a cluster of tiny freckles on her nose that Belinda suddenly wanted to touch. Her laughter caught in her throat as desire replaced her amusement.

Ali forgot her eager hunt for fossils. The hammer slipped from her hands, but neither of them moved even when it clattered to the rocks. They stood looking at each other, scarcely breathing, for many minutes. Eventually, Belinda raised her hand and gently touched the most prominent freckle on Ali's nose and then ran her finger from one to the next, tracing a pattern.

Ali savored the moment, absorbing the sensations of Belinda's touch. She kept her eyes steadily on Belinda's. Understanding flared between them far more accurately than if they used inadequate and stumbling words. Belinda grew a little bolder and let her finger press more firmly against the softness of Ali's skin. She opened her hand and cupped Ali's cheek and then trailed her fingers over her mouth.

Ali finally moved, echoing Belinda's gentle movements. She raised her hand slowly and outlined Belinda's face from her temple to her chin. Belinda drew in her breath and her eyes wavered as desire heated her body. Her touch faltered, but Ali, emboldened by her own illicit desires, pressed the corner of Belinda's mouth and brushed her fingers over her soft lips. Belinda shuddered and Ali was aware of how her friend's breasts swelled beneath her light linen dress.

Ali pressed her fingers more firmly on Belinda's mouth, gently tugging the lower lip. Belinda's mouth opened slightly and Ali pushed the tip of her finger into the heat of Belinda's mouth. Belinda sucked, gently at first, and then drew more of Ali's finger into her mouth, tasting her with her tongue.

Ali moved closer until her body was merely a whisper away. She could feel the swell of Belinda's breasts against her own which were tight and heavy. Her nipples had bunched into hard peaks and were pressing against her corset painfully. It wasn't an unpleasant pain, though, and she rubbed herself against Belinda to find either some relief or pleasure. She wasn't quite sure which.

Ali pulled her finger out with a soft pop and placed her hand behind Belinda's neck, spreading her fingers into her hair. She tilted Belinda's face downwards and raised her own face up so that their lips met. Belinda slid her hands around Ali's neck to keep her balance and to draw them closer.

Ali drew Belinda's lips between her own and sucked and nibbled the soft, smooth flesh as it yielded to her. She pushed her tongue deeper into Belinda's mouth and explored the softness of her mouth.

The initial uncertainty and awkwardness dissipated as the two women surrendered to the heat of passion. The beauty of the day, the sounds of the sea, faded as they expressed their love. After many moments, they parted, breathless and gasping for air but laughing. Ali picked up her fallen hammer and the two made their way back to the sandy place where Belinda had left the picnic basket.

Belinda opened the basket and pulled out a flask of tea, As she handed it to Ali, she said, "Your kisses are different from Jasper's. His are hard and possessive while yours are gentle and tender. I like both."

Ali sipped some tea. "I like both as well. I think it's wonderful that the three of us found each other. It almost makes me believe that fate is real and it guided us."

Belinda sat down next to her, close enough that their legs touched. "If Peter had not fallen into difficulties, we would never have met. I had met Jasper and so had you, but it was the coincidence of both he and I seeking help from the earl that brought us all together."

Ali laughed. "It is a good example of Newton's law. To every action, there is an equal and opposite reaction."

Belinda laughed and packed the flask back into the

basket. "Come on, let's go and find some fossils." She held out her hand and Ali took it, letting Belinda pull her to her feet.

The two of them spent the next two or three hours exploring the beach and finding fossils.

"Oh, look. I think I've found a good specimen here," Ali called as she scrambled over a rock that had been worn flat from the pounding of the sea through the eons. To reach it, she had to step on another larger one, but a clear outline of a spiral mollusk was caught in the stone and she was determined to get the specimen.

Belinda eyed her friend and laughed, but her smile faded as she looked out to sea. The tide was coming in quickly and the waves were edging higher and higher up the beach. To make matters worse, a storm was brewing. Belinda shivered at the ominous clouds that roiled in the sky and blocked out the sun, threatening to spoil the perfect day. Perhaps the universe was warning her, warning them, that their behavior, their desire for one another, was dangerous. Belinda shook her head. She was not a fanciful, romantic miss with superstitious notions about the world. But it would be better if she and Alicia made their way back to her house as soon as possible if they wanted to avoid being drenched. The wilder the sea became, the more difficult it would be to row the little boat back to the town.

"Ali, we need to go. Leave that one. It will still be there next time we come."

Ali half-turned and her right foot slipped on a piece of slimy seaweed. She gave a little yelp and stretched out her arms to get her balance. But she tilted her chin stubbornly. "I might not find the exact spot again and someone else could come along and nab it. It really is beautiful."

"Careful," Belinda paused in her stowing of the picnic

basket in the rowing boat to caution Ali, "it isn't very steep there, but it wouldn't be very pleasant or comfortable to fall."

Ali, once again sure on her feet, shot her a laughing look. "No. I've fallen a few times in search of specimens I'm after, but never on such hard rocks. But this is really the best I've seen all day and I really do want it."

"Do come down," Belinda coaxed. "We don't want to spoil the day by getting soaking wet and catching the death of a cold."

Ali gritted her teeth, but before she could answer, big drops of rain began to splatter onto the rocks and the sea. One landed on her glasses. She wiped it away and blinked to clear her vision. "I guess you're right." She tucked her little hammer into the shoulder bag she was carrying and turned around with a last reluctant glance at the specimen that remained just out of reach.

Her foot caught a piece of slippery seaweed and she lost her balance. Her arms flailed wildly and she tumbled. She gave a sharp scream and then there was silence.

Belinda stood frozen for a horrified moment. Ali did not move, her body lying still on the rock where she had landed. Only the pale blue of her dress fluttered in the wind that was blowing harder and harder by the minute.

Belinda dropped the rope she had been rolling and dashed across the beach, her feet also sliding on the now-slippery rocks. When she almost fell on a piece of seaweed, she paused and then continued more slowly. She would not be able to help Ali if she, too, fell. It was only a few minutes before she reached her friend, but the journey felt like Odysseus' epic journey home from Troy.

Her heart was pounding and her hands were shaking. She knelt next to Alicia. "Ali, Ali, can you hear me?"

Ali did not stir. She had not fallen far, but the angle was an awkward one. Her leg was bent strangely and a trickle of blood seeped from where she had hit her head on the sharp edge of a rock. She was pale and her lips were bloodless. Belinda straightened Ali's glasses.

Belinda blinked back tears that, together with the drops of rain, were making it difficult to see. She shook Ali's shoulder and was relieved when she emitted a low moan. At least she was alive. Belinda's heart began to beat again. "Ali, Ali," she called. But Ali's eyes remained closed.

Panic began to rise in Belinda's mind. How was she going to lift Ali and carry her to the boat over the rocks that were more and more dangerous as the rain fell harder and the waves began to crash over them? One wave swept up to the rocks where Ali had fallen and drenched the bottom of Belinda's dress and washed over Ali. Belinda grasped her shoulders and lifted her face above the water. Ali groaned again. Belinda looked around her wildly, trying to think of a way to get them both to safety.

She gasped back a sob and tried to stand, lifting Ali with her, but the weight of her limp body was too heavy and Belinda stumbled.

"Give her to me." Belinda looked up, startled to see Jasper Keeton standing on the rocks as steadily as if he were in a drawing room, even though the waves lapped at his knee-high riding boots.

"Move aside and let me take her. You go ahead and get yourself to safety." His voice could be clearly heard above the wind and rain. Belinda had never seen him look more powerful or heard such command in his voice. Meekly, she gave way to him and, with a quick glance over her shoulder when Ali groaned, scrambled to the shelter of the over-hanging cliffs where Jasper had left his horse just where a path wound its way to the top.

She shivered and wrapped her arms around herself as she watched Jasper stride over the rocks as easily as if he were dancing the minuet. Ali lay in his arms, her head lolling to the side and her arms hanging loosely. He was balancing her legs with his left arm. Belinda shuddered when a particularly large wave rushed over the rocks and Jasper paused as it knocked against his calves. His face was set in a grim expression as he made his way steadily towards her.

When he reached the horse, he spoke brusquely. "Hold the reins while I settle her." He hoisted Alicia onto his saddle and tucked her dress up so he could examine her leg. He ran his hands down her calf and tugged off her boot. The ankle was swollen and beginning to bruise. He pulled off his neatly tied cravat and wrapped it around Ali's foot. "I don't think she has broken any bones." But as he examined her head, running his fingers sensitively over the small wound, his eyes were very grave.

He covered her with his great coat. She had roused briefly while Jasper was bandaging her ankle but fell into an unconscious swoon once more. Belinda chaffed her wrists while Jasper tipped a mouthful of brandy from his pewter hip flask into Ali's mouth. Most of it dribbled down her chin which he wiped away with his thumb, but she imbibed enough of it for it to rouse her a little. Her eyes flickered and then closed and her lips lost their bluish tinge.

Jasper handed the flask to Belinda. "You'd better have some, too."

She took the flask and gulped a large mouthful before handing it back to him. Only then, did he look at her properly. Belinda was annoyed that tears were sliding down her face and her nose was blocked. She gave a loud sniff. Jasper cupped her chin and brushed the trail of tears. His voice softened. "It's all right. She will be fine. If you sit behind Alicia and hold her, I will lead Monty. It will probably take us half an hour to reach the house."

It was impossible to talk on that long and weary journey

and Belinda never forgot the agony of every moan that Ali emitted or the coldness of the rain that trickled down her neck. Jasper was drenched. His light hair was darkened and lay flat against his head. His coat clung to his body in wet folds but he trudged tirelessly along the path and over the fields, only occasionally pushing the hair off his forehead or glancing back to see if the women were fine.

Belinda had fallen into a semi-slumberous state. She did not know how long she had been on the horse with Ali in her arms and the rain falling down. She was shocked into consciousness when Ali was lifted off the horse and someone helped her down. She stood in the foyer of Jasper's house, dripping a large puddle of water onto the floor. She blinked her eyes and shivered. Jasper was carrying Ali upstairs and calling out orders to servants who were moving swiftly to fetch hot water and blankets.

Mrs. Rudd, the housekeeper, was clucking as she followed Jasper up the stairs. One of the senior housemaids bobbed a curtsey to Belinda. "Miss, if you would follow me, I will show you where you can have a bath and change into some warm clothes."

Belinda followed her numbly up the stairs and was soon soaking in a tub filled with steaming water. She laid her head against the back and breathed deeply as the heat seeped into her cold body.

Half an hour later, wearing a dress loaned to her by the housekeeper, she made her way along the corridor to the room where Alicia had been taken. The door was ajar and she could hear the low rumble of the doctor's voice as he discussed Ali's condition with Jasper and Mrs. Rudd. Symes, the under butler, was standing just inside the room, ready to do the bidding of the doctor or Lord Keeton.

"Her leg needs to remain bound and raised. That will heal quickly as no bones were broken. However, not only is her head injury of concern, she has developed a fever from being out in the rain for so long. She will need constant care."

Jasper was holding Alicia's hand, and as the doctor spoke, he ran his other hand over her forehead, brushing aside the long dark strands of hair. "I will send for her sister."

Belinda stepped into the room, her hands clasped in front of her. "There's no need for Jane to come. Cecilia needs her at the moment. I can look after Ali." She hesitated as Jasper raised his eyes to her. She had never seen him look so distant, so remote, even when he had accused her brother of murdering his father.

The doctor, oblivious to the undercurrents, nodded. "That sounds like a good idea. She cannot be moved."

She took a step back and her voice faltered. "I'm sure Nell will come as soon as she hears, and so I will only need to be here for a day or two."

Jasper frowned. "Is there any urgent reason for you to return to your house?" His eyes swept over the grey gown she was wearing which hung loosely on her thin frame. "Except to fetch some clothes for you and Ali."

Belinda let out a long breath and moved slowly towards the bed. "There is nothing at home that needs my attention. I want to make sure Ali is well."

"Good, good," the doctor said as he packed away his instruments and gave Belinda and Mrs. Rudd instructions for Ali's care. When he left, Mrs. Rudd and Symes went with him.

There was silence in the darkened room for a while, broken only by Alicia's labored breathing. Eventually, Jasper held out his hand. "Come and sit here beside the bed where you can see her better."

Belinda walked up to the bed, but her eyes were on Jasper, rather than Alicia. "I am sorry."

Jasper frowned. "Sorry for what? This isn't your fault."

"No. It was an accident. But you seem angry."

Jasper took a deep breath and took Belinda's hand in his. "I am worried, not angry. I apologize if I came across as abrupt."

A housemaid brought in a tray on which a pretty teapot and teacups had been arranged together with a plate of sandwiches and some pie. Jasper drew a little table and two chairs close to the bed. He held out one chair. "You need to eat and I am hungry, too."

Belinda sank gratefully onto one of the chairs and poured them each a cup of tea. When she had eaten one of the ham sandwiches, she asked, "How did you happen to be on the beach just when Ali fell?"

Jasper ate half a sandwich before he answered. "The timing was purely coincidental. If one believed in fate, one could say I was destined to be there when you both needed me. What were you doing there? Do you know that it is private land?"

Belinda blushed. "Private? To whom does it belong?" When she caught Jasper's eye, her blush deepened. "I did not know it was your land. I didn't mean to trespass. We were fossil hunting."

"You're welcome to collect fossils there at any time as long as you are careful. Perhaps next time, it would be better if I accompanied you."

Belinda bristled. "Why is it that men do not think that women are capable of looking after themselves. We are not fragile dolls that need to be kept on a shelf behind glass doors."

Jasper laughed. "I know, but even you must admit that you did need my help today."

Belinda looked at Ali and subsided. "Yes. I would not

have managed to get her off the rocks on my own. Thank you."

"It is just as well that I was returning from visiting one of my tenants and that the cliff path was the quickest way home for me. I heard Ali's scream." He paused as he recalled that blood-chilling moment. "I thought both of you were in danger. If anything happened to either of you, my heart would never recover."

Chapter 10

"LETTERS FOR EVERYONE TODAY," Nell sang out as she waltzed into Ali's room, still dressed in the breeches and shirt she had worn when she went for a walk after breakfast. She had arrived three days after Ali's fall and stayed on even when the doctor announced that Ali was out of all danger.

The curtains were open and the sunlight brightened the colors of the flowers on the windowsill and the cushions on the daybed where Ali was resting. Belinda, seated on the window seat, put down the book she had been reading and took the letter that Nell handed her. Her hands were slightly clammy as she recognized her brother's handwriting. Why was Peter writing to her? His last few letters had been very strange and it had been a while since she had heard from him.

Jasper had followed Nell into the room and, after checking that Ali was comfortable and dropping a kiss on her forehead, sat down next to Belinda. "You don't seem to be happy to have received a letter. Are you expecting bad news?"

She shook her head and tried to smile but her eyes were clouded with worry.

Her need to answer was interrupted by a shriek from Nell. "Cece's had her baby! A little girl. How gorgeous. Her name is Sarah-Jane. That is pretty and Jane will be delighted."

Ali took the letter from her twin's hand and scanned it. "Oh, I am glad that I am strong enough to travel. I so want to see our first niece."

Nell hugged her twin. "We'll go in a day or two. I'm sure the doctor will say it's all right for you to travel if we take it easy. In the meantime, I want to write a poem to honor her birth. What rhymes with Sarah-Jane?" she mused as she wandered out of the room to find her notebook.

Ali smiled at Jasper and Belinda. "Do you have any exciting news in your letters?"

"Not as exciting as a new baby," Jasper laughed. "I have a lot of business letters and one from Lord Halstead."

Ali sat up straight. "Have they found anything useful?"

Belinda gritted her teeth and her fingers curled tightly over the letter from Peter. Ali looked at her, a question in her eyes, but she said nothing more. Jasper smoothed out the pages on which Halstead had written in his clear, flowing script. "They have not found any definite evidence of a plot against Wellington, although there are some disgruntled members of the militia who complain that there is no glory to be found during times of peace. Perhaps we were tilting at windmills after all." The only indication of his disappointment was the resignation in his tone and a slight sagging of his shoulders.

Ali leaned over and took his hand in hers. "I am sure your father would be happy that you have honored him and I believe, from what you have told us of him, that he would be pleased that there is finally peace in Europe."

The grim expression on Jasper's face faded. "Yes, indeed." He glanced at Belinda who was still sitting very quietly next to him. "Would you like some privacy to read your letter?"

The gentleness in his voice stirred her but she could not look him in the eyes. "It is from my brother." She sounded stilted as if the words came from a wooden toy that had learned to speak.

Jasper stiffened and she flinched and then rose quickly to her feet. "Alicia is so much better now that there is no need for me to remain here. She will be leaving soon anyway." Pain made her words sharper than she had meant them to be. "We dreamed of an idyll that cannot be. There are too many difficulties, too many differences and divided loyalties." She gave a stiff bow. "I wish the two of you well."

"Belinda, no!" Ali cried out. "You can't just leave like that. These last two weeks have been the happiest of my life and we can find a way through this if we talk about it." She looked imploringly at Jasper, whose eyes were filled with anguish.

He rose and took hold of Belinda's arm. "I am sorry. I know we have not talked much about your brother, and perhaps we should do so now."

Belinda stopped moving towards the door, but she was still stiff. She looked straight ahead of her. "I know you believe Peter had something to do with your father's death. I cannot split my heart between my brother and those who oppose him."

Jasper tugged her arm. "Come and sit down. Perhaps if you told us the story from the beginning, we would have a better understanding." Belinda sat down again and he sat beside her, close enough for her to know he was there but not close enough to actually touch her. Ali poured a glass of water and handed it to Belinda, brushing her hands with her fingers as she did so.

Belinda looked up with a watery smile. "I'm not usually such a watering pot."

"You also don't usually make such impulsive decisions," Alicia declared. "Now, if you are feeling more yourself," she continued as Belinda drank the glass of water, "perhaps it would do well to share what is troubling you." She gave Jasper a stern look. "If we are to find a way for our unusual liaison to work, then we will need to be open and honest with each other at all times and accept that we might have differences of opinion but that we are strong enough to work through them."

The other two laughed. "You are right," Jasper agreed. He took Belinda's hand in his. "Tell me about your brother. He was my father's secretary for only a few months and I never met him."

Belinda took a deep breath. "Peter was excited to be employed by the late Lord Keeton. I know your father and he disagreed on some philosophical ideals but, essentially, they wanted the same thing, peace and a chance for all citizens of England to prosper. He did not want to be a soldier but he did want to do what is best for our country."

Her explanation was interrupted by the entrance of Symes who, after a light knock on the door, entered the room, carrying a small silver salver. "My lord, Colonel Mannering has left his card. He has asked you to dinner on Thursday night. He is a man I respect very much, a true hero who fought bravely for the honor of this country, not like so many cowards who refuse to fight because they are not manly enough."

Belinda gasped and Jasper tilted his head. "Thank you, Symes. You need not have brought the message up to me. It is not urgent, and I do not think I will attend anyway.

156

Mannering is not a man whose company I enjoy. He talks of nothing but war."

Ali was startled to see the under-butler's face twist into a grimace of dislike and his eyes fill with disdain. His usually impassive appearance returned so quickly that Ali wasn't sure if it had been a trick of the light, especially when he answered blandly, "Very well, my lord. Will you be lunching in this room?"

Jasper glanced at Ali who was looking energetic and very healthy. "I think we will come down to the dining parlor. You may tell Mrs. Rudd to have luncheon served in half an hour."

Ali watched Symes as he left the room, his back straight and his shoulders set in rigid lines. "He is a strange man," she mused. "Did he serve your father for long?"

"They were in the same regiment, my father was a colonel and he was a sergeant. When my father took up a position on the peace council, Symes, who had been injured, came with him."

Ali's mouth twisted as she thought about it. She pushed her glasses more firmly onto her nose. "He does not seem to favor peace."

"Indeed, he doesn't," Belinda agreed. "He and Peter did not get on very well."

"What does Peter say in his letter? You do not seem very eager to open it." Ali tried not to let her curiosity color her voice.

Belinda looked at the letter, now slightly crumpled where she had held it so tightly. "I am uncertain. His last few letters have been strange, not like him at all, and each time he writes, he begs me to help him but I do not know what more I can do."

"Oh, I do hope it is nothing serious. Would you like me to read it for you?"

The grateful look Belinda gave Ali was full of warmth, but she said resolutely, "No, thank you. I am not a coward, and neither is Peter, no matter what Symes might believe." She slid her finger under the flap of the envelope and carefully opened the letter. It was crowded with small, cramped handwriting and Belinda had to squint to make sense of it. She skimmed the letter while the other two watched her. When she took a deep breath and murmured, "Oh, no!" Jasper slid his arm around her shoulders and she was grateful to lean against him.

"What is it? Is he hurt?" Ali asked.

Belinda shook her head. "No, at least I hope not. He says that someone broke into the cottage where he is staying and stole some things. I am sure I have misunderstood what he has written, but it seems as if, rather than taking anything, the person left some papers behind."

"That is odd," Ali agreed.

"What do the documents say?" Jasper asked.

Belinda glanced at him hesitantly. "Again, his handwriting is difficult to read, but it seems as if they refer to some plans to harm Wellington."

Ali gasped. "But that must prove his innocence."

"Not necessarily," Jasper said. "There is only his word to say the papers were left there. It could be a way for him to cast suspicion away from himself."

Belinda shook her head. "When it seems as if everything is going to work out, something else occurs to make Peter look guilty."

Jasper slid his arm around her and drew her closer to his side. "Was there any indication in the letter about where he is staying?"

Belinda turned the letter over and looked at it closely. "It looks as if he's near Painswick."

Ali gave a little gasp. "That's in Gloucestershire, near

Daniel's estate. If we went there, we could look for Peter. And see Sarah-Jane."

Jasper smiled at her. "That would work well." He pulled Ali closer and she bent down to press a kiss on his lips.

"Thank you. I really want to see Cece and the new baby." She tumbled onto his lap and kissed him again. Jasper was still holding Belinda and he turned to her, bringing her into the kiss. Ali was right. A strand of three cords would not easily be broken.

———

Lord Keeton's comfortable open landau rumbled slowly along the lane and turned onto the post road that led through the village nearest his home. Ali leaned back against the dark blue squabs and stretched her leg out in front of her. Nell, sitting opposite her, was peering at every person they passed, hoping to catch a glimpse of Lord Summerson who was still, so she believed, in the neighborhood, although they had not seen him at all during Ali's convalescence.

Belinda moved a little closer to Ali and pulled the blue and green plaid rug straight. "Are you comfortable, my love?"

Ali smiled. "Yes, thank you. I am so glad you decided to come with us. Robbie and Daniel will be able to help, I know." Her eyes wandered to Jasper who was riding alongside the carriage. "Everything will work out well."

Nell made a startled sound. The other two turned to her. "What is it?" asked Ali, somewhat alarmed.

"Look, isn't that Lord Keeton's grumpy butler?" She pointed as the carriage passed through the town center.

Belinda and Ali looked in the direction in which she was pointing. Just outside the haberdasher's, two men were in earnest conversation. One wore the bright scarlet of the militia, and even at this distance, the girls could see his insignia was that of a colonel. The other man, dressed in sober black, was definitely Symes. Jasper slowed his horse, also watching the two men. "Mannering." He identified the colonel. "I wonder what that's about." As they moved past the men, Jasper remembered that Mannering was a known crony of Brigadier Wallace and shared some of his ideas about war and Wellington. As they drove past, Jasper noticed Symes give Mannering a folded piece of paper.

Traveling was very pleasant, as the weather was sunny and the roads were in good condition. Even Belinda was able to relax and forget her anxieties about Peter and her uncertainty about the future with Ali and Jasper. The posting inns where they stopped were comfortable and the company was amiable.

The sun was beginning to set, two days after they left Dorset, when the landau turned into the long drive that led to Daniel Eliot's manor house. The golden stones glowed in the afternoon light and the wide wooden door was standing open to allow the afternoon breeze to keep the house cool.

As soon as the carriage pulled up in front of the big main door, Jane and Messy came running down the steps, Ruffles rushing in circles around them. Lord Robbie and Daniel Eliot were just behind them. The twins descended quickly and ran to greet their sisters, stopping to pet the little brown dog who was barking a welcome at them. Belinda sat in the carriage, watching them and Jasper, who was handing his horse over to a groom.

Suddenly, Ali broke away from Jane and ran over to the carriage, laughing. "Come on, Belinda. Let's go and get changed and then we can go to Daniel's herbarium. His gardener has some wonderful ideas about plants and he was keeping some specimens for me."

Jasper saw to the stabling of his horses and then also went upstairs to change out of his riding breeches. He joined Robbie and Daniel in the library where the windows looked out over a long sweep of lawn surrounded by colorful flower beds. The setting sun cast a low light into the wood that was usually dark because of the paneling that covered the walls between the heavy bookshelves.

"You are very welcome here," began Daniel, as he poured brandy for each of them, "but your letter didn't give much explanation for why you needed to come to Gloucestershire."

Jasper turned from the window where he had been watching Ali and Belinda wander across the lawn arm-in-arm and took his glass of brandy, which he drained before sitting down and leaning his hands on his knees. Briefly, he filled the others in on the burglary that had taken place at Peter Bennet's cottage. "He has been living in this area since he left London, in a remote cottage that belongs to a friend. We might be able to track him down, and then, if we talk to him, then perhaps much of this will begin to make sense."

"I think it is time to speak to him," Daniel said. "There is more going on here than meets the eye." He sat up even straighter and looked at Jasper; his face was impassive but his eyes were hard. "Everything is centered in your house, and we have, I believe, missed something vital. We must consider all your servants as under suspicion until we know who Bennet's contacts are."

Keeton bristled but bit back his retort. Eliot's point was valid but he couldn't think of any of his servants who could not be trusted. They had all been with the family for many years and had always been loyal. But even as he tried to relax, he remembered how Symes had been talking to Colonel Mannering.

He took a deep breath. "Belinda has given me the letters she has received from her brother and you have the ones he sent her earlier about Turner." He passed them over.

Robbie took them. "I was able to find out that Turner inherited a cottage from his godmother in this district."

Eliot shot him a glance. "Why have you only mentioned this now?"

The earl shrugged. "I only had the information confirmed just before Keeton arrived."

"Then we will pay a visit to Mr. Peter Bennet tomorrow morning."

Chapter 11

"OH, SHE SMILED AT ME!" Ali exclaimed as she rocked her newborn niece in her arms.

Nell reached over her shoulder and little Sarah-Jane gripped Nell's finger in her tiny fist. "She's strong. And beautiful. She has such big eyes." The baby stretched and yawned but then suddenly her little mouth scrunched up and she let out a yell that filled the room.

"What's the matter? Have I hurt her?" Ali asked.

Cece laughed. "She's hungry, that's all. Here, give her to me." Gingerly, Ali handed her over and soon the little one was noisily drinking milk from her mother's breast. Cece looked at her sisters, admiring how striking they were with their similar features and dark hair. "You've let your hair grow, Nell. I like the way you are arranging it now. Those curls are very pretty."

Nell blushed. "Yes. I like this year's fashion of dressing hair. It is romantic and pretty."

"And there are a number of gentlemen who have particularly admired your new look," Ali teased.

Nell's blush deepened. "They are simply being polite.

Besides, there are none of them whom I particularly admire and, unlike you, I have no intention of forming any particular attachments this year," she deflected. "You're the one who is hearing the sound of wedding bells chiming, whereas the only ones that are chiming for me are in my book."

Cece cocked her head to the side. "I believe that Lord Summerson has been among your admirers and I distinctly remember you saying that you considered him the model of a perfect man."

Nell tossed her head. "He is good-looking and charming, but he has no interest in me. I am nothing like the women with whom he prefers to keep company. He treated me as if I were an object of vague amusement, a strange kind of creature he had never encountered before and which he had no real desire to see again." She couldn't keep the hurt and feeling of rejection out of her voice and her sisters knew her well enough to understand that her admiration for the rake had not diminished. Ali slipped an arm around her waist and Nell shifted the conversation. "You're the one who has formed strong connections and found love."

Ali's smile was quite smug as she answered Nell. "I never believed that my heart would govern my head. It is a glorious feeling to love and be loved."

Jane, accompanied by her two sons, entered the room in time to hear the last part of this conversation. Her sons scrambled up onto the bed to look at their cousin but Jane turned to the twins with a smile. She was concerned about Nell's continued infatuation with Lord Summerson but hoped that a summer in the country, away from his influence, would send her thoughts in a different direction. Nell was still chasing after rainbows and was likely to fall hopelessly in love with all kinds of men before she found her one true love.

Ali was a different matter. "Are we going to be planning

another wedding before the year is out?" Jane, the ever-practical, wanted to know.

Ali's smile faded a little and she bit her lip, pushing her glasses up her nose as she looked at each of her sisters in turn. "Before we can begin to discuss what might happen, both Jasper and Belinda need to solve the issues in their families. Besides, our situation is so odd that I don't really know how we will resolve it. Jasper might choose to marry Belinda rather than me."

"You really are in a difficult situation," Nell agreed. "It has been most interesting watching the three of you interact. It is clear that each of you loves the others. It would be thrilling to write your story in one of my books but no one would accept it."

Ali joined the laughter of the others, but she admonished her sister. "Real-life people are not as easy to control as the characters in books. We can't wave a magic pen and change the world to suit our reality."

Nell laughed as well even as she defended herself. "The characters in my book do not always behave the way I want them to."

The door burst open and Messy stumbled in, followed by a rambunctious Ruffles who raced twice around the room, stopping to sniff at all the corners and bark when he thought he had found an interesting scent that needed investigation. Sarah-Jane, who had just been nodding off to sleep, began to howl.

"No dogs near my cousin!" Little Lord Gregory sounded very stern. "She's too little to play and dogs can be rough," he dutifully repeated the scolding he had received from his nanny when he had brought his own dog, Brutus, to be introduced to the baby.

Messy caught hold of Ruffles and sent him outside. "I'm so sorry. I didn't mean to wake the baby. But I wanted to hear all about the twins' news." She looked around the room with a grin. "It's been a long time since we were all five together, just like old times. Growing up is all very well but it's horrid that we can't stay together just because some of you wanted to get married. And now it looks as if only Nell and I will still be at home." There was a tinge of wistfulness underneath her humor.

Her sisters laughed at her muddled speech. "It would be easier to see each other more often if traveling didn't take so long, or if we lived a little closer to each other," Jane said. "Although we will all be together in London for the Season."

"Not really," Nell argued. "Cece wasn't there this year and who knows whether you'll be having another baby next year." Her lip trembled as she slipped her arm around Ali's waist. "And Ali will be all the way down in Dorset, hunting for fossils and plants with Jasper and Belinda, and maybe having babies of her own."

Ali hugged her sister. "No matter how far I am from you, you'll always be my twin. Besides, you might form an attachment soon and we could have a double wedding."

"Oh, do!" Messy enthused. "Then I will only have to be a bridesmaid one more time. I wonder if the saying is true— three times a bridesmaid, never a bride? Because then, I won't ever get married if I'm your bridesmaid."

Jane tugged the loose curl that hung over Messy's shoulder. "I don't think you need to worry about old superstitions."

"A double wedding would be fun, but that's completely unlikely unless you're prepared to wait for years until I find someone to love who loves me too, and who fits my idea of an ideal husband," Nell said.

"What about Lord Blackstone?" Ali prompted. "You spent a lot of time talking to him at Mrs. Carter's soirée and you danced twice with him at the Blackstone's ball."

Nell pulled a face. "He is pleasant but so dull and ordinary. There is nothing exciting about him, nothing wild and adventurous. He is reasonably good at all he does but doesn't excel at anything. Besides, he spent most of the time explaining why young ladies should be demure and obeisant. I think he would have a fit if he saw me in breeches."

"I can't imagine that many gentlemen would not be alarmed by your choice of clothes," Jane said dryly.

Nell ran her hands over the fitted breeches she was wearing. "Which is why I cannot marry someone like Lord Blackstone. I would never be able to be myself, not all the time. I seem to be so many different people, that it's confusing at times, even to me. One moment, I'm a demure débutante who delights in wearing pretty dresses and who's flattered when a handsome gentleman asks me to dance, but then I want to run wild and free across the fields, climb trees, and swim in the rivers near Lamercie. And besides, gentlemen might enjoy reading novels by lady writers, but they do not want to marry the author."

Ali gave her another hug, while Jane said, "We're none of us particularity conventional, and yet Cece and I found men who love us and accept us as we are, and Ali is likely to be married soon in a very unconventional liaison. I'm sure you will find the man meant for you who will love every facet of your character and help you to flourish."

Nell kept her arm around Ali's waist as she turned the conversation back to her twin's dilemma. "If I were writing your story in a book, I would arrange it so that Jasper married both you and Belinda, but society would never approve and so another way must be found for you to find your happily-ever-after."

Ali laughed. "It is complicated, but I will wait until Jasper actually proposes before I begin making my wedding clothes."

"What's this?" Lord Robbie's cheerful voice echoed through the room as he and Daniel Eliot entered. "So Jasper Keeton has spoken, has he?"

Ali shook her head in frustration, not wanting to explain the whole situation yet again. She was glad that Gregory and Michael, excited to see their father who had promised to take them fishing, rushed to him, shouting excitedly. Ali slipped out of the room in the hullabaloo, to find Belinda and Jasper.

Lord Keeton turned from his position at the window where he had been watching Belinda and Alicia stroll arm-in-arm in the delightful pleasure gardens that surrounded Lord Eliot's house. Lord Halstead, who had recently arrived along with Barlow and Bellingham, was watching him with a smirk. "I see there are more important matters for you to consider than the possible plots of traitors and assassins."

Jasper colored slightly but answered with his usual polite manner. "I do apologize. Did you ask me something?"

Simon Barlow chuckled. "We've been trying to get your attention for the last five minutes," he exaggerated. His face became more sober. "Do we understand correctly that Peter Bennet is cloistered somewhere in this district?"

Keeton gave a quick nod. "A friend of his, Captain Turner, has a cottage just over ten miles from here that is quite secluded, miles from the nearest neighbor."

Lord Halstead leaned forward. "Perhaps it would be best for you and Belinda to go. It is likely to attract less attention and you will be able to bring him back here."

Bellingham looked up from the page he had been reading to say, "I would like to see how the person broke into the cottage and talk to Mr. Bennet about some of the points in these letters. I think there might be some clues among his own papers that will help us unravel this mess." He tapped the page in front of him. "Eliot and I have made some progress, but we will have a more complete picture if we see those documents, too."

"I doubt that we could learn much about the person who broke in from seeing the cottage. It was a few weeks ago, and any trace of him will have vanished by now," Barlow said.

"But still, there might be something of interest. In fact, Bennet himself is of interest and I would like to go," insisted Bellingham.

Robbie said, "I think that is a good idea. Also, it might be a good idea to have an unbiased observer keep an eye on Bennet. You might notice something that the others miss."

Halstead raised his eyebrow and looked questioningly at Daniel Eliot who was standing near the fireplace, his foot on the fender. "Can you accommodate one more person? We have taken over your house."

Eliot looked as impassive as usual but his voice was dry with irony as he said, "I suppose the price of so recently becoming a father is that my home must, of necessity, draw all kinds of guests to it. By all means, bring Peter Bennet and any other strays you might find on the way. We have plenty of room."

The others laughed.

When they were quiet, Jasper said, "There is something else I need to mention. I've given some thought to who in my household might have been passing on information. It is difficult to imagine that there is someone I cannot trust, but I believe that it is possible for people to become so fanatical about an ideal that they will forsake all other values to promote their cause."

The others nodded and Robbie waved his hand, urging Jasper to get to the point.

"My father's valet, Symes, whom I kept on as an under-butler, is an old soldier and we saw him talking to Colonel Mannering, an acquaintance of Brigadier Wallace."

Halstead looked at Barlow. "Can you find out more about him?"

Barlow nodded, and with a reluctant glance at Bellingham, said, "I will have to return to London for that."

Belinda was silent as the barouche made its way down the overgrown, rutted lane. The sun, which had been shining brightly for the last three days, was sulking behind grey clouds. Ali had also fallen silent, but she slipped her hand around Belinda's and squeezed lightly. Belinda kept her eyes on the road but squeezed back and moved slightly closer to Ali. Jasper, seated on the opposite bench with Bellingham, watched them, and a slight smile creased the corners of his mouth.

The carriage rounded a bend and turned into a short driveway. A ramshackle cottage with ivy growing up its walls and thatch badly in need of repair stood at the end of the lane. The windows were all closed and everything was still. Not even the birds sang. Jasper brought the barouche to a standstill but no one moved. Fear gripped Belinda's heart and her stomach was in a knot.

After a moment or two, when they all sat in silence, Bellingham said, "Well, we're not going to achieve anything sitting here." He swung down from his seat behind the horses and Jasper opened the door, letting down the steps. He held out his hand and Ali took it as she descended. Belinda was still sitting frozen in the far corner. Jasper leaned over the seat and took her hand. "Come, love. Let's see where Peter is."

She looked into his eyes and, comforted by the tenderness she saw, she let him guide her down and to the front door where Bellingham had already sounded the brass knocker. The banging echoed hollowly into the house. No answering sound was heard. Belinda clutched Jasper's hand and leaned against Ali who was standing close behind her.

Bellingham tried the knocker again, but again, the only response was silence. He turned around and walked past the others to a diamond-paned window. He rubbed the glass with his gloved hand and peered in. It was dark inside but he could make out a desk on which papers were scattered as if someone had been looking for something but not found it. Some papers had fallen to the floor.

He stood back and shook his head. "Something is not right. I am going to see if the kitchen door is open."

Belinda gave a little gasp and Ali tightened her hold on her. Bellingham made his way around the cottage. The others followed silently. Belinda shivered when a crow cawed nearby.

The kitchen door was closed, but a gentle shove against it made it swing open with a rusty creak. Bellingham patted his coat pocket in which he had placed his pistol. He didn't want to alarm the others but he did want to be prepared in case they encountered trouble.

The house was silent as the grave. A plate and wine glass were on the kitchen table and a pot had been left on the hob, but the fire was ice cold and the stew congealed. It had been a long time since the fire had been lit. Quickly, they made their way through the small cottage. It did not take long. The kitchen opened into the front room where the desk Bellingham had seen was near the window and a small sofa stood in front of the small hearth place. A narrow staircase led to a low-eaved bedroom. The covers of the bed were neatly arranged and clothes were in the wardrobe. But Peter was nowhere to be found.

Belinda began to clear away the dishes in the kitchen,

blinking back tears that stung her eyes. Ali helped her silently while Bellingham and Keeton gathered together the papers in the study.

Bellingham paused as words on one page caught his eye. "Now, that's interesting," he murmured softly, but Keeton, only a few feet away, heard him.

He straightened from his task of collecting the papers that were on the floor. "What is?"

"A letter. It could explain why Bennet left in such a hurry."

Belinda, who had put away the cleaned dishes, came to the doorway. It was difficult to speak. She tried once but no words came out. She cleared her throat and began again. "Where is Peter?"

Bellingham glanced at her and his face softened. Perhaps she truly had no knowledge of her brother's plots. She was shocked and fearful.

"He has gone to London to join the other conspirators."

"No!" The word was hoarse and caught in her throat, but the others heard it. Ali placed her arm around Belinda's waist and led her outside.

The two men looked at each other wordlessly, gathered the papers, and followed them.

When they arrived back at Brockworth Manor, Belinda excused herself and went to her room to lie down. A headache was throbbing behind her eyes and she felt dizzy. Ali brought her a cup of chamomile tea, pulled the blankets over her, kissed her forehead gently, and then left her to try to sleep away her troubled thoughts.

In the meantime, Jasper and Bellingham joined Halstead and the other gentlemen in the library. Barlow was at the desk sorting through the papers they had brought from Bennet's cottage. The others all looked very somber as they perused the documents that were already sorted.

Jasper sat down near the desk and picked up a dossier which he began to flip through.

Lord Halstead leaned forward. "Why would Bennet leave some of his clothes behind and all these papers?"

"Perhaps he no longer had need of them," suggested Barlow.

"He does not strike me as a man of fashion, but it is odd that he did not take his clothes. He might no longer have need of the documents, but surely, he is not going to buy a whole new wardrobe."

Eliot looked thoughtful. "He might if he were attempting a disguise of some sort. Let me see that letter again." Halstead handed it to him and Eliot read the words aloud. *"Bennet. The duke will be in London this week before he returns to France. Now is the time to take action. W."*

"Who is W?" asked Bellingham.

"Wallace?" Lord Robbie suggested.

"Perhaps," said Halstead, "but he likes to use his title. I doubt he would be on such familiar terms with Peter Bennet."

"He might not if he did not want to be identified."

"Then why use Bennet's name?" Lord Robbie argued.

"He is not as well known. But at the moment, our priority is trying to work out what their plan is," Eliot said. "Some of these papers are written in code. I have made some progress with the previous ones and if I apply the same techniques to these, I might be able to understand them."

Halstead rose. "I think it is imperative that we return to London as soon as possible. Eliot, can you bring yourself to leave your wife and daughter for a few days? Any delay might prove fatal."

Chapter 12

ALI TILTED her chin and crossed her arms across her chest. "We're not staying here. It's Belinda's brother and she needs to go to London to find him. I wouldn't stay here if you were missing."

Jane raised her eyebrow. It was not like Alicia to behave so petulantly or so emotionally. "I would, perhaps, trust an *adult* to be in London, but such childish behavior arouses deep concerns about your ability to behave sensibly."

Alicia blushed and dropped her arms and head. "I'm sorry, Jane. It just doesn't seem fair that men can always dash off wherever and whenever they want to but we have to stay meekly at home as if we would just be in the way."

Jane resumed sewing Michael's new nightshirt. "I do understand your frustration, but I wonder if it would not be better for Belinda to be here, rather than in London."

Ali sat down next to her sister. "She would fret and worry. She needs to feel that she is doing something."

Jane was thoughtful. "I believe you are right, but I would feel less anxious if there was someone steadier with you."

"What about Louisa Halstead? Is she staying here or returning to Derbyshire?"

"I believe she will go to London with Hugh."

Ali smiled. "She can keep an eye on me."

Jane pretended to groan. "I will go and warn her."

Belinda read Peter's letter for the hundredth time, at least. Nothing really made sense. She had expected to find him here in London. His previous letter had prompted her to go to Gloucestershire, but then he had disappeared. Now the paper trail led back to London. But London was a big city where people could easily vanish. She shook her head. Surely, Peter was not hiding from her? And how could he be involved with anything as ignominious as an assassination plot? She had to find him so that he could clear up all the misunderstandings but no one knew where he was. The earl and Lord Halstead had tried various places where Peter had boarded in London previously but no one had seen him. They had also not been able to track down Captain Turner who had not been seen in his barracks for at least five days.

She stared at the letter again. It contained no hint that Peter had been thinking of coming to London and Belinda had no idea where to begin looking for him. Jasper leaned forward and took the letter out of her hands. "A walk in the park will clear the cobwebs from your brain."

Belinda attempted a smile. She gave the letter one more glance and then folded it and tucked it into her reticule. She and Ali were having an early luncheon at Jasper's uncle's town house where he was staying. It was rude of her to keep focusing on her letter instead of joining the conversation but she had lost track of the discussion of toxicology and medicinal plants that had kept Jasper and Ali so enthralled.

Ali handed Belinda her straw bonnet with a laugh. " Come on. Jasper's gone to arrange for his carriage to take us to Hyde Park." Neither of them noticed the sneer that quickly crossed the face of Symes, the under-butler, as he handed them their gloves.

A little while later, Belinda breathed deeply as the quiet and beauty of Hyde Park brought a little peace to her troubled mind. Jasper and Ali chatted about inconsequential matters and Belinda almost began to relax, although she wasn't really listening to the others.

They turned down their favorite path that ran along the banks of the Serpentine and were strolling slowly, enjoying the warmth of the day and admiring a pair of swans as they glided on the smooth water when, suddenly, Belinda stopped. It took the other two a moment to realize they had left her behind.

Ali turned around. "Come along, slow coach." She laughed. But then she caught sight of the expression on Belinda's face and all her levity evaporated. She hurried back to where Belinda was still standing and Jasper was close on her heels.

"What is it, love? What's happened?" Ali put her hand on Belinda's arm.

Belinda blinked as if she were just waking up. She was still staring at a spot farther along the path although there was nobody there. "I-I saw…" Her voice trailed off.

Ali jiggled her arm but her voice was very gentle as she asked, "Belinda, who did you see?"

Belinda blinked again. "P-Peter. He was there." She pointed vaguely.

Ali looked around in bewilderment. "Where? There's no one there to alarm you, only a nanny and some children."

Belinda looked distraught. "He was there. I saw him," she insisted.

"Did he see you?" Jasper asked.

"He looked right at me and then turned away as if he had no idea who I am." Belinda's voice was so brittle that Ali shivered. Even though they were in a public place, she hugged Belinda hard and kissed her cheek.

Jasper was standing very close to the girls, shielding them from the curious eyes of passers-by. As they talked, he scanned the people around them. He had only ever seen a portrait of Peter Bennet, but he was certain he could recognize him. However, the only people he could see were nannies and governesses with their charges. This was not the fashionable hour for the park as most members of the *haut ton* were either still asleep or shopping in fashionable Bond Street.

After a few moments, he placed his hand on Belinda's shoulder. "Let's go back to the earl's house. We can talk there."

Each of the ladies took one of his arms, and a quarter of an hour later, they were sitting in the small blue drawing room, which was the favorite place for the family to relax. The earl ordered refreshments and they were soon sipping hot tea, although none of them touched the little lemon cakes that the housekeeper had sent in with the teapot.

Lord Robbie asked, "What, precisely, did you see this morning?"

Belinda scowled. "I've already explained. Peter was walking along the path and then he disappeared."

The earl raised an eyebrow and his usually affable demeanor vanished. "If you expect us to help you and your brother, who is looking more and more suspicious, then a little cooperation will go a long way."

"I'm sorry, my lord."

The earl gave a brief nod and turned to Jasper. "If you are serious about taking on these two ladies in a permanent arrangement, then now might be the right time to establish how things will work. They both need a strong hand to guide them."

Alicia and Belinda were stunned for a moment. Jasper smiled at them, straightened his shoulders, and answered Robbie. "As soon as we've finished here, I will ensure Belinda learns how to show a little more respect to others. Ali, too."

Ali, who had been sitting quietly in a deep armchair, spluttered. "I'm the epitome of amenability and compliance!"

Lord Robbie quirked an eyebrow but said nothing to his ward. He turned his attention back to Belinda. "Now that we have that sorted out, let's get back to the more pressing matters. Any little detail of what you saw this morning, even if you don't think it's important, might help us to unravel the mystery."

A faint flush colored Belinda's face, but the last few minutes had reassured her that she belonged here with these people even though she had been raised to despise the aristocracy. Living with them, had convinced her that not all of them were idle and selfish. And she was definitely falling in love with Ali and Jasper which meant she would be spending much more time with members of the *haut ton*. She gave the earl a quick nod and then began. "Peter was walking towards us along the path. He was with two other men, one of them in the uniform of the Horse Guards."

"Did you recognize either of them?"

Belinda swung her head around. Lord Halstead, and the other gentlemen who made up the elite group of spymasters, had arrived while she was speaking. They quickly sat down and Lord Halstead nodded to Belinda to continue.

She swallowed. "I did not see the officer clearly but he didn't appear familiar. He was of average height and his hair was light brown. The other person was taller and thinner. He had a long, lean face and was wearing clothes that were not well cared for." She blinked and took a deep breath. "I didn't really notice much other than Peter. I'm sorry." She took a deep breath. "Peter looked more disheveled than usual. His hair was messy and uncut and his cravat was askew. He wasn't wearing a hat."

Robbie leaned forward. "And he saw you? You're sure?"

Belinda tightened her mouth. "Yes. He looked directly at me and then he turned away. I tried to call out his name but it was difficult to speak. I closed my eyes for a moment and then when I looked again, they were gone. They must have gone into the grove of trees nearby. When we followed the only path they could have taken, there was no sign of anyone."

"In which direction did they go?" Lord Halstead asked.

Belinda glanced at Jasper and Ali. She was not very familiar with London and wasn't sure of the different areas. Jasper smiled reassuringly at her. "The path leads towards Uxbridge Road and Tomlins Town cottages."

"That's where workers from the waterworks are housed," Lord Halstead commented.

"Not the most salubrious place in London," Eliot said.

Belinda looked alarmed and Ali leaned forward to take her hand. "It's all right," she whispered. "There must be a perfectly good explanation. Peter could have just been leaving the park that way."

The earl looked at her and nodded encouragingly. "They could be anywhere. Don't give up hope."

Daniel Eliot's mouth straightened into a thin line. "It is best not to allow personal sentiment to overrule clear objectivity. That way, something important could be overlooked."

Ali glared at her brother-in-law, but the earl nodded.

"Something about this does not feel right," Halstead

mused. "Who knew that you were going to take a walk there this morning?"

Ali shook her head. "No one. It was a spur-of-the-moment decision."

Jasper sat up straighter. "We did use my landau to get there, which means that my servants knew something of our movements." He clenched and then unclenched his fists as the others watched him quietly. He took a deep breath. "A footman or groom would have had time to send a message to Bennet. We had been in the park for quite a while before Belinda saw her brother."

"We usually walk along the banks of the river. It's one of our favorite places," Ali said, sitting up straighter and looking concerned. "They could have been waiting for us and appeared just in time to make sure Belinda would see Peter. " She paused. "But why? It doesn't make sense."

Jasper's expression became even more somber. "It is beginning to look more and more as if someone on my staff is in league with the traitors."

Halstead nodded but looked sympathetic. "We have been gathering information on some of your staff. You haven't taken on any new people since your father passed, except for two housemaids and a scullery maid, who are back in Dorset. Of course, you brought some of your own staff with you to London because your uncle is in Brighton for the summer." Jasper nodded, and Halstead continued. "We have taken the most interest in your valet and your secretary."

Jasper frowned but Halstead continued before he said anything in their defense. "We believe that they are loyal to you and the country." He gave a quick smile.

Barlow picked up the thread. "There are, however, two or three people who do concern us. The first is a footman who wanted to enlist, but his father, who is a vicar in a small country village, would not let him. Joe is outspoken about the glory of war and the heroism of soldiers. He wants the war to start again so that he can become a soldier."

Jasper thought of the earnest young footman who had been reprimanded more than once for his aggression towards other members of the staff. He nodded. "He is here in London. Who else is on your list?"

"Your under-butler, Symes, was your father's valet." Barlow said. "He fought in the Peninsula and did not want to leave the army, but he was injured. He believes that Napoleon must be properly defeated, not left to his own devices on Elba."

"Many people think that, but most are not considering a treasonous act to see it happen," Eliot said dryly. He picked up a dossier in which neatly arranged documents had been placed. He flipped through them carefully and then extracted two pages. "I've worked out the code." His voice was as bland as if he were mentioning that he had drunk a cup of tea for breakfast. He ignored the surprise and satisfaction on the others' faces and glanced at the pages. "The different codes were variations of a basic one in which a keyword is used." He glanced up at the others with a slight twist of his mouth that didn't quite turn into a smile. "Once I realized that one keyword was *Napoleon*, I simply tried names of other generals and now all the coded information is clear."

Halstead gave a quick laugh. "That's great. So, are you going to let us know, or are we expected to guess what the message says?"

Daniel flashed a rare smile that made him look much more approachable. Belinda could see why Cecilia had fallen so hopelessly in love with such an apparently emotionless man.

Daniel's smile disappeared. "It is a very serious matter. The earlier letters are not of much import right now, but the ones that were in the cottage where Bennet was hiding need immediate attention." When Halstead made an impatient gesture, Eliot's eyes flickered and his mouth tightened. He smoothed out the pages he had selected from the dossier and began to read the first one. "*We have a narrow window. The most propitious moment will be during the re-enactment of the Battle of the Nile on the Serpentine during the Grand Jubilee celebrations. You all know your roles.*"

There was silence for a few moments. The earl shook his head. "That doesn't give us much to go on. We believe that Wellington is the target, but we don't have any actual proof so we can't ask him not to attend."

"He wouldn't stay away, even if he thought he was in danger," Halstead said.

"We need to stop the traitors before then." The earl's voice was much more somber than usual.

"But we don't even know who is in the group, except Bennet," Barlow pointed out.

Belinda gave a startled gasp. "No, someone is trying to make him the scapegoat! Peter is not a murderer."

The others all looked at her but no one said anything. Ali squeezed her hand tightly. Jasper rose to his feet. "Perhaps it would be best if Ali, Belinda, and I left you to strategize and discuss what must happen now."

Ali responded to his cue by standing up and yanking Belinda to her feet. Belinda started to splutter a protest but Jasper raised an eyebrow and she followed meekly.

When they had left, Halstead looked at his team, his face grimmer than usual. "Our best clue is the unexpected appearance of Bennet this morning. If we can find out where he is staying, we might have a chance to put an end to this plot before it goes much further."

"I will organize our street brigade, to see if they can find out anything about where Bennet is staying," Barlow said.

Over the years, Halstead had established a network of eager young delivery and errand boys who knew the streets of London and who were excellent at picking up tidbits of information from all over the city. They had proved very useful.

"And we need to go back to our original investigation of Wallace and his nephew," Halstead said.

"And Turner. He is involved, without a doubt." He nodded at the earl. "Can you find a way of inveigling your way into a card game or something like that with the brigadier?"

Robbie nodded. "I'll go to White's this evening."

"Eliot, Bellingham and Barlow need to continue working through the documents. There might be something there we've missed."

Barlow suppressed a low groan at Lord Halstead's words, and Bellingham squeezed his hand sympathetically. "When you finish with the brigade, we can go for a ride out to Richmond. That will clear the cobwebs and help you concentrate when we tackle the documents."

Barlow kissed Bellingham's hand. "Thanks."

The others gathered their things together in preparation for their various tasks.

***

Jasper led Belinda and Ali to the earl's library. He closed the door and turned to look at them. Standing side by side, they made a very alluring picture, Belinda's fair hair contrasting with Ali's dark curls and her lean figure setting off Ali's more obvious curves. They both wore green dresses, but Ali's was a deeper moss and Belinda's was a paler spring green. Ali took hold of Belinda's hand, entwining their fingers, but they both looked at him with wide eyes.

He had to hold back a chuckle at how apprehensive they looked. He wanted to help them. He would never hurt them. Apart from the sting of his hand on their buttocks that was more stimulating than sore. He folded his arms. "Well, Miss Bennet, do you understand why we are here?"

Belinda's first impulse was to give a pert answer but she raised her eyes to Jasper's and something inside her melted. "I was rude to Lord Medwell." Real remorse made her voice husky. She didn't want her foolishness to get in the way of the bond the three of them were forming.

Jasper dropped his arms to his side and stepped towards her. He placed his left hand at the back of her neck and spread his fingers, holding her firmly. "My love, you have a tendency to become defensive when you feel uncertain of yourself. Your emotions become erratic and your instinct, understandably, is to protect yourself because there has never been someone in your life who cares for you." Belinda started to protest, but he covered her lips with the index finger of his right hand. "Your father and brother cared for you in a vague, remote way that left you believing that you do not quite belong anywhere or that you do not really matter. I want to help you find a way to release your emotions so that you can feel more secure, more sure of yourself, when you are faced by something or someone you perceive as threatening." His smile was full of tender affection. "Because you do matter. Very much. To me and to Ali."

Ali nodded enthusiastically in agreement and slid her arm around Belinda's waist and kissed her cheek. "You have brought something into my life I didn't even know was missing. Nell and I have always been extremely close, but with you and Jasper, there is something deeper, something more powerful than I have ever known, even with my twin sister."

Belinda felt tears prick her eyes and she blinked rapidly. She never cried. Yet over the past few months, as she had grown closer to Alicia and Jasper, her heart had become softer and she felt herself on the verge of tears more often than she ever had previously in her life. She breathed deeply as Jasper kept his eyes focused on hers. He had the ability to see beyond the shields she held up and understand what she felt deep in her heart. And Ali was able to express the feelings of all their hearts.

After a few moments that felt like a lifetime in which she evolved into a better version of herself, Jasper removed his hand and stepped away. He moved a large leather chair with no arms into the middle of the room. Then he removed his coat and rolled up the sleeves of his fine linen shirt before sitting down, his legs slightly apart. "Come here, pretty Belinda."

Belinda hesitated, but Ali squeezed her hand and encouraged her to move to where Jasper was waiting. Ali was right behind her. Her arm was around Belinda's waist. Belinda drew strength and comfort from Ali's closeness and from the memories of how Jasper had spanked Ali that day on the beach. It has been far more arousing than Belinda could have imagined. And now she was going to be spanked. But her misdemenor was much more serious than Ali's playful teasing of Jasper. And this punishment was sure to match the severity of Belinda's bad behavior.

Jasper steadied his legs, his knees slightly apart, his hard thigh muscles forming a perfect place for Belinda. He held out his hand. "Come, my love."

With one desperate glance at Ali, Belinda let go of her hand and stepped towards Jasper. She clenched her hands tightly and looked at him, both wanting to please him but unsure how to place herself on his waiting lap. He took her hands and guided her to his right side and then gently bent her over his knees. She braced her arms at the sudden loss of control and desperately kicked her legs in an effort to get her balance.

She had not noticed Ali kneeling down in front of her and was startled to hear her say, "Relax, Belinda. Don't struggle." Ali took hold of her face and smoothed her fingers over her cheeks. Belinda let the sensations flow over her. She relaxed and placed her hands on Ali's shoulders, drawing her closer. For a moment, she forgot her awkward and uncomfortable position on Jasper's lap. It was only when Ali sat back on her heels that she became aware of Jasper's hand in the middle of her back. She tried to twist her head to see his face but it was difficult, so she dropped back and looked at Ali instead. Ali's eyes gleamed and the corners of her mouth twisted up as she tried to suppress a smile. She stroked Belinda's hair with her left hand while the other caressed her arms.

Belinda relaxed, dropping her head down and leaning into Ali's body. Her muscles softened against Jasper's thighs. His hands had been roaming over her back ceaselessly and now he moved lower, rubbing her bottom through the layers of her dress and petticoat. She liked the heat that soaked into her and she sighed gently.

Finally, after what seemed like hours, Jasper spoke quietly. "My love, do you remember why we are here?"

Belinda nodded and then said, "You're going to spank me because I was rude to the earl."

Jasper's answer was to ease the material of her dress up, baring her legs and bum. She stiffened, but Ali tugged her hair gently, and when she could think clearly again, Jasper was already dropping light smacks all over her buttocks. The light tingling was pleasant and she wriggled her bottom, trying to encourage him to touch her in places his hand hadn't yet found.

"Belinda, my love, this is not so much a punishment for

your rude behavior, as a way to help you release the emotions that you have buried for so many years. I am not going to decide on a certain number of smacks but watch how you respond. When I believe there is a breakthrough, I will stop."

Belinda stiffened. "What if there is no breakthrough?" Her voice was hoarse, as if she had already been sobbing.

"Then I will stop when I know you have had enough." With that, he raised his hand and brought it down sharply on the middle of her left bum cheek. She cried out at the sting but Jasper ignored her and repeated the action on her left side.

He quickly developed an uneven rhythm, covering her bottom with hard smacks that quickly turned it pink and then a deeper red. Each strike of his hand was placed in a different place, making it impossible for her to predict where the next would fall. She tried to bite back the cries that rose in her throat, but after a while, she surrendered. Everything around her faded and her world consisted only of the burning sensations on her bottom. At first, she resisted allowing the tears that bit the back of her eyes to fall. She could hear the echo of her father's scornful voice scolding her eight-year-old self when she had fallen and scraped her knees. "Tears are a weakness indulged in by those who have no control over themselves. There is no reason to cry, and intelligent, rational people control their emotions." She had not fully understood his words then, but as she grew older, she had tried to please him by never indulging in displays of emotion. Until now. Until she had met Alicia and Jasper.

She gasped as Jasper's hard hand landed on the sensitive place between her thighs snd her bottom. He smacked her again in exactly the same spot and her gasp turned into a loud cry. All thoughts of her father's disapproval dissipated like grains of salt dissolving in warm water. All that mattered now was Jasper's approval and Ali's love.

Her bottom was sore but the pain seeped into her body, softening the crusty layers that had covered her heart for so long, allowing her emotions to flow spontaneously. Suddenly, she gulped, and the large lump that had formed in her throat dissolved into loud sobs. A flood of tears was released from her eyes and cascaded down her cheeks. She cried noisily because of the pain of the spanking, but soon, she was crying for the loneliness of her life, for the little girl who had been forced to act like an adult, for her brother who had lost his way.

The longer she cried, the lighter and lighter Jasper's smacks became, until he was simply caressing her sore bum and murmuring softly to her. Ali's arm was around her shoulders and she rested her head against Ali's breast.

Belinda had no idea how much time had passed. She was exhausted, but her heart felt oddly content and at peace even though her throat was raw. She was snuggled against Jasper's chest, seated on his lap, but she did not remember moving from the position she had been in earlier. But she was too filled with a deep satisfaction to care. Ali was sitting next to Jasper, pressing closely against his side. Her hand was resting on Belinda's thigh.

Both of them were surrounded by Jasper's large body. Belinda had never felt so safe or loved. She sighed softly.

"How are you feeling, little one?" Jasper's voice was like the first ray of sunshine after a spring storm.

She breathed deeply again. "Good. I'm feeling good."

Jasper chuckled. "You are good, sweetheart. Very good. You took that spanking well."

Belinda attempted to sit up to look at him but he kept her pressed close to his chest. "I feel clean inside, as if eons of rubble has been cleared away. But I made a mess of your shirt and Ali's dress."

"They'll wash." Ali smiled at her. "You look so peaceful, so lovely."

"Lovely, with my eyes all puffy and my face red from crying," Belinda protested but she, too, smiled. She twisted to look at Jasper. "Do you really think I will no longer be defensive and rude after today? I don't like being at odds with the people around me."

He dropped a kiss on her hair. "Little one, there is a lifetime of beliefs and habits that won't vanish overnight, but it's a start." Belinda's face fell. "But Ali and I are here to help you through it all."

"Does that mean you're going to spank me again?"

Jasper laughed outright. "I rather like having the two of you over my lap. I'm sure even if you are completely cured of rudeness to the earl, I'll find some reason to have you here again." His eyes darkened with desire. "Besides, both of you show distinct signs of being aroused by spankings, and that increases my desire to kiss you, and do much more." He rocked his hips slightly so that Belinda could feel the hardness of his cock. She giggled and kissed the only part of his face she could reach.

Jasper turned her so he could take her mouth more fully with his own and Ali maneuvered herself onto his lap as well to join the kiss. It was many minutes before any of them was ready to stop.

Chapter 13

BELINDA TUGGED her cloak closer to her body in spite of the sweltering humidity of summer in London. The large peak of her bonnet shaded her face, making it difficult to identify her, not that anyone in this part of the city was likely to recognize her.

When a cart rumbled past, throwing up muck from the road that splattered her skirt, she questioned, not for the first time, the sanity of her spontaneous decision to seek out Jenny Smith, who had been their housekeeper in Dorset before marrying and moving to London with her husband. Jenny had always had a soft spot for Peter, and Belinda wondered if her brother was staying in the boarding house Jenny and her husband ran.

The farther Belinda wandered from the elegant and fashionable areas of Mayfair and Grosvenor Square, the noisier and dirtier the streets were. She turned a corner and wrinkled her nose at the mingled odor of rotting cabbage and horse manure. She was now near the docks and, impossible as it might have seemed, the noise grew more raucous.

She turned a corner and a man bumped into her,

uttering expletives as he moved on, not bothering to help Belinda, who skidded on an unidentifiable patch of slime. The man who had almost knocked her over nodded at another man with scraggly hair and a wicked-looking grin that revealed a row of yellowed teeth. The second man, who had been following Belinda since she left the earl's house, passed the other a gold sovereign and moved on, leaning against the grimy wall of a building to light a pipe, when Belinda stopped.

She paused in front of a narrow building next to a small courtyard where carts were being loaded with goods. She looked at a piece of paper she had been clutching in her gloved hand. Cautiously, she pushed the door open and entered a dark, narrow entryway. A faint aroma of boiled meat and cabbage permeated the house. Belinda shuddered. She could not imagine cheerful Jenny living in such a squalid, dark place after the wide open spaces of the coun-tryside. It took a few moments for her eyes to adjust to the darkness. The entry was empty, but she noticed a small brass bell on a narrow counter. She rang it and waited as the clang echoed through the house.

After a minute or two, a short, round woman bustled in, wiping her hands on a clean apron. When she saw Belinda, her face broke into a broad smile. "Miss, how good it is to see you. This is a surprise." She embraced Belinda in a tight hug.

"Jenny, you look happy."

The former housekeeper nodded. "This isn't Dorset, but Micky and I are independent and the business is doing well." Her eyes narrowed as she looked carefully at Belinda. "Why are you here? Not that it's not good to see you, miss, but you look a little worried and this is not the kind of establishment young ladies like you frequent."

Belinda sighed. "It's a long story, Jenny."

"Come into the kitchen, dear. A good cup of tea will

refresh you while you tell me all about it."

Belinda blinked back tears as she followed Jenny into a large, warm kitchen where a big pot was on the hob and a side of beef was cooking over the fire. She sat down at the long wooden table and was soon gratefully sipping a cup of strong tea. Jenny continued peeling potatoes and cutting carrots and turnips while she listened to Belinda's story. She said nothing until Belinda brought her tale of woe to an end. Only then, did she sit down at the table.

"You and Master Peter always had your heads screwed on right. I can't believe that either of you would get yourselves involved in anything wicked. I would stake my life on his innocence."

Belinda smiled for the first time since she had left the house that morning. "The problem is we don't know where he is now, and unless we find him, we cannot help him."

Jenny nodded. "Why did you come here today?"

Belinda put her empty cup in its saucer. "I wondered whether Peter had come to see you, or if you could suggest where he might be staying in London? I know he visited you when he first moved and I thought you might know some of his acquaintances."

Jenny shook her head. "I haven't seen him for a long time now. And after the story you've just told me, I understand why he didn't come to me for help." She was quiet for a moment and Belinda watched her, waiting. Jenny placed her hands on the table. "There might be a possibility that he is staying in a small house in Ludgate." When Belinda raised questioning eyes, she explained, "Master Peter took lodgings in a house there when he was working at the Foreign Office. He might have sought accommodation there again."

Hope brightened Belinda's face. "I didn't think of that. Do you still have the directions? My letters from him are still at home and I don't remember the address."

Jenny rose and opened a drawer in a large, solid oak dresser. She rummaged for a few minutes and then pulled out a box, which she opened. "I keep all the letters you and he send me in here." She pulled out one and handed it to Belinda who could not stop tears from trickling down her cheeks. Ever since she had sobbed her heart out over Jasper's lap, tears seemed to be ready to fall at the slightest provocation. She held the letter for a moment before she opened it. At first, the words were blurred, but after a moment, they cleared and she could read what her brother had written.

Half an hour later, she put on her cape again and left Jenny's house. She glanced up at the sky where clouds had gathered. Rain showers were not usual in late July, but those clouds looked ominous. It would take half an hour or more to get from the docks to Ludgate. But the sooner she found Peter, the better it would be. With a determined tweak of her cape, she walked to a stand where hansom cabs waited for passengers.

She did not notice the yellow-toothed man who had been leaning against a door on the opposite side of the road from Jenny's house saunter up to the hansom cab driver and talk to him quietly before slipping away into the shadows.

Belinda descended from the cab when it stopped in front of a tall, narrow building. Belinda's heart felt lighter. This was a more pleasant environment than Jenny's. Peter was likely very comfortable here. She stood on the pavement for a moment before knocking on the door.

A thin woman with greying hair opened the door just a slit. The scowl on her face deepened when she saw Belinda. "Yes?" she asked without preamble. Her voice was as thin and sharp as her appearance.

"I am Peter Bennet's sister and have come to see him." Belinda had decided that a direct approach would bring about the best results, but the woman's eyes narrowed.

"Likely story. He's not here, and my lodgers are not permitted to entertain female guests." The slight emphasis of her words and the way she looked Belinda up and down suggested something salacious.

Belinda gave her a hard stare. "I do not like your insinuations about me or my brother. You say he is not here. When is he expected back?"

The landlady had begun to close the door, but Belinda took hold of it and held tightly.

"How would I know? I'm not his mother or his nursemaid."

Belinda took a deep breath. She had tracked down her brother and now that she knew where he was straying, she could come back every day until she saw Peter. She gave a curt nod. "Tell him that I called and will return soon." She handed the landlady a card on which she had quickly written the earl's London address. "He can find me here."

As she descended the stairs in front of the house, a man in the showy uniform of an officer of the Horse Guards pushed past her on his way into the house. Her thoughts were so taken up with how close she was to finding her brother that she took no notice of him, although he paused at the top of the stairs, turned around and looked at her, a smirk on his face, before opening the door and calling out, "Aunt, did Bennet keep quiet and out of sight while she was here?"

Belinda was trembling and still feeling shocked when she returned to Lord Medwell's house. Ali came flying down the stairs. "There you are! I've been so worried. You've been gone for hours and I had no idea where you were." Her voice dropped lower as a footman took Belinda's cape and bonnet.

"You're not upset with Jasper, are you? With what happened last night?"

It took Belinda a moment to remember the spanking Jasper had administered. She could still feel the slight sting from where his large hand had struck her bottom, and at the reminder, she felt moisture trickle from her pussy, dampening the space between her legs. "No, I'm not upset about that at all." She felt blood heat her face as she confessed that his spanking had made her feel stronger and more in control of events.

The two ladies walked arm in arm towards a little sitting room that looked out over the garden. When they were seated on a pretty loveseat, Ali took Belinda's hand in hers. "Where have you been?" she asked.

Belinda looked down to where their hands were joined. She rubbed her thumb over Ali's wrist. "I thought I might know a way of finding Peter."

"And did you find him?"

Belinda bit her lip. "Not exactly." She looked into Ali's eyes. "Can I trust you? I might know where he is staying."

Ali looked worried. "I think you should let Robbie know what you have found out. He will help. If we do something careless, we might endanger ourselves."

Belinda withdrew her hand and shifted to the edge of the small sofa. "No. Lord Medwell and the others are convinced that Peter is involved with the traitors and is going to try to assassinate the Duke of Wellington. If they find him, they won't give him a chance to explain what is really happening."

Ali was not deterred by Belinda's pulling away from her. If one of her sisters was caught up in a similar conspiracy, she would do all within her power to help them, no matter what anyone said. She placed her hand on Belinda's back, glad when she leaned closer. "If Robbie and the others were able to speak to Peter before anything bad happens, they could help him far more than if things just proceed at their own pace."

Belinda turned around, her hazel eyes a little clearer than they had been. "You might be right. I'll think it over and decide in the morning."

Ali smiled. "Tomorrow, everyone will be celebrating the Grand Jubilee. There'll be time enough after that to talk to Robbie."

The first day of August was bright and sunny and people were already thronging the streets very early, eager to enjoy the festivities that celebrated peace in Europe and the centenary of the ascension of the Hanoverian monarchy to the throne of the United Kingdom. Most of the festivities were scheduled for the late afternoon and evening, but many visitors from the country thronged Hyde Park to wander among the hundreds of stalls and booths that had been set up and marvel at all the sights of one of the biggest cities in the world.

The Goodwins and their friends were making up a party for the evening and so the day was a relaxed one. Nell, Ali and Belinda were reading in the ladies' sitting room, Messy was trying to teach a new puppy how to fetch items that were a little too big for it to carry, while Ruffles got in the way, darting in front of the little interloper and snatching the old shoes Messy was tossing for the puppy.

Jane was listening to Gregory's lessons in the schoolroom while little Michael was playing with a set of alphabet blocks, building a tower and laughing delightedly whenever it toppled.

The earl looked up from the papers on his desk when his butler knocked on the door of his private bookroom and announced, "Lords Halstead and Eliot, Sir Bellingham and Lord Keeton."

Simon Barlow rose from his desk as the group of gentlemen entered. He gave Bellingham a quick kiss before they all sat down. Halstead wasted no time getting down to business. "If we have correctly understood the coded letters, then the assassination attempt is scheduled for sometime today."

Eliot nodded. "When people gather in the parks this evening, it will be difficult to keep track of our suspects."

The others agreed. "How certain are we that the note indicates the attempt will be this evening in Hyde Park?" Bellingham wanted to know.

Eliot shook his head. "It is the best information we have, but I have my doubts. There was something just a little too easy about the code." The others made sounds of disbelief but Eliot insisted. "The clue was too obvious. It's almost as if someone wanted us to know this plan. It could be a way to misdirect us."

Jasper leaned forward. "It was found with Bennet's things. Do you think he is deliberately leading us astray?"

Eliot shook his head. "I'm not sure but, remember, the original notes were found in your house, with your father's papers."

Halstead sat up straight. "We do not have time for specu-lation. We have to make some decisions. I think our best option is to act as if the note was not a diversion and prepare for something to happen during the last reenactment on the Serpentine, at six o' clock this evening. But we also need to ensure that we are prepared for any other eventuality."

"That would be easier if we had a whole brigade of men. There are only six of us." He gave Jasper an apologetic look. "Seven, if we include Keeton."

"Perhaps keeping our eyes on Wellington will be the best

solution," Barlow suggested.

Halstead nodded. "Robbie, will you try to stay in the duke's vicinity? The assassin will need to get quite close to ensure he can aim at his target, and if you are nearby, you could intervene."

The earl nodded, but his heart was tight. He was prepared to put himself in danger for his country, but his immediate thoughts were for his wife and sons. As he considered the implications of possible danger to himself, his butler, Tomlinson, knocked lightly on the door. "My lord, I apologize for the interruption, but there is a person who insists on speaking to Mr. Barlow." The usually implacable butler gave such a grimace that Robbie almost laughed. Clearly, the visitor was not a gentleman. Barlow left quickly and was back within five minutes, bringing with him the same yellow-toothed man who had followed Belinda Bennet the day before.

He leered at the group of men and licked his lips but doffed his cloth cap and ducked his head in the vaguest semblance of a bow.

"Gentlemen, this is Stanley. He organizes the brigade of errand boys we use as our eyes and ears in the streets of London. He has some information that could be useful."

Stanley showed no sign of being overwhelmed by his surroundings or by the presence of such illustrious gentlemen. He ran his fingers through his hair and said, "This guv 'ere asked me to keep an eye on a young lady from this 'ere house."

Robbie glanced at Barlow, who nodded briefly, indicating that he had arranged for Belinda to be followed. Stanley, enjoying his position of bearer of important tidings, continued his tale. "Most of the time, she did nuffin' unusual, jus' the usual things young ladies do. Shopping and walking in the park and such like."

Halstead gave an impatient grunt and Stanley grinned but did move to the point of his story. "Yesterday, though, she acted most peculiar. She left the 'ouse by the side door, all on 'er own, wif no companion, all wrapped up in a big cloak like she din't want no one to see 'er." He was clearly enjoying the drama of his story and the effect it was having on his audience, but when Halstead made a growling sound at the back of his throat, Stanley bared his yellow teeth in what could be considered an apologetic grin. "Anyways, one of my ovver coves and I follo'd 'er to a boarding ' ouse near the docks an' then to a 'ouse in Ludgate." He paused for dramatic effect. "Turns out, 'er bruvver is stayin' in that there 'ouse." He grinned at the effect these words had on the gentlemen.

Halstead was the first to regain his composure. "And have you seen Peter Bennet? Is someone keeping an eye on his movements?"

"I seen 'im. The gennelman is still there. Oi've left me son and a couple of other lads to watch. They'll alert me when 'e leaves the 'ouse. So far, 'e's never gone out or in." He gave another of his grins. "Oh, an' it might intr'st you gennelmen to know that the 'ouse b'longs to an aunt of a certain cap'n in the army, also one of those you's said you was interested in knowing about."

Each one of the gentlemen was ready to shake the information out of Stanley but before they needed to resort to such measures, he said, "Cap'n Saunders, as is nevvie to a grand military gennelman 'as been there more than usual this week."

Halstead handed a bag of coins to Stanley before he left, with the promise of more if he and his lads kept their eyes on Peter Bennet and Captain Saunders .

Feeling much more positive about being able to prevent

any catastrophe that day, the spymasters completed their plans.

———

Alicia looked around dubiously. She and Belinda were standing against the wall in a narrow alleyway from which they could see both the basement door and the front door of the house in Ludgate where Peter was staying. "I do wish we had told someone where we were going," Ali said softly.

Belinda gave an irritated flick of her head. "My brother will never allow any harm to come to me."

"Yes, but he doesn't know me and, besides, I am a little unsure about his companions." She was beginning to wish that she had not allowed Belinda to convince her to try to see Peter Bennet.

Belinda took a deep breath. "I think I am going to knock on the door again. After all, I did tell the landlady that I am his sister and that I want to see him. She would probably expect me to try again."

Alicia shook her head. "We don't know if he's actually there. We've only seen Captain Saunders and one other gentleman leave the house, apart from the maid who went out a while ago."

Belinda looked at Ali thoughtfully. "It might be best if they don't see you. Wait here, and I will go and ask to see Peter." She placed her hand on Ali's arm. "Please."

"All right. I'll wait here, but if you don't return within fifteen minutes, I am going to alert Robbie." She gave Belinda a quick hug before she crossed the road and ascended the four shallow steps that led to the house.

Neither of the girls noticed the young boy who was leaning against the railings surrounding the house next door to the one they were interested in. He was whistling softly, his hands thrust deep into his pockets and his cap pulled down over his eyes, hiding the alert way he was taking note of everything around him. Another two lads were playing a game of jackstones on the pavement across the street. None paid any apparent interest to the passing traffic or the two ladies who thought they were well hidden in the alley.

Belinda raised the iron knocker and rapped it loudly. The sound echoed through the house but only silence greeted her. Belinda banged the knocker once more. This time, she heard footsteps and the landlady's irritated voice calling out, "I'm coming. No need to be so impatient."

When the door opened, Belinda pushed against it to prevent the landlady from slamming it in her face. She smiled politely. "You might remember me. I came yesterday looking for my brother. Is he here now? I would like to ask him to join me for the festivities today."

"Ha. I can imagine just what sort of festivities you would want to indulge in. He's not here. Went out early this morning. He probably won't be back until very late."

Belinda let go of her hold on the door and the landlady slammed it triumphantly. Slowly, Belinda made her way back to where Ali was waiting for her. Ali slipped her arm around Belinda's shoulders. "Never mind. I'm sure we'll find him soon. Let's go back home and get ready for this evening. I'm looking forward to seeing the hot air balloon being launched. And I have an idea that Peter will want to be there too."

As the two of them turned to leave, the lads who had been watching the house whistled to each other but stayed where they were. They only left an hour later, when Captain Saunders, his friend Colonel Wilfred Aslett, and Peter Bennet left the house and headed towards St. James's Park. One of the lads scooted off towards Mayfair while the others sauntered casually behind the three men, keeping them in sight all the time in spite of the growing crowds.

Chapter 14

BELINDA WAS NOT ENJOYING the various entertainments that were being presented for the pleasure of the crowds in London to celebrate the jubilee. She hardly noticed the music that was playing or the performances of actors on the stages set up in the parks. When the people around her laughed raucously as one actor aped the dandies who liked to parade along Bond Street, she hardly smiled. She scanned the crowds, hoping to catch a glimpse of her brother, but it was almost impossible to see anyone in this crush.

Jasper looked at her anxiously from time to time and kept her close to his side. Ali was walking on his other side as they wandered through the crowds, making their way to the space that had been cleared in Hyde Park for Mr. Sadler to launch his hot air balloon. Jasper maneuvered his way through the crowds until he and his two ladies were in a good position to see the engine that would power the great silk balloon which was spread out in a glorious array of the red, white and blue of the Union Jack. The basket was smaller than Jasper had thought it would be, but three people would probably be able to fit into it fairly comfortably. The gas release interested him the most. If that could be controlled, the height and direction of the balloon could also be controlled. He pointed out some of the mechanics of the burner and Belinda forgot her troubles long enough to ask questions and make her own observations as the huge silk balloon began filling with air and rising above their heads.

They watched for a long while as the balloon ascended into the clear evening sky and drifted away on the wind currents.

Eventually, when the crowds began to disperse in search of more amusements, Jasper led the three of them towards the Serpentine, where a spectacle of two enemy fleets engaged in battle was about to begin. With a frown, Jasper realized that they were near the spot where Belinda has seen Peter that day when they had been walking in the park. He scanned the area, noting how easy it would be for a marksman to find a good spot beneath the trees. The Duke of Wellington and his entourage had prime positions near the bank of the river. Jasper noted that Robbie and Jane were amongst those surrounding the Iron Duke and that the earl, while appearing to be relaxed and thinking of nothing but the spectacle being played out, was actually keeping a sharp lookout for any trouble.

At six o'clock, the battle commenced, with each small fleet firing cannons at the other as they maneuvered closer. The battle was fiercely fought amidst the cheers of the onlookers. Just after dark, the British forces descended on the enemy fleet that had set anchor on the bank and set fire to the ships. The conflagration was magnificent and gratified the onlookers who cheered loudly.

Even Belinda had been mesmerized for a while, almost forgetting that she wanted to find her brother. Just as the display of a new kind of water-rocket firework, invented by Congreve, began, she saw her brother towards the back of the crowd. She gave a sharp cry that caught the attention of both Jasper and Ali.

"What is it?" Ali asked.

But Belinda had pulled away from Ali and Jasper and was pushing her way through the crowds. "Peter! Peter!" Her voice was lost in the hullabaloo of the crowds cheering on the British fleet on the river, but Ali and Jasper could hear her as if they had some unique sensor that could identify her voice out of the thousands around them.

"Belinda, wait," Jasper instructed, but she paid no heed. Exasperated, Jasper was torn between following her or alerting Robbie. Ali had no hesitation. She was following in Belinda's wake as quickly as she could. With a grunt, Jasper went after them both. His primary concern was to protect the two women he loved. And he could only do that if he was near them.

Peter Bennet looked up as he heard his name being called. He scowled when he saw his sister coming rapidly towards him, pushing her way through the mob that was trying to get closer to the banks of the river. He had to stop Belinda from interfering in something that had nothing to do with her. She was going to ruin everything, and what was worse, she was going to put him in danger. He swore under his breath. He knew that writing to her about the accusations raised against him and the trail he had deliberately left to entice that inter-fering group of self-righteous prigs to follow a false trail had been a bad idea. Belinda would never simply express her sympathy. She would insist on being involved. She had always been like that. Even as a little girl, she had followed after her older brother, hauling herself up the same trees he climbed and running as fast as she could, to keep up with him as he played with his friends.

His frown deepened as he noticed another young lady right behind Belinda. She placed her hand on Belinda's arm and said something, to which Belinda shook her head and continued walking towards him.

"I do like it when everything works out perfectly," drawled Saunders, who was also watching Belinda and her friend. "People are so very predictable. It is so easy to get them to do what you want them to do if you place the right lure in front of them."

Peter tried to catch his sister's eye, but there were so many people around her that she was watching her steps rather than him. She slipped past a burly farmer and his sonsy wife who were cheering loudly as a British ship captured an enemy captain and then she was only a few paces from him.

When Belinda had made her way to a clearer spot, she looked at her brother, grim determination and consternation clear in her hazel eyes. "Peter, at last. How are you? I have been so worried." She stepped right up to him, not noticing as Captain Saunders deftly moved away, leaving Peter alone with his sister and the ward of Lord Lamercier. They were making enough of a scene to attract the attention of some passers-by. Any of them would be able to give a good description of Peter Bennet if they were questioned, but none of them noticed him in spite of his uniform. And when the spectacle on the river began, all of them lost interest in the people at the back of the crowd.

"Belinda," Peter choked out. "Go away. I don't want to talk to you."

Belinda flinched and gasped. "Peter, what is going on? People are saying the most horrendous things about you."

He moved his hand towards his pocket and snarled, "You're in the way. You need to move. Now."

Ali, who had come up behind Belinda, slipped her arm around her waist. "He's got a gun," she said.

Belinda was as pale as moonlight. "No. Peter, think. Don't do anything foolish. Please."

He gritted his teeth. "I have to. You don't understand." He took a few paces forward. The little rise in the path gave him an advantage and he aimed the pistol that he had withdrawn from his pocket. Ignoring his sister and Alicia, he focused on the Duke of Wellington who was standing on the bank, resplendent in his crimson coat. Alicia's gaze followed the direction of his aim. Her throat was dry as she saw Brigadier Wallace maneuver the people around him until the duke was an easy target. Without looking in Peter's direction, he gave a discreet signal.

Ali held her breath as she saw her brother-in-law's much taller figure move closer to Wellington. She looked around wildly, trying to see where Jane was, but she needed to keep close to Belinda, who was wavering on her feet as if she were about to faint. Ali had no idea where Jasper was in the melee.

One of the boats on the river fired a mini cannon just as Peter Bennet fired his gun. There was such turmoil as people milled around, trying to decide if they had actually heard a gun or if it had just been the show.

Ali lurched forward, crying out loudly. "No. Don't." Her words were lost in the babble, but Jasper Keeton, a few paces away, heard Ali's cry above the noise of the crowd and pushed his way through the spectators.

Peter Bennet didn't wait to see if his shot had reached his target. He spun away and began walking quickly down the path, away from the scene. Belinda stumbled after him, her feet heavy but determined to find a way to help her brother, even now. Even after she had seen him try to kill the Iron Duke.

Bellingham came up alongside Keeton. "Over there. They went that way." The two pushed their way through the surging crowds but by the time they reached the quieter area, there was no sign of Belinda and Ali or Peter Bennet.

Peter tightened his jaw, thrust the gun into his pocket, and slipped away through the crowd. Just beyond the crowd of people, Saunders was waiting for him. Without a word, the captain fell into step alongside Peter, matching his steps stride for stride. Both walked faster and faster as they left the crowds behind them. Peter did not turn around and so did not notice that Belinda and Alicia were hurrying after him.

Belinda could not speak. Her throat was dry and tight and her eyes burned. She wiped her damp hands on her dress. She could not make sense of anything that had happened but she had to speak to her brother. She was vaguely aware that Ali was with her but nothing mattered except catching up with Peter and finding a way to protect him from the consequences of an act of treason.

The sun had set and the streets outside the park were dark and full of shadows. The two girls stumbled behind Peter, Captain Saunders, and another man who joined them as they walked rapidly along the now empty streets. Ali looked around, alarmed that they had not headed towards Ludgate. Instead, they made their way to St. James's Park, where elegantly dressed ladies were being rowed on the canal by dapper gentlmen, looking for the best positions from which to watch the firework display that would take place once it was fully dark. She had no idea what had really happened back at the Serpentine. She felt tears sting her eyes and her heart was tight. Had the bullet hit anyone? Was the Duke of Wellington alive and uninjured or lying wounded on the banks of the river? And, more importantly, were Jane and Robbie safe? But Belinda could not be left on her own. Her face was set in a wooden expression and her eyes were cloudy. She was breathing heavily as she tried to match her pace to the faster one of the group of men they were following.

Booths and stalls had been set up in this park and, as elsewhere, crowds were milling in search of refreshments and souvenirs. More and more of the men were showing signs of inebriation from consuming too much of the freely flowing ale. Some sang loudly, but others were becoming aggressive and bolshy. One or two leered at Belinda and Ali, making lewd comments. One particularly obstinate man stood directly in front of them, breathing beery breath over them as he tried to convince them to slip down a side path so that he could show them how a real Englishman celebrated.

Ali drew herself up to her full five foot three inches and tilted her nose in the air. "I am sure my guardian, the Earl of Medwell, would be very interested to know your intentions."

The man swore loudly and lumbered out of the way. The two girls hurried in the direction in which they had last seen Peter walking, but there was no longer any sign of him or his companions.

Belinda stopped and looked at Ali, despair and anxiety clouding her eyes. "He's disappeared. We'll never find him in this crowd. What if someone else saw what he did and even now he has been arrested? Where is the nearest magistrate's court?"

Ali looked around. Lanterns hung from the trees and lamps were affixed to the bridge and seven-story Chinese-style pagoda that had been built over one of the canals. The scene was magical but she hardly noticed the beauty of the

decor. She scanned the crowd, but there were so many officers in uniforms of different regiments that it was impossible
to distinguish one fairly slight officer and his companions
who had melted into the mass of people from any of the
others. The rapid walking had left her out of breath and she
drew in a lungful of air. "Perhaps we should return to the
others," she suggested.

Belinda tilted her chin at a stubborn angle. "No. I have to
find Peter."

Ali caressed Belinda's arm slowly. "Dearest, he said he
didn't want to speak to you. He ordered you to leave him."

Tears stung Belinda's eyes. "It doesn't make sense. Why
did he send me a letter saying he was in trouble if he doesn't
want my help?"

"You saw him draw the gun and shoot. Perhaps his letter
was a last-ditch effort to reach for his more noble ideals."

Belinda could not prevent the tears that had been
burning her eyes for the last hour from running down her
cheeks. Ali hugged her. "Perhaps if we enter the pagoda, we
would have a better view of the crowd and we might spot
him. And then we can see if he will talk to you and explain
his actions." Ali was grasping at straws as she tried to keep
Belinda calm. She didn't really believe that Peter Bennet
would be able to provide a satisfactory explanation that
would keep him from being hanged for treason. But she
loved Belinda and she was not going to let her go off on her
own and lay herself open to accusations that she had abetted
Peter.

Belinda nodded her agreement and the two women
made their way to the booth to purchase their entrance tickets. The pagoda, made entirely of wood, was sturdy, and the
two of them soon climbed to the fourth level from where
they could look out over the park. They took a minute to
admire the beautiful scene, the paths edged with lights, the

people in bright colors and the colorful tents and booths that were selling a wide variety of food and drink as well as engraved views of the wonderful sights that the crowds were enjoying. As they leaned over one balustrade, Ali pondered something that had been troubling her. "Why did they come here? I would have thought that after attempting to shoot the duke, they would have found somewhere to hide, not come to such a public place where they might be found and arrested."

Belinda blanched. The punishment for treason was public hanging. For one horrid moment, she envisaged her bother swinging from the hangman's rope on Tower Hill. She tried to breathe but the very simple action made her splutter and cough. Ali patted her back. When she had regained some of her composure, she said, "It is all very confusing. I don't think we will understand anything until we speak to Peter."

Ali drew in a deep breath. "I hope Jasper isn't too angry with us for running off the way we did."

Belinda smiled wryly. "Perhaps he will forgive us if we explain that we were following Peter." Her smile faded. "I will explain that it is my fault. He must forgive you. If he chooses not to forgive me, then I will have to accept that this was never meant to be."

Ali hugged her and then they fell silent and watched the people below them. Boats were gliding along the canal, lit with pretty lamps of various colors. Chinese lanterns, fancifully painted, glittered among the foliage, and the bridge on which the pagoda was built was profusely hung with lamps and decorations, creating a scene of enchantment. From their position, they could see the numerous fireworks that had been attached to the bridge and pagoda and which were going to be set off around ten o'clock. They would have a magnificent view from where they were, but neither of them was thinking about such frivolities right now.

"Look, over there!" Ali called out suddenly.

"Is it Peter?" Belinda asked, anxious to see her brother.

Ali shook her head. "No. It's Jane and Robbie, with Nell and Messy. And Jasper." The tightness that had strained her heart since Peter had fired his gum loosened and she had to hold on to the railing to stop herself from falling.

Even from this distance, the women could see just how furious Jasper was. Every line of his muscled body was rigid. His jaw was clenched and both of them had no difficulty imagining just how hard the amber of his eyes was glinting. Jane was clutching her husband's arm and talking rapidly and Nell's shoulders were slumped. Guilt flooded Ali. She hated to worry her sisters. And Robbie looked just as angry as Jasper. She and Belinda were not going to escape the consequences of their heedlessness. But before Ali could suggest that they leave the tower and apologize to the earl and Jasper, Belinda gripped her arm. "There he is."

Ali did not need to ask who. Belinda's voice was tense and eager and she spun away, ready to dash down the stairs and rush to her brother's side. Ali grabbed hold of her arm. "Wait a minute. He's coming this way. With his friends."

Belinda stopped and watched as Peter, Saunders, and the third gentleman headed for the bridge and crossed to the entrance to the pagoda. "You're right. If we go to the staircase, we will meet them."

This time, Ali let Belinda lead her to the stairs that gave visitors access to the different levels. A family that had clearly come in from the country for the festivities blocked their way, making it impossible for them to descend as quickly as Belinda wanted to. It took all her good manners to stop her from pushing past in her haste to reach her brother. She waited impatiently for the woman, who was carrying a wriggling infant while two other young children clutched her skirts, to follow the slow-moving man down the stairs while, at the same time, a party of young men, who had clearly indulged liberally of the ale available in many booths around the park, ascended rowdily.

Ali shuddered when two of the young men spotted her and Belinda and moved in closer, making suggestive comments. She wanted to retch at the smell of beery breath that, combined with unwashed bodies, created a sickening stench. And then, just as she was contemplating shoving the most persistent man down the stairs, a gentleman in the uniform of a captain of the Horse Guards appeared, coming down from one of the higher levels.

"Ladies, may I be of assistance?" His clear voice rang out over the slurs and stammers of the two drunk men and Ali looked up, gratitude and relief flooding her face.

"Captain, if you could ask these gentlemen to move on, it would be better for all of us." Ali tried to keep her voice steady.

The captain bowed. "My pleasure, ma'am." He placed a hand on the scruff of the collar of each of the men and dragged them away. "Come along, you wouldn't want to spend the rest of this auspicious day languishing in a prison cell." The two men swore but allowed themselves to be moved on.

The captain smiled at Ali and Belinda, but a faint hint of disapproval darkened his eyes. "There now, ladies. You are safe to return to your chaperone. All the other visitors who were here have gone outside. The fireworks are about to begin."

Belinda bristled but Alicia was keenly aware that young ladies, even ones who were in their third season, should not be without a suitable chaperone in such a public place. "Thank you kindly, sir. May I know the name of the person who so gallantly rescued us?"

"Captain Wilfred Aslett at your service, ma'am." He bowed smartly.

As Belinda and Ali turned towards the stairs yet again, thankful that no further obstructions were in their way, Peter Bennet appeared with Saunders on one side of him and the third gentleman on the other. Saunders focused on their rescuer but adroitly blocked the way downstairs, effectively trapping the ladies on the platform.

"Aslett," he said curtly. "I see you've made it here before us. Have you cleared the galleries?"

Aslett shrugged. "No need to think I wouldn't arrive. Everything is ready." He walked to a place near the back of the pagoda and lifted a loose floorboard so quickly, it was clear he knew that it was there. He rummaged inside for a moment and withdrew some sacks, a couple of coils of rope, and a long rifle.

Saunders nodded. "Good. At least the workman we bribed did his job well."

Belinda was hardly aware of the actions of the other men. Her entire focus was on her brother. "Peter." Her voice was faint from the strain of emotions she had endured for the last few hours. She moved towards him, her arms outstretched.

He turned towards her, his face grim. "I told you to leave me. This is no place for you. Don't blame me if you get hurt."

Belinda flinched and Ali tugged her hand. "Come, Belinda. Lord Medwell and my sister are waiting for us." She deliberately used her guardian's title to let the men know they were not without protection.

But Saunders smirked and came closer. "Do you think the earl and his little group are able to prevent well-trained soldiers from achieving their carefully thought out campaign? He and his do-gooder friends will be seen as fools when we succeed and the earl's niece is implicated along with her friends."

The pagoda was now empty except for the four men and two ladies. Ali was aware of the voices of revelers in the distance, but here in the pagoda, all was quiet. Again, she tugged Belinda's arm and headed for the stairwell, but Saunders stood in their way.

The captain gestured towards the women. "Tie them up, Turner," he instructed the fourth man. "We don't want these little brats running off to tell anyone that we are here. Not yet, anyway."

Belinda stared at the fourth man. She had never met her brither's school friend and she didn't like the look of him. Why had Peter made friends with such a person? Turner's thin nose and sharp chin made him look like a weasel. His eyes were small, hard buttons. She shuddered and once again tried to reach Peter, who moved into the shadows at the back of the pagoda.

Ali straightened her shoulders and glowered through her spectacles. "You will not get away with your nefarious plans. Peace and goodwill must triumph over war and chaos. Evil is always thwarted by good."

Saunders laughed outright at this. "This world has no place for high flown philosophies. You should go back to reading your fanciful novels." Then his face hardened. "We have spent many months planning this. The war ended too soon because Wellesley, now the grand Duke of Wellington, favored peace and a quick outcome." His voice was hard with scorn.

"Twenty years of war is hardly a quick outcome," Ali pointed out, even as Turner was tying her hands behind her back and fastening the end of the rope to one of the railings.

"It was too soon for us to prosper, for us to make our fortunes through prize money," Saunders bit back.

A sob choked in Belinda's throat. She addressed her brother, who had fallen into a sullen silence. "Peter, surely, you haven't abandoned all your ideals? If you did become involved in a plot involving assassination and treason, I would have hoped it was because you were motivated by higher ideals. Father would have been so disappointed to learn that money has led you down this path."

He grunted and muttered, "You're a girl. This is not something you could be expected to understand."

Belinda flinched as if her brother had stabbed her with a knife. Turner finished tying Belinda's arms behind her and pushed her down next to Alicia, who leaned as close as she could, offering what little comfort she was able to.

Captain Aslett turned from the balustrade where he had been scoping the terrain on the left bank of the canal and watching the movement of the boats on the water. "Girls are incapable of understanding the necessity and glory of war." Ali spluttered, but he continued. "Those fools believe they have defeated Napoleon by giving him an island to rule when he wanted the world. He will not be satisfied with the toys they have given him to play with. And we are helping to prepare the way for his victory and our fortune."

Belinda looked at her brother, her eyes filled with horror and despair. "Peter, surely, you don't sanction murder and mayhem. You have always cherished peace and tolerance. That's why you wanted to work with Lord Keeton."

Peter flinched at the mention of his former employer. "Belinda, I told you to stay out of this."

Ali had been thinking hard. "You didn't succeed at the Serpentine. Why do you think you will be more successful now?"

Saunders sneered. "That little show was a diversion to put those interfering bastards off our trail and to ensure that Bennet is clearly the main suspect. Our plan was always to kill Wellesley during the firework display here. Not even a trained soldier would have been able to make that shot easily, let alone a flabby, timid coward like Bennet."

"Here comes the general," announced Aslett from the place where he had been keeping watch. "Let's hope that your uncle can keep him in our line of fire at the right moment."

Saunders and Turner joined Aslett at the balustrade and Belinda looked at her brother, who was still hovering in the shadows at the back of the pagoda. She studied him closely for the first time. His face was gaunt, his clothes disheveled and his eyes heavy with despair.

She shifted closer to Ali and whispered, "I think Peter has been forced into this. He doesn't look happy at all, not as if he wants to be here."

Ali nodded but said nothing. Aslett and Turner were discussing the best angles and positions for shooting Wellington. Aslett was lovingly priming the rifle and looking down the scope, his finger playing with the trigger. Saunders was listening to his co-conspirators but he kept his eye on Peter.

Peter's hands were clenched and his jaw tight. He was watching the men but Ali stared at him until he moved his gaze to her and his sister. Ali gave him an encouraging smile and he moved slowly towards them. His expression was one of regret and hopelessness. He shook his head at his sister. "I told you to stay away. I'll never be able to live with myself if anything happens to you because of all this." He gestured with his head towards the other men and lowered his voice. "It's a long story, but I have been manipulated so that I will be accused of their crimes."

"But if you tell the truth, they will not get away with what they're doing." Belinda sounded more hopeful than certain.

Ali nodded vigorously. "Especially now. We can corroborate anything you say."

Peter shook his head. "Who will believe me? If you tell the truth as you have seen it today, you will confirm that I am guilty. You saw me with a gun near the Serpentine."

Belinda frowned. What Peter said was true. Even she had found herself wondering about his actions, and she knew Lord Halstead believed Peter was willingly involved in this plot. "If you make a run for it, you will get away from them and still be able to redeem yourself and save the duke," she urged.

Peter laughed bitterly. "I've tried to run a few times, but each time, they stop me and haul me back." A sorrowful look crossed his face. "And now that you are here, if I get away, they will harm you." He swallowed the lump that had been blocking his throat.

Ali sat up straighter. "But we cannot allow them to succeed. We must warn Lord Robbie and the others." Her voice was louder than she meant it to be and Saunders heard her. He gave a scornful laugh and stalked across the room.

"Peter is too much of a coward to try anything reckless. He cares more for the safety of his own arse than anyone or anything else."

Peter flushed at this accusation and glanced behind himself to the staircase.

"Don't even think of it," Saunders snarled. He grabbed hold of Belinda's hair and gripped so hard that her scalp ached. She bit back a cry even though tears burnt her eyes from the pain.

"Don't!" both Ali and Peter cried out at the same time.

Saunders just laughed again. "Turner, if you've finished over there, I think we might want to restrain Bennet, too. He has suddenly grown a backbone and might just decide to sacrifice himself for his sister and her friend." He still clutched Belinda's hair but not quite as tightly as before.

Turner stalked across the room and, soon, Peter was tied up some feet away from Ali and Belinda. The smugness on Saunder's face increased. "We will let Bennet go later, with more evidence against him to prove that this plan was all his idea. He will hang and we will prosper. The trail we have laid over the last few months will implicate him thoroughly."

Ali looked from one to the other of the men. Her glasses had slipped and she couldn't reach to push them up so she wrinkled her nose and peered at Saunders. "There's something I don't understand."

His scornful laugh was filled with derision that made Ali grit her teeth. "There's a lot you don't understand. Girls should stick to embroidery and watercolors. Their brains are not sufficiently evolved to handle issues of war and politics." He gestured to the sky that was almost fully dark. "There's a while to go before the fireworks begin, so I will entertain you with a bedtime story. What specific details would you like me to explain to you?"

"How did Peter become involved? It is clear that he does not share your philosophy on war."

Saunders aimed a kick at Peter's calf. "He has no idea what it is to be a real man, a man who seeks glory in war. He spends his time with books and talking about ideas."

Ali gave Saunders a hard look, and he shrugged. "However, he conveniently placed himself in a position that made it easy for us to divert attention from us. We have been striving to achieve our goals for years, and Bennet conveniently started working as Keeton's secretary. He was another fool who wanted peace, and when he began making progress, it was imperative that he be removed, which we successfully did and prolonged the war." He took a swig from a silver hip flask.

Turner, who had been mostly silent until now, picked up the narrative. "I was at school with Bennet and I made sure I met him, quite by chance, of course, in Lyme Regis. His outspoken views on Napoleon's reforms in France made it easy to position him as someone opposed to Keeton's peace talks." He sneered. "The fool was so blind, he didn't notice when we planted documents amongst his papers and made sure his interests in flowers aligned with the method of Keeton's death. Of course, it did help that someone who worked closely with Keeton actually supported our cause."

Ali sat up straighter. "Symes."

Saunders looked grudgingly impressed. "Yes. He had been an aide-de-camp in my uncle's regiment but when he was injured, he took up a position as Keeton's valet."

Belinda had been slumped against Ali for most of this conversation. Now she sat up and looked at Peter before saying, "So it was Symes who poisoned Lord Keeton and made it seem as if Peter was guilty."

Turner gave a nonchalant shrug. "Keeton's death delayed the peace talks and, for a while, all went well, until this year, when the war ended and we had to find another way to prolong the hostilities. It wasn't difficult to bring Bennet back into the picture. A few threats and a week or so incarcerated in a basement made him very compliant."

"You're despicable," Belinda spat out.

All three of the conspirators laughed. "Your opinion doesn't matter. After tonight, we will be heroes, Bennet will be accused of treason, and you will be dead."

Aslett, sho had been leaning against a wall in the shadows, looking out over the park, straightened and lifted his rifle. "The fireworks are about to begin."

Chapter 15

JASPER KEETON'S emotions were in turmoil. Anger, anxiety, and concern rioted in his heart and mind. He had lost sight of Belinda and Alicia when they entered St James Park and he had no idea where to look for them. He should have held onto them tightly, not letting them leave his side.

The sun was setting and lights blazed in the park, but there were so many people jostling for good positions from which to watch the fireworks that it was impossible to look for anyone.

"Lord Keeton?" Jane had to call his name three or four times before he heard her.

"I beg your pardon, my lady. I was distracted."

She gave a grim smile. "I understand. My sisters seem to think that causing me as much concern as possible is their mission in life. First, Cece rushed off to France after traitors and now Ali runs off after assassins and murderers. I am sorely tempted to lock Nell and Messy in a tower at Lamercier Manor so that I know where they are at all times."

Nell, who had been looking very dejected and teary, rose up at this. "*We've* given you no reason for concern." She bit her lip. "Do you think Ali is in real danger?" Her voice was hoarse with fear.

Lord Robbie turned to her. "Buck up, lass. You're not helping anyone with your moping. We will find her. And heaven help her when we do."

Nell blinked back tears and looked around. "They are almost ready to begin the fireworks. It is very pretty, like a forest decked out for a fairy ball. The pagoda is like an enchanted tower. But, oh, I can't help feeling that an ogre has captured Ali." She blinked again and Jane slipped her arm around her sister's shoulders.

Messy looked in the same direction and suddenly gave a little cry. "Look! There are people up on the fourth level. I thought everyone had been asked to leave the pagoda for the fireworks."

"Nonsense, Messy. There's no one there," Jane countered.

"I saw someone," Messy insisted. "Look. There he is again."

The others all looked to where she was pointing. A shadowy figure could just be seen within the interior and then a second figure farther back was visible for a brief moment. Light glinted on something metallic and Robbie clenched his jaw. "That is odd," he agreed. He gestured to Bellingham and Barlow who were standing nearby. "We need to investigate that. They do not look like workmen."

Jasper joined the earl and the other men as they made their way through the throng of people. Nell began to follow as well, but Jane caught her arm. "Stay here. I've enough to worry me without you running headlong into danger as well."

As the men moved towards the pagoda, Eliot said, "I knew there was something not quite right about the event at the Serpentine. Any half-decent marksman would not have missed. It's as if Bennet didn't actually want to shoot anyone."

Robbie answered his brother-in-law as they reached the entrance to the bridge. "Who were the other men with him in Hyde Park?"

Bellingham shook his head. "It was difficult to see. They kept themselves in the shadows, but one was definitely in the uniform of the Horse Guards."

"It is odd that Bennet allowed himself to be seen so clearly," observed Barlow as they arrived at the bridge that had been built across the canal.

Halstead, who had been nearer the bank, had also noticed the presence of people in the pagoda and was already waiting for the others. He studied the boats on the canal, taking note of where Wellington was positioned. He swore when he noticed that Brigadier Wallace was one of the passengers. There appeared to be uncertainty about where the boat was planning to rest for the fireworks display. The captain of the boat was arguing with someone and the boat was rocking from side to side. Some of the ladies looked alarmed but, at last, it steadied and the revelers sat back to sip champagne and nibble on delicacies as the fireworks began. Halstead gauged the position with concern. Even a poor marksman would be able to fire directly at the duke from the fourth floor of the pagoda. He contemplated hailing the boat and warning the great general, but they were just too far away, on the other side of the river, for him to be heard.

The first firework exploded into the dark night like a fiery dragon seeking its treasure. They blinked against the brightness of the light. A sigh of delight swept through the crowd as they focused on the colors and patterns filling the sky, leaving the spymasters an opportunity to dart across the bridge and into the enclosure of the pagoda.

The delighted *oohs* and *ahs* of the crowd suddenly turned to gasps of horror and shocked cries. One firework had burned down where it was attached to the facade and the dry timber of the construction burst into flame.

Ali had been wriggling her hands in her bonds for the last half an hour but she could not slip them through the tightly knotted ropes. Her skin was raw and chaffed and she could feel blood dripping down her wrists, but she had to get free. She gritted her teeth against the pain. She had to find a way to stop these men from assassinating the Iron Duke—and to save Belinda and herself from this danger. She looked across to where Peter Bennet had been tied up. He had been kicked so often by Saunders and the others that he was gasping for breath as he slumped to the floor. He would not be of much use. Irritation and anger surged through her. She was not going to risk her safety for him. He could stay here and face the consequences of his actions. It was his fault that they were caught in this way. He might have been duped by Turner, but when he realized what was happening, he should have spoken to someone in authority, someone who could have helped, rather than going into hiding and leaving his sister to find a way to help him out of the mess.

She stopped wriggling and heaved a sigh. "We might not be able to free ourselves," she murmured to Belinda who was leaning against her, "but if we create a disturbance, a distraction, we might be able to prevent them from assassinating the duke."

Belinda turned her head slightly to look more closely at Ali. She swallowed, trying to get rid of the dryness in her throat. "You are far braver than I am. Aren't you even a little bit scared? They said they are going to kill us."

Ali gulped. "Of course, I'm scared. I don't want to die." A dark shadow filled her eyes. "I have only just begun to live and love, but thinking of ways to stop these men, helps to distract me."

Belinda nodded. She glanced at her brother who was staring blankly at the far wall of the pagoda. He looked completely defeated. "I think our father did both of us a disservice. He taught us to think and question ideas, but he never encouraged us to be practical and take action."

Ali looked over at Belinda. "It's not too late to do something with all the knowledge you have garnered. What kind of action can we take now?"

Belinda looked around. "We've tried talking to them, but they didn't delay what they're doing to engage in conversation. And they won't be persuaded by clever arguments. The fireworks are too noisy for anyone to hear us if we begin shouting and screaming."

Ali straightened up and scrunched her nose, trying to prevent her glasses from slipping farther down. "Fireworks. There's our answer." Belinda looked at her as if the stress of the situation had robbed her of any sense. Ali giggled in spite of the danger. "I'm not ready for Bedlam. But think, the walls of this structure are not very solid. If we could jostle them sufficiently to unsettle some of the fireworks that have been attached to the facade, we could dislodge some of them, and then the spectators will know something is wrong and come and investigate."

"But we could cause a fire, and that might kill us," Belinda objected.

Ali nodded grimly. "It seems that we have two options. Either we sit here meekly and wait for those men to kill us, or we do something that will lead to their demise and save the duke, and die that way." She gulped. "Jasper will be furious with us." She blinked rapidly and Belinda also drew in her breath sharply.

"He will be." Both women were silent for a few moments. Then Belinda sat up straight. "Well, if we're going to do this, we'd better start."

Both women braced themselves and then Ali counted softly to three. They bashed themselves against the wall as hard as they could. The wall shuddered. Peter looked up for the first time. "Hey, stop that. What do you think you're doing?"

Neither Belinda nor Ali heeded him, nor a furious Saunders who spun round to stare at them. They continued their rhythmic banging of the wall. Saunders strode across and grabbed the shoulders of both of them but their work had been successful. Some of the fireworks had been dislodged and two of them caught the dry timber, causing a small trail of fire to lick the birch siding. It was only a matter of minutes before the trickle of fire became a flame that devoured the brittle wood hungrily.

"Damnation!" Aslett had stepped back from the edge and lowered his rifle. "We have to get out of here." Turner had already started down the stairs and the other two quickly followed, leaving their prisoners to their fate.

Peter glared at his sister and Ali. "This is your fault. We're going to die."

Ali bit her lips and nodded. "But we saved the duke and the country."

The smoke was already filling her nose and lungs and the heat of the flames was making it very uncomfortable. She tugged her ropes, hoping against hope that they would finally loosen. Facing death was much more frightening than she had imagined it would be. She cried out and shifted as close to Belinda as she could. "I love you."

"I love you, too." Belinda's voice was raspy from the

smoke. "And I love Jasper."

Ali made a sound that was half sob, half laugh. "I do, too. He will be so angry and sad."

Jasper stopped on the bridge to take a deep breath. He looked up at the pagoda and was surprised to see it shake. Someone was rocking it deliberately. He cursed as some of the fireworks were dislodged. A few dropped harmlessly into the water, narrowly missing some of the boats, but two tilted dangerously and set the soft wood of the pagoda on fire.

Suddenly, he knew without a doubt that Ali and Belinda were in there and he had to rescue them. He rushed after the other men who were already at the entrance. As they entered the pagoda, three men tumbled down the stairs, pushing one another in their haste to escape the conflagration. Barlow, Bellingham, and Halstead caught hold of them, twisting their arms behind their backs and quickly stopping their flight.

The fire had not reached the bottom sections and workers were hastily dowsing the bridge and lower sections in water. Chaos had erupted amongst the spectators who were pointing and shouting, although some had joined the workers to form a line that was passing buckets of water to those closest to the blaze.

Jasper made his way to the stairs.

"Where are you going? We've caught the bastards who were trying to kill Wellington," Eliot said.

Jasper shook his head. "They're up there."

"Who?"

A faint cry was heard above the crackling of the fire. Daniel, Robbie, and Jasper ran up the stairs. It was only a matter of minutes before they came out onto the fourth floor platform. Jasper darted across even as a burning beam crashed down in the corner. Ali looked at him through bleary eyes. "I knew you'd come," she rasped out.

Belinda had passed out and was slumped against Ali. Jasper tried to lift her and swore when he realized ropes were holding them prisoner. Robbie pushed him aside, wielding a knife he had pulled out of his boot. Jasper said nothing as the earl cut through Belinda's ropes. As soon as she was free, he scooped her up and made for the stairs, trusting Robbie to take care of Ali.

As he made his way across the room, he heard Peter Bennet, who was near the back and farthest from the burning wood, call out, "What about me? I don't want to die."

Jasper threw him a dirty look and carried his precious bundle downstairs into the cooler night air. He was met by Jane and Louisa Halstead, who quickly took charge of Belinda, rubbing her temples and chafing her wrists. Jane tilted a flask of brandy to her lips and a few drops trickled into her mouth.

Nell was standing close by, wringing her hands. "Where is Ali?"

Jasper nodded his head towards the pagoda. "The earl has her."

Nell began to dash towards the bridge but Jasper stopped her, even though everything inside him ached to return, to ensure Ali's safety. "Be careful. Don't add to the trouble."

Nell was torn between tears and wanting to scream, but Lord Robbie appeared just then with Ali leaning against him. She began to rush forward, but Jasper was quicker, and she stopped. She would need to let her twin go. Ali now had a man and a woman who loved her, and her twin would no longer be the most important person, although there would always be a special bond between them.

Chapter 16

BELINDA WOKE UP SLOWLY. Her throat ached and her wrists were sore. For a moment, she couldn't remember what had happened and then, suddenly, it all came rushing back. She could see the flames licking up the side of the pagoda, smell the acrid smoke and taste it as it filled her mouth. She should be dead, but somehow this cool, dark room was not how she had imagined the afterlife to be.

She needed a sip of water, to ease the dryness of her sore throat. She tried to form the word but it sounded only like a gasp, then a gentle voice answered, "Here, take a sip. Don't gulp too much at once."

She managed to open her eyes, which were also dry and felt burnt. "Lady Medwell," she choked out.

"Hush, don't try to talk yet," Jane said.

Obediently, she sipped the water, but as soon as the coolness eased her throat, she managed one more word clearly. "Ali?"

"Ali is sleeping. She is well, but her wrists are severely chafed and she sustained a slight burn on her arm." Belinda gasped, but Jane reassured her. "It is red and sore but will hardly leave a mark when it is healed."

"Can I see her?"

"Later. Now, I'm going to bring you some chicken broth and fruit juice and then you are going to sleep again."

Belinda nodded, relieved to have someone take care of her. Jane straightened her blanket and plumped her pillows before ringing the bell which brought a housemaid with the promised light meal. When Belinda had eaten most of the soup, she remembered something else. "What happened to Peter?"

Jane frowned slightly. "He is downstairs, talking to Robbie and Halstead."

Belinda nodded again and soon drifted back to sleep.

Ali sank back against the soft cushions of the sofa. Her head had stopped aching and it no longer felt as if she were breathing in a lungful of smoke with every breath. Her arm still hurt and her wrists were uncomfortable. She smiled at Belinda, who was sitting next to her. They were both alive.

Robbie scowled at them, but Jasper was the first to speak. "You two were very foolish, rushing off like that." He swallowed hard. "You could have died." The rawness of his voice conveyed all the emotions that had been flooding over him the last few days, since the fire.

Ali grinned. "But we didn't, and we stopped the assassination. I think that makes us heroines." Nell had been begging her for details over the last few days, determined to use the incident in one of her stories, and her twin's praise had puffed her up until she was quite proud of what she and Belinda had done. Messy had also contributed, begging Ali to retell the story and acting out parts of it, to the thrill of little Lord Gregory, until Jane put a stop to it, reminding her son that true heroism was born from sense and logic, rather than impulse and chance.

Jasper stopped his pacing and strode across the room, stopping in front of his two loves. His eyes were hard and his jaw clenched. "Flippancy is not going to get you out of the trouble you're now in."

Ali looked up into his eyes, which were the color of whiskey. "I am sorry. I am still having nightmares about it, and trying to make light of it prevents me from becoming hysterical." Her voice trembled and Jasper's eyes softened.

Jasper cupped her cheek and she nestled against his strength and warmth, shuddering as she remembered how close they had come to never feeling his touch again.

"Besides," Belinda said quietly, "Ali is not to blame. She tried to stop me, but I would not listen to her."

Jasper used his other hand to trace the shape of Belinda's mouth. "I understand, my love, but you are never again to put yourself in such danger, or lead Ali into a place where she thinks sacrificing her life is a valid choice."

Ali giggled and placed a quick kiss on Belinda's cheek. "Our mission is to ensure Jasper never becomes bored or staid."

Robbie put down his empty tea cup and shook his head with a little laugh. "You'll have your work cut out with those two."

Peter Bennet had been slouching against the wall next to the window and now, he stood up and walked closer to his sister. "I do not know what kind of people you have become involved with, Belinda, but I am now here to look after you."

"Belinda has looked after herself very well for many years, and I do not believe she will welcome your control of her life," Jasper said as he sat down next to Belinda and placed his arm along the back of the sofa so that he could reach Ali's shoulder.

Belinda shook her head but snuggled closer to Jasper. "I am also here and able to speak for myself. Peter, I am glad that you are safe and that your name has been cleared, but it is time for me to live my own life."

Peter tried to look authoritative but managed only to look like a bullfrog puffing out its chest. "It would be remiss of me to allow my sister to ally herself with people of dubious morals. We have always believed the aristocracy to be corrupt and dangerous, and your current behavior proves that you are too easily influenced by them." His voice dropped a little and he coaxed her. "Do come with me, Belinda. When we were young, you always said that you would trust me to care for you and you were never interested in love or romance."

"You didn't care very much for your sister when we were all in danger," Ali pointed out. "Before we started the fire, you were ready to let us be killed by your friends."

Peter flushed. "There was nothing I could do. I was in rather a pickle."

Lord Halstead leaned forward. "Ah, yes, indeed you were. Your friends are all facing a court-martial, but *we* need to decide what will happen to you."

Peter spun around. "What do you mean? You make it sound as though I were somehow culpable in all of this, instead of being a victim. It is my notes and reports that will prove the guilt of Saunders and the others."

Halstead raised his eyebrow at Bennet's churlish tone. Bennet backed away and his mouth opened once or twice but no sound came out.

"Good. Now that you are prepared to listen, I will explain the situation. While it is true that you were lured into an involved and intricate plot, you did not behave with integrity or wisdom. As soon as you realized what was happening, you should have revealed the information you had, thus avoiding years of worry for your sister and months of work for us."

Peter looked as if he wanted to protest, but Halstead continued smoothly. "I know that it was difficult to know just whom to trust, but if Belinda could find the right people, you could have too. Of course, your crime is one of foolishness, rather than actual wrongdoing, but it is well known within London circles that you were acquainted with Saunders and Turner and there will always be an air of suspicion surrounding you."

"What do you propose I do about that?"

For an answer, Lord Halstead turned to Simon Barlow who was sitting at the earl's desk. "Do you have the documents ready?"

Barlow nodded and pushed back the chair. "Yes, here they are. All in order. *The Sea Queen* sets sail at the turn of the tide tomorrow."

Halstead took the proffered documents, glanced through them, and handed them to a stupefied Peter Bennet. "A new life awaits you in America."

Belinda rose from the sofa and took her brother's hand in hers. "Peter, this is the best for all of us. You can make new choices in a country whose government is based on republican principles. You will flourish there. As for me, I have a different life to pursue." She glanced at Ali and Jasper. "My work is to ensure that the next generation of aristocrats is less self-interested and more willing to accept the changes this century will bring."

Epilogue

ALICIA SANK down on the window seat and looked out over the gardens as the rays of the setting sun caressed the top of the trees. In the distance, the darker blue of the sea touched the rosy clouds on the horizon. She was tired but happy. The last of the wedding guests had left an hour or so ago and she, Belinda and Jasper were relaxing in the spacious, airy sitting room that linked Jasper's bedroom with hers. A smile curved her lips. She was now Lady Keeton.

And Belinda was going to be with them, ostensibly a companion for her, but in reality, a very necessary member of their coterie. Ali turned her head to look at Belinda, who had leaned her head against the back of a comfortable blue brocade chair, her eyes closed and her hands lying loosely on her lap.

The door opened quietly and Jasper walked in, loosening his cravat and pulling off his grey jacket. He smiled at Ali as Belinda slowly opened her eyes and turned to watch him. He stopped behind her and leaned forward to kiss her forehead.

Ali's skin flushed and her breasts felt swollen. She shifted on the cushions of the window seat and Belinda held out her hand, beckoning her to join her and Jasper. Ali rose, smoothed her hands over her white dress and straightened her glasses. It took her only a moment to be at the side of her husband and lover. She slid her arm around Jasper's waist and placed her hand on Belinda's shoulder. Jasper leaned down and found her lips, kissing her gently at first, but as she responded, he pulled her closer to him so that her body was pressed against his. She opened to him and his kisses became harder, more possessive, more insistent. She rubbed her aching breasts against him and twisted her fingers in his hair to bring him as close as possible.

After many minutes, she pulled back to take a breath. Her glasses were askew and steamed up. She laughed breathlessly and turned slightly in his arms. "Belinda." She said nothing more, but Belinda was quickly at her side. Ali shifted, making a place for her. With Jasper's arm around her, she brushed a kiss against Belinda's lips. Belinda steadied herself, by sliding her arms around Ali. Their kiss deepened and she swiped her tongue along Ali's lips and then pressed into the warmth of her mouth until their tongues stroked each other's.

Jasper watched as Belinda began to work the buttons of Ali's dress loose. He settled his hand over hers and helped her slip the soft material off Ali's shoulders, which he then kissed. The three moved together, seamlessly, harmoniously. When Ali's dress had been removed, they began to take Belinda's off her.

She turned her back to Jasper so he could more easily work his way down the row of little buttons while Ali slid her hands under the top of her bodice and began to loosen her stays. Then, Belinda tugged at Jasper's shirt, urging him to remoove it. He raised his arms and lifted it over his head, revealing the firm muscles of his chest and the light covering of hair that tapered in a V that disappeared below the waistline of his breeches. She ran her hand over his skin, lingering at his nipples that had puckered into hard points.

When Belinda's dress lay in a heap at her feet, Jasper stood back. "I think we should move to the bedroom." His voice was low and raspy with desire. Ali peered up at him, her blue eyes wide behind her glasses and her face flushed with longing. She was finding it difficult to speak, but she nodded and took hold of Belinda's hand as they followed him.

On the threshold, the two ladies paused. They had never been in Jasper's bedroom before, yet this was where they were to fully commit themselves to one another, where they were to give themselves to each other forever. It was a large, comfortable room, with wide windows that looked out over the gardens and down to the sea. The evening light poured in, casting a golden glow over the dark mahogany of the bedframe and the deep blue of the bed covers. A small settee, just big enough for all three of them, was near the window, with two armchairs, creating a pleasant sitting area, and various tables and chests of drawers were arranged along the walls. Books were piled haphazardly on the tables and pleasant paintings of the sea hung on the walls.

Ali took a deep breath and then focused on Jasper who was standing near the bed, his arms folded, as he waited for his two loves to come to him. Ali grinned and tilted her head saucily as she and Belinda slowly crossed the room, their hips swaying in a tantalizing way. Belinda's loosened bodice revealed the gentle swell of her pert breasts.

They stopped a few feet in front of Jasper. Ali let go of Belinda's hand and, keeping her eyes on Jasper's, raised her arms, loosening the pins that had kept her elaborate coiffure in place. Her glossy, dark hair tumbled over her shoulders as she tossed her head.

Jasper sat down on the edge of the bed, his cock hard

and aching with longing, as he watched Ali turn to Belinda and kiss her. At the same time, her fingers pulled the pins from Belinda's hair, letting the silky tresses cascade down her back. Ali tangled her fingers in Belinda's hair, using her grip to position Belinda's mouth where she had the best access. Belinda entwined her hands in Ali's mass of dark curls and they kissed each other for a long time. Finally, they drew back, breathless and tousled.

They seemed to have forgotten that Jasper was there until he leaned forward and said, "Alicia, remove Belinda's petticoat and stays." Ali gave him a quick glance, grinned, and then turned Belinda to face their lover. Belinda crossed her arms over her breasts but Ali swiped them down to her sides and loosened the ties that held her garments in place. She pulled the white linen down, baring Belinda's breasts and stomach. She reached around and cupped the breasts and offered them to Jasper, taunting him by running her fingers over the soft skin and hard, raspberry pink nipples. Jasper responded by coming to them. He lowered his mouth and took one of Belinda's breasts in his mouth, sucking on the tasty morsel and letting his tongue explore the contrasting textures.

Belinda reached for his bare shoulders and gripped tightly as sensations washed over her in increasingly fierce waves. Jasper let go of her first breast, to give the other the same attention. She moaned softly and caught her lip between her teeth. She shifted from side to side and then stilled as Ali's delicate hand shoved itself between her legs and began stroking the petals of her folds. Her fingers worked busily, moving up and down but always avoiding the nub where all her sensations were gathering.

When Jasper's hand joined Ali's, Belinda groaned and shuddered, widening her legs so they could reach the places that longed to be touched. Jasper's large fingers were rougher than Ali's but they were just as clever at finding the places that brought her the most pleasure. He circled her hole, increasing the pressure as his finger slid into her, filling her with its thickness. She gasped and held on to his arms more tightly, rocking herself on his hand and sending waves of pleasure ricocheting through her. His finger moved in and out, faster and faster, while Ali's flicked her engorged clit.

The waves became rougher and more powerful. She could no longer contain the torrents that crashed through her. With a loud cry, she threw back her head and shuddered, allowing the pleasure to cosume her.

She took a deep breath, enjoying the comfort of a firm mattress beneath her. She was completely naked and lying in the middle of Jasper's bed. Only vaguely, did she remember him scooping her up into his arms and bringing her here. She turned slightly on her side to look at Ali, who was now also completely naked. Ali smiled and brished a strand of hair off Belinda's face. "That was wonderful."

Belinda frowned. "But I was the only one who was pleasured," she protested, running her hand over Ali's face and down her neck to the swell of her breasts. "What about you? And Jasper?"

Jasper leaned over from behind Ali. "Loving one another, means finding delight in giving each other joy. "Besides," he added with a brief kiss to Ali's shoulder, "we're far from done." He slid his left hand down Ali's body, lingering over the breasts and stomach, until he reached the top of her mound where his fingers caressed the soft hair that covered her maidenhood.

Ali blinked and pressed closer to Belinda. Jasper continued his caresses by sweeeping his hand up Ali's body again and cupping her face. He turned her head so that he could capture her lips in a kiss. Belinda pulled herself up and laid one hand on Ali's body and her other on what she could reach of Jasper's chest. As she stroked them both, she placed kisses wherever she could reach on both of them.

Ali rolled onto her back, her legs splaying open as she welcomed the touch of her lovers. Jasper removed her glasses and placed them on a table next to the bed. "You won't be needing those for a while." He leaned on his elbow and watched the two women he loved.

Belinda ran her hand down Ali's body in long, firm strokes and slid her hand between her legs. His eyes lit with eagerness as Belinda's fingers played with Ali's folds and teased her clit. Ali squirmed and twisted on the bed, trying to draw as much pleasure as she could. Her hands cupped her breasts and toyed with the puckered nipples.

Jasper leaned forward and kissed Belinda, urging her to quicken her movements. He covered her hand with his and guided her to breach Ali's opening. Together, his large finger and Belinda's slimmer one stretched the tight muscles of Ali's pussy. Ali panted at the pain and then subsided as she accepted their penetration. Their fingers rammed into her and slid out, faster and faster, until she was crying out and thrashing on the bed. She arched her body, reaching for the height of pleasure that was just out of reach.

Jasper twisted his finger and rubbed against a particularly sensitive place inside her. Her back rose off the bed and she clutched the sheets as pleasure swept her to heights she had never imagined. Jasper continued sliding his finger and Belinda's in and out of Ali's pussy until the ripples subsided and she lay back on the bed, soaked from the pleasure, her eyes glazed and her mouth open. Her dark hair was damp and tangled over the pillow.

Jasper raised Belinda's finger to his lips and licked Ali's juices slowly, savoring the taste. Then he undid his breeches and shucked them. His cock sprang out, jutting from his body towards Ali, swollen, red, and eager, the head pushing out from the foreskin and a drop of clear liquid gleaming at the slit.

He knelt on the bed, maneuvering Belinda to sit up against the pile of snowy white pillows and arranging Ali against her. Belinda opened her legs and twisted her ankles around Ali's, splaying her open for Jasper to see. He sat back on his heels for a moment and admired the abundance of loveliness before him. Ali's dark hair was spread over Belinda's pale skin and wandered down over the two bodies, lingering on the place where their splayed legs revealed the petals of Ali's folds. Two exquisite flowers were ready for him to pluck, red and swollen, wet with their juices and lusciousness.

Jasper traced first Belinda's, and then Ali's, pussy with his finger, enjoying the way each of them squirmed at his touch. Ali's hands gripped Belinda's thighs, digging into the soft flesh, making red marks. Belinda's hands tightened on Ali's breasts.

Jasper shifted so that he was between their legs. His cock jutted out proudly, dripping with excitement. He took the hard rod in his hand and stroked himself a few times. Both women's eyes were riveted on his cock. He leaned forward and swiped his cock between Belinda's folds and then did the same to Ali. As he did so, he kissed each of them lightly.

He kissed Ali again, deepening it as he prepared to make Ali fully his wife. Belinda would have her chance later. Ali responded to his kiss by wrapping her arms around his neck and pulling him closer. He shifted the weight of his body, sliding his cock up and down her slit. He pushed against her hole that had been stretched earlier. She tensed as it stretched the muscles and he paused, waiting for her to get used to the size and heaviness of his member.

She took a deep breath, caught her lip between her teeth and gazed at him. "Yes," she said. "More."

He grinned and pushed another inch in, holding the rest of his throbbing shaft in his hand as he controlled his movements. Belinda helped Ali by distracting her with kisses on her neck and shoulders and by kneading and stroking her breasts. Jasper paused in his minitrations to Ali, to give Belinda a kiss.

Ali relaxed as she adjusted to the heavy weight of Jasper's cock filling her. He moved another inch forward and pushed against her maidenhead. With a quick thrust, he broke through and entered her more deeply. She uttered a cry at the sharp pain and her muscles stiffened. Jasper whispered soothing words and dropped kisses on her mouth until she relaxed.

She felt so full, so stretched, as her husband's manhood took possession of her. She smiled up at him and curled her hands around his arms as he began pulling out and then sliding into her, using the copious juices of her pussy to ease his movements. He settled into a regular rhythm and Ali widened her legs to accommodate him fully. Each time he thrust into her, his balls slapped against her pussy. All three of them were breathing hard and Ali was moaning loudly. Jasper moved Belinda's hand to between Ali's legs and encouraged her to rub Ali's clit. Ali rocked from side to side as sensations overwhelmed her. Her nipples were deep red and tight and she tried to rub them against Jasper's chest.

Jasper moved faster and faster as his balls tightened. It was no longer possible to control his movements. He thrust in and out rapidly, relishing the tight grip of her pussy muscles around him.

Ali could not contain the sensations that filled her body. Every inch of her skin was tight and tingling. Her breath was coming in hard gasps, She clung to Jasper as her body joined with his in seeking the peak of pleasure. Blood raced through her body. Her muscles tightened and her back arched. She screamed as she tipped over the edge and plunged into a pool of pleasure. Her muscles rippled and her pussy gripped Jasper's cock as he, too, found his release and, with a cry, filled her with the hot seed that pulsed in jets from his cock.

The three of them lay in a satiated pile, satisfied with the expression of their love. When Jasper had recovered from his first climax, he had focused on Belinda. Happy and exhausted, he fell into a light sleep.

Belinda did not know how long they had been lying there, the three of them, limbs tangled and bodies warm from pleasure. Through the window, she could see stars filling the night sky, and the glow of the rising moon gave just enough light to the room for her to be able to determine the outlines of both Jasper's and Ali's bodies, Jasper in the middle and she and Ali each snuggling against the warmth of his body. She gave a deep sigh of contentment. "I am glad for all that we went through, even the dangers and fears. If not for Peter's foolishness, I would never have found the two of you and learned just how wonderful love is."

Earlier that day…

Lord Alexander Summerson raised his champagne glass to his lips and then scowled as he realized it was empty. He waved a footman over and took another glass. As a rule, he didn't attend weddings. He considered them morbid displays of social necessity in which women smugly paraded their triumph and men grimly accepted the inevitable. One day, he would need to marry. It was his duty to his family name and far preferable to leaving his title to his cousin Harry, who was weak and selfish. But he was not ready to settle down. The thought of being wedded to one of the brittle, superficial ladies eligible to marry an earl horrified him.

He swallowed half his glass of champagne and tried to look as if he was interested in the comments Lady Phylis Montgomery was making about other guests. One name penetrated through the dark clouds of his thoughts.

"Oh, what a fright Eleanor Goodwin is! No wonder you have been staring at her." It was only at these words that Summerson realized he had spent most of the morning watching Alicia's twin sister. He did not reply, and Lady Phylis continued with a very annoying titter. "That air of distractedness she has is such an affectation, and her hair! I have never seen such a riot of disorder. And she has none of the accomplishments that befit a young lady of quality. To be sure, she does speak French, but a little too well to be quite decent. She plays neither the harp nor the piano and the watercolor she presented the other day was worse than anything my younger sisters create in the schoolroom."

Lord Summerson's eyebrow rose laconically. "And you, my dear, are truly accomplished. Your future husband will indeed be fortunate to decorate his house with your water-colors and needlepoint cushions."

Oblivious to the scorn in his voice, she fluttered her eyes flirtatiously and tapped his arm with her folded fan. "Oh, Lord Summerson, you are a cad."

Her titter made his teeth ache, but her words had sent his thoughts in a new direction. With a polite nod, he moved away from her and scanned the guests who were mingling on the long terrace, enjoying the banquet that had been prepared. His friend, Jasper, was grinning broadly, his light brown hair almost golden in the sunshine as he leaned closer to his bride, Alicia. Belinda Bennet was standing close to them. Summerson's mouth twitched. Most of society would not know anything about or understand their strange rela-tionship, but it was clear that they all loved one another. And he wished them happiness. Jasper deserved it.

His eyes wandered farther until they found his target. Eleanor Goodwin had deftly avoided being anywhere near him all day, but he was determined to catch his prey. He was fascinated by her for all the reasons that Lady Phylis despised her. Over the last few years, he had grown bored of the supercilious women who had nothing to recommend them beyond the modistes who dressed them in silks or the mediocre skills they had learned from their governesses and which they called accomplishments. He had dismissed his last mistress when she began to show signs of jealousy and possessiveness, demanding his time and insisting he provide her with expensive gifts, but it was when she began to hint at marriage that he had broken off all contact with her. He had no desire to replace her with another grasping, greedy woman.

He paused near the edge of the crush of guests and leaned against a column to watch Eleanor. He was close enough to hear her conversation with Lady Hester, the wife of the local squire.

"How I do love a wedding!" Lady Hester exclaimed. "Alicia, or rather I should now say *Lady Keeton*," she giggled, "makes a beautiful bride. And you will look just as lovely when you marry." She looked around conspiratorially. "Do you have a beau?" She did not wait for Nell to answer. "A lady should not wait too long before finding a husband. Sitting on the shelf, is not a comfortable place for any woman."

"Thank you for your advice, Lady Hester." Nell smiled politely but Alexander Summerson could hear the tension in her voice. Her fists were clenched tightly at her sides and her eyes did not echo the smile on her lips. "I have no beau and I am determined that I will not marry a gentleman who wants nothing more in his bride than for her to find pleasure in honoring and obeying his every whim. I want my husband to be a nobleman in every sense of the word, who will fulfill his marriage vows to love and cherish his wife and family."

Lady Hester huffed. "A lady in her third Season cannot be too fussy. Men are not known for their commitment to their families. A wise wife allows her husband the freedom he needs and focuses on her home and children." With that, she stalked away, leaving Nell seething.

Summerson, whose views on marriage had, for most of his life, agreed with those of Lady Hester, for a moment, felt an unexpected twinge of regret for his attitude to women and marriage. It was an unusual feeling for him and he quickly banished it. Smoothly, he approached Eleanor. She scowled at him. He raised an eyebrow. "Good day, Miss Goodwin. You are looking remarkably well." His words were more than an empty compliment. She really did look lovely in spite of the scowl that creased her forehead. Or perhaps that somehow added to her charm.

She was too well-bred to refuse to reply but every line of her body was stiff with disapproval. "My lord," she muttered.

His hard, dark eyes glinted but his voice was as suave as usual. "So, three of your sisters are now married, but from what I overheard you say to Lady Hester, you will not be following them into the bliss of married life any time soon."

Her scowl deepened. "A *gentleman* would not have listened to that conversation, nor would he comment on it."

The corner of his mouth tweaked in the beginning of a smile. "Ah, yes. I certainly do not meet your romantic notions of a noble and honorable gentleman."

Nell drew on all the dignity and iciness she could. She tilted her chin, and her mouth thinned. "I am glad that I could provide you with amusement, my lord. Now, if you will excuse me, my sister has need of me." She swept away as regal as a princess and as haughty as a queen.

Summerson watched her go, admiring the grace of her

walk, the lushness of her dark hair, the curve of her hips and bottom. But the smile that lingered on his lips held regret, rather than triumph.

***

Nell held the book up to her face and breathed in deeply, relishing the smell of new pages. She ran her fingers over the binding and then opened it carefully, staring at the title page. *An Unexpected Heiress* by Miss Ellen Medwin. She traced her finger over the letters and then chuckled at the clever name she had chosen as her *nom de plume*, taken from her surname Goodwin and her guardian's earldom Medwell. She turned the page and read the first sentence aloud. *Love was not in Constantina Mallory's thoughts as the large traveling coach lumbered slowly up the pass to the wrought iron gates of Castle de Scillie.*

She sat back on her heels and pushed her hair out of her face. She had not meant to model her heroine on herself, but as she had written, her own dreams and expectations, her own desire for romance and adventure, had poured out onto the page. But her own life was not a novel and it was not as easy to bring about a happy ending for herself. She sighed deeply. She was delighted for Ali's happiness, and the wedding had been such a romantic occasion in the gardens of Jasper's house, overlooking the sea. But at moments like these, she needed her twin with her, to share her joy and celebrate with her. But Ali had other priorities now and she would have to learn to let her go.

The sense of loneliness left a void in her insides. She wiped the back of her hand over her eyes and blinked back the tears that had gathered there. She looked down at her book again. The deep satisfaction at her achievement was not quite the same as sharing her life with someone who loved her, someone she could love—someone who would rejoice in her success and comfort her when things did not go well.

Her desperate desire for love had been further stirred by the presence of Lord Alexander Summerson at Ali's wedding. Nell had tried to banish thoughts of his dark, inscrutable eyes, his well-defined features, and firm, full mouth, but while she wrote, details of his appearance, of his mannerisms, of his deep voice and tall, muscled body had informed the descriptions of her hero. And her heroine had foolishly fallen in love with him. Although, in her book, she had given her hero a kinder heart and softer character than the dismissive and arrogant man she knew in real life. But, contrary to all good sense, she still admired Lord Summerson and wished that she had been more sympathetic to him when he approached her at the wedding.

She took a deep breath. Maybe living in her dream world with characters she created in her imagination would need to satisfy her desires. She held the book in one hand while her other slid between the buttons of her shirt and caressed her breast slowly. She closed her eyes and bit her lips as she pinched her nipple until it was tight and hard. Then her hand slid lower, over the smooth planes of her stomach, until her fingertips teased the top of her mound. She shivered as the sensations rippled quietly through her body.

As her finger reached her nub and her pleasure rose to a climax, the image of Lord Summerson's face filled her mind.

Kathy Leigh

Kathy Leigh has loved books and writing since she could first follow the stories in her bedtime tales. She began writing stories in old school notebooks when she was eight years old but only recently thought that others might want to read her stories, too.

A romantic at heart, she is inspired by thunderstorms, sunflowers, and the belief that every princess deserves to find her prince. Recently she moved to a small village in France where long walks in the meadows and woods are wonderful inspiration for her writing.

She loves curling up on her couch with a good book, a glass of wine and her cats for company. As a young girl she particularly enjoyed the novels by Georgette Heyer and Jane Austen, and sighed over Mr. Rochester in *Jane Eyre*. She now enjoys historical and contemporary romance with an edge. She also enjoys fantasy, especially if it has a touch of romance.

Visit her website here:
https://kathyleighauthor.wordpress.com

Don't miss these exciting titles by Kathy Leigh and Blushing Books!

The Wards of Lamercier
Jane's Conquest
Cecilia's Victory

Alicia's Feat

Lords of Voluptas Series
A Wife for the Duke
An Heiress for the Marquess
A Paragon for the Viscount
A Companion for the Earl
A Ward for the Barron

To the Manor Born Series
Arabella's Journey
Dorothea's Quest
Lilian's Journey
To the Manor Born collection

Blushing Books

Blushing Books is one of the oldest eBook publishers on the web. We've been running websites that publish spanking and BDSM related romance and erotica since 1999, and we have been selling eBooks since 2003. We hope you'll check out our hundreds of offerings at http://www.blushingbooks.com.

Blushing Books Newsletter

Please join the Blushing Books newsletter
to receive updates & special promotional offers.
You can also join by using your mobile phone:
Just text **BLUSHING** to 22828.